PRAISE FOR *HORIZON*

"A thrilling and fast-paced science fiction story that takes depth of feeling as one of its core principles and combines that with pyrotechnic grace. I like here the ability to rethink genre trope, to add something new—to tell Caeli's story in a way that makes the whole enterprise feel fresh and invigorating instead of just going through the same old motions."

—*Writer's Digest*

"Tabitha Lord weaves a tale of moral strength and courage under fire. As an added bonus the action scenes will leave you breathless!"

—*Heather Rigney,*
Amazon Bestselling author of the
historical fantasy Waking the Merrow

"Starting a new book is like boarding a ship destined for unknown waters. As such, you want to make sure you trust your captain. Tabitha Lord is a captain who warrants such confidence."

—*Book Club Babble*

INFINITY

BY

TABITHA LORD

ISBN 13: 978-1-63489-945-1
eISBN: 978-1-63489-944-4

Library of Congress Catalog Number: 2017938250
Printed in the United States of America
First Printing: 2017

21 20 19 18 17   5 4 3 2 1

Cover and interior design by Steven Meyer-Rassow

Wise Ink Creative Publishing
837 Glenwood Ave.
Minneapolis, MN 55405
www.wiseinkpub.com

This one's for my dad, who first showed me the stars.

PART I — HORIZON

DEREK

CHAPTER 1

He was being followed. The small hairs on the back of his neck stood on end, and he felt eyes boring into his back. The shadow was discreet, cautious, but Derek knew someone was there. Years of field experience had taught him not to ignore his gut. He scanned the room as the crowd pressed in on itself. Bodies melded together on the dance floor; more pushed their way to the bar, and still others sat in groups at perimeter tables.

He leaned forward to catch the bartender's attention and ordered a drink. His contact hadn't arrived yet, so he sat on the high stool and sipped the caustic liquid. It burned his throat going down and then sat like a hot coal in his belly, but he'd acquired a taste for it these last few weeks. The Baishan system harbored an interesting subculture of illicit scientific researchers, and, Derek imagined, the chemistry of good distillation benefited from their attention.

Twirling the data chip in his jacket pocket, he glanced at the exits. A short, wiry-haired individual entered through the side door. Derek caught the young man's eye and then nonchalantly turned back to his drink. A few moments later, the same man bellied up to the bar next to Derek.

They ignored each other for a while until finally, Derek spoke. "I'm being followed, Cas."

"What?" The young man's eyes darted around the room.

"Stop that and relax," Derek said.

"Don't tell me to fucking relax. They'll kill me if they know I'm working a side deal. They own this shit," Cas said, and with a shaking hand raised his glass to his lips.

"I have the transfer codes, and the funds are untraceable. Give me the key card and we'll be finished here," Derek said.

"If they're following you, they'll get to me," Cas said.

Derek knew Cas was panicking, and he still hadn't turned over the key.

This deal would *not* go south. Derek wouldn't let it. Not after getting so close. "Cas, this is enough money for you to get out of here and live underground pretty comfortably for a long time. Give me the key," he said.

Cas rocked on his feet. If he bolted, Derek was screwed. He tried a harsher tactic. "It's too late if they're on to you. Take the damn chip and get out of here, now. I'll do the same."

Staring straight ahead, Cas fished around in his pocket and placed a small, plastic-coated data stick on the bar. Derek covered it with his hand and slid it in front of him, and then he placed the chip containing the routing codes on Cas's napkin.

Cas downed the remaining liquid from his glass and, without a word, left the bar.

Derek blew out a long breath. He had the key codes. Now, he had to get to his ship and get out of the Baishan system in one piece.

He sat for a few more minutes, sipping his drink, and contemplating the fastest route to the docking bay where his ship sat waiting. Scanning the room once more, he got up and left in the opposite direction of Cas, out of the bar and into the street. There was a subway entrance a block away, and Derek hurried in that direction.

The streets of Baishan's capital city bustled with people, and he eased his way into the anonymity of the crowd. A light breeze didn't provide much relief from the sweltering Baishan air. Even at night, it was thick and humid. Sweat prickled between Derek's shoulder blades and his shirt clung to his back.

Ducking down the stairway into the subway, he glanced backward. No one passing through the entryway looked familiar, but then again, he hadn't really gotten a look at the person following him. He moved to the very end of the platform and stood where he could observe the staircase. In moments, the alarm blared announcing an incoming train.

The sleek silver cars whooshed past him, and the smell of metal and damp earth assailed his nostrils. When the train came to a silent halt and the doors slid open, he stepped in and took a seat near the exit.

Reaching around his back, he discreetly removed his sidearm and held it tucked hidden between his knees. The train remained with its doors open for several moments as passengers trickled onboard. He searched the faces, knowing he wouldn't recognize anyone in particular, but unable to shake the nagging feeling that he was being pursued.

The last person to step onto the train was a woman. Tall and slender, with her dark hair tied back efficiently, she sat directly across from him, hands folded in her lap. When they made eye contact, she blinked once and then held his gaze with cold indifference. A chill crept up his spine and he gripped his gun tightly. Although he didn't recognize her, he'd felt this strange *otherness* once before, in the presence of a Drokaran prisoner.

He swallowed hard, fighting to keep the dread he felt in his gut off his face. The woman turned her head and looked out the window, her body perfectly still. As the train sped away from the platform and through the network of underground tunnels, Derek waited, counting his own breaths.

His stop was next. As soon as the doors slid open, he bolted out of the train car and ran full speed toward the exit. Taking the stairs two at a time, he maneuvered easily around the few people in his way. When he cleared the stairway, he glanced backward to see that the woman was, in fact, chasing him.

When he saw her arm move out of the corner of his eye, he threw his body sideways, around a corner, and behind a building. But his fraction-of-a-second pause gave her enough opportunity to raise her gun and take a shot at him. The searing round grazed his shoulder.

"Fuck!" he shouted to no one in particular.

Clearly, she was willing to fire at him in the open, among civilians. Even at this hour of the night, if he kept running through the streets, he'd be putting an awful lot of innocent people in harm's way. And she had to know where he was heading. The main hangar for visiting ships was on this side of the city, about three blocks away.

He zigzagged through back alleyways between the tall buildings, staying out of the city lights and in the shadows, and slowly and circuitously made his way toward the hangar. Breathing heavily, adrenaline still coursing through his body, he stopped when he reached the outskirts of the city. Backing into a dark doorway, he waited. His own heartbeat thudded against the silence.

When he'd stood for several minutes, alone and in the dark, he finally stuck his head around the corner. Nothing. He exhaled the breath he was holding and surveyed the hangar from his spot between the buildings.

The structure was brilliantly constructed, with several large circular platforms miles in circumference floating out over a bay. The platforms were divided into individual hangar compartments, able to house shuttles and other spacecraft from single occupant vehicles to moderate sized ships. Visitors would notify the control tower that they needed a space, and one would be assigned. Once landed, a magnetic lock secured the ship, and the pilot was assigned a security code. The ship would only be released when that code was entered and when the appropriate fees had been paid.

The glowing lights around the base were as bright as the daytime sun. Derek wasn't keen on exposing himself, but he had no choice. There was one main entry point, and then a network of automated shuttles and lifts that would take him to the hangar bay where his ship was docked.

He figured he'd be less conspicuous walking briskly than if he barreled inside at a run, so he held his gun hidden in his jacket pocket and crossed the street. Commerce and interplanetary travel didn't recognize the time of day, and the main entryway bustled with people. He felt safer in the crowd, but only barely. Searching the sea of faces, he made his way toward one of the shuttle ports. A flashing timer above the doorway signaled the car's approach, and he queued up with the crowd waiting to board.

His heart still hammered in his chest as he stepped into the compartment. He gripped the safety bar and waited for the doors to slide closed. As they did, he saw her. From across the station, her eyes locked on his. She stared at him until the shuttle began to move, and then she simply turned and walked away.

***

He'd cleared the docking port and was through the planet's upper atmosphere when a proximity alarm blared in the cockpit.

The ship he was using wasn't the sleek fighter he most enjoyed, but rather a modified shuttle, missing any Alliance insignia and outfitted with various weapons, mostly non-Alliance issue as well. It looked like a typical unaffiliated vessel, fast and well-armed.

But it was no match for the cruiser that now had a missile lock on him.

"Shit," he said as the larger ship came within visual range.

He recognized the design. His com blinked, and he opened the channel.

"Power down your weapons and prepare to be boarded," an icy voice said.

"Who is this and what's your jurisdiction?" he asked, buying time while he inserted the data stick into his ship's main computer system.

"Power down your weapons and prepare to be boarded," the voice repeated. And then, "Comply or we will open fire."

"I'm taking weapons off-line now," Derek said. As he powered down the weapons, he booted up the stealth shield. Nothing obvious happened when he authorized the activation code, but feedback from the small display monitor indicated the field had been deployed. He'd never had a chance to test it. Silently, he begged it to run.

When the system showed a green light, he engaged his thrusters and banked hard to port. He'd know in seconds if it had worked. Either he'd force the Drokarans to blow him out of the sky or he'd escape. Being boarded and taken prisoner wasn't an option.

The Drokaran ship fired, but the errant shots missed him. They couldn't see him. The stealth shield not only hid him from the naked eye, but it also rendered him invisible to their sensors. He leaned back heavily in his chair and rubbed his hands over his face. And then he sent an encrypted message to *Horizon* requesting rendezvous coordinates.

CHAPTER 2

"Bay doors are open, and you are cleared for landing. Welcome back, commander," the familiar voice said through his com.

"Thank you, *Horizon* control," he responded. "It's good to be back."

He maneuvered his ship easily into the docking bay, smoothly set it down on the deck, and powered it down once the containment doors had closed.

He'd patched up his shoulder while in flight, but it sent him an angry reminder when he slung a bag over it. In addition to his own personal belongings, he had a significant amount of gear to unload, including an impressive array of side arms that needed to be returned to the weapons locker. Both hands full, he winced before stepping out onto the flight deck.

"Can I give you a hand with that, sir?" a familiar voice asked.

"Yeah, I'd love a hand. How's it going, Drew?" he asked.

Drew Chase was one of the pilots in his squadron, an explosives expert with serious skills, and someone he considered a friend. On their last mission, Drew had single-handedly disarmed a number of devices which, if detonated, would have taken out an area the size of a city block.

"Rough mission?" Drew asked, eyeing Derek's bloody shirt and torn sleeve.

"Got a little dicey at the end."

As they walked to the armory, Derek glanced sideways at Drew. "How's Kat?" he asked. Kat had been flying with Derek since they'd both first joined the Alliance. Tough and loyal, she was one of his best friends.

He caught the small, almost embarrassed grin on Drew's face and knew things must still be fine. "She's good."

"Glad to hear," Derek answered, and he was. Drew and Kat made an interesting pair—polar opposites in many ways, yet they had what appeared to be a meaningful and healthy relationship. As their commanding officer, he knew he should discourage them, but as their friend, he decided he would just be happy for them. Shit happened out here, and life was short.

"Have I missed anything interesting?" Derek asked lightly.

Drew didn't answer and shrugged uncomfortably.

"What's up, Drew?" Derek stopped and turned to face the younger man.

"Donovan wants you for de-briefing in an hour." Drew shifted on his feet, not meeting Derek's eyes. Usually, Derek had a little more time to settle back in after a mission. Something else was going on.

"Tell me."

"Don't you want a minute to catch your breath?"

Derek merely raised his eyebrows. Patience wasn't one of his stronger attributes. "What end of the galaxy is falling apart this time?" he joked, but with a note of seriousness in his tone.

"That sensor you dropped in the Almagest system picked up a ship. We've been gathering intel on it and monitoring the situation. It's come and gone from the planet twice in the last six weeks. Kat knows more," Drew finished.

Almagest. Caeli's home world. He'd only spent a few days there, but they'd felt like a lifetime.

This was not what he'd expected, and the information made him feel slightly ill. While he knew rationally it wouldn't be long before someone found Almagest, he had been holding onto a purposefully self-deceptive hope.

There really wasn't anything more to say about it. Derek could worry over the implications, but at the moment there was absolutely nothing he could do. And Drew knew him well enough, and understood the situation well enough, not to try and placate him with meaningless words.

***

The captain and Kat were waiting in one of the smaller conference-style rooms just off the tech deck. Kat smiled widely and with genuine warmth when she saw him, a rare expression for her.

Captain Donovan welcomed him back on board and they all sat. Derek would have to prepare a written report for Alliance records, but Donovan always wanted the whole story, including the things that would never be entered into an official document.

"My take is that the Drokarans developed the initial stealth shield prototype and then brought it to the Baishan for further development. It was supposed to stay proprietary, but the Baishan figured they could turn an extra profit by selectively marketing it elsewhere," Derek said.

"We should assume the entire Drokaran fleet is now using this shielding," Donovan said.

"If they aren't yet, they will be soon. It's out of the testing phase and into full production," Derek agreed.

"The Drokarans would have had a huge advantage with this shield. We needed to get our hands on it. Excellent work, commander."

"Thank you, sir," Derek said, running a hand through his too-long hair. It seemed like they were always one step behind the Drokarans. But this was a victory. The Alliance now had a shiny new piece of stealth technology in its possession.

"Reece is already salivating over it," Kat said.

Reece was an experimental physicist who specialized in . . . well, Derek wasn't actually sure *what* Reece specialized in, but he designed micro-drones, was an encryption genius and had a brain that worked faster at solving technical problems than any others Derek had ever encountered. Young and enthusiastic, he was a valuable asset to the *Horizon* crew. And despite his annoyingly talkative nature, Derek very much respected his skill.

Donovan sighed and sat back in his chair. Derek waited, knowing the conversation was about to take a turn.

"A ship has been coming and going from the Almagest system," Donovan said.

Kat furrowed her brow and looked at Derek.

"What do we know?" Derek asked.

"The signal you were tracking when you crashed on Almagest is still transmitting. It must have attracted this new ship." Kat began.

Last year, *Horizon* discovered a radio signal coming from a planetary system thought to be uninhabited. Derek was sent to investigate the source of the signal and drop a sensor in the sector. But he'd been shot out of the sky by a ship using the same stealth tech he'd just purchased on behalf of the Alliance.

On Almagest, he'd found Caeli. Or rather, she'd found him.

Risking her own safety, she dragged Derek from the crash and saved his life. Once he understood the political situation on Almagest and the danger Caeli faced, he couldn't leave her behind when he was rescued. Well, that and he'd fallen completely in love with her.

"Our sensor grabbed a lot of data for Reece to analyze," Kat continued. "First, we knew whoever responded to the signal was obviously not Alliance, and based on the information about the ship itself, we knew it wasn't Drokaran."

Derek breathed an audible sigh of relief at this, and Kat nodded. "I know, right? That would've really sucked." A mercenary ship was bad, but a Drokaran ship would be far worse. There would be no trade deals with the Drokarans, no negotiations. When the Drokarans set their sights on a planet, the results were deadly. The Alliance had already lost two member worlds to full-scale Drokaran invasions.

"Based on information you and Caeli shared about the resources on Almagest, we made a few assumptions. The fact that this ship has returned to the planet twice already suggested to us that some kind of commercial agreement was established between them and Marcus, if Marcus is still in power. Most likely they're a mercenary crew."

Derek agreed with the assessment so far.

Kat continued, "We asked ourselves what kind of products they could be buying, selling, or trading, and where would they go to do that after leaving Almagest?"

Derek interrupted, answering Kat's mostly rhetorical question. "The Amathi were mining. There would be real money to be made selling ore to the Baishan or the Sibiu out of Elista."

Kat nodded vigorously. "So, that's where we focused Reece's attention. And we were not disappointed."

She tapped the tabletop, and a three-dimensional screen appeared in front of them. After a little manipulation, the image of a moderately sized ship, with no revealing insignia, floated and turned in front of them. There were some similarities to the modified shuttle Derek had just returned on, but this ship was larger and appeared better armed.

"Definitely room for cargo." Derek stood and moved closer to the holographic image. "And their weapons show they can defend themselves."

He sat back down. "Okay, they sold ore. What did they buy and bring back to Almagest in return? Do we know?" he asked, looking at Kat.

She gave a hesitant nod. "We know weapons for sure. I was able to communicate with one of our agents on Elista and get him to do some very cautious digging around. A large transaction definitely happened between that ship's crew and a major weapons dealer on Elista." She pointed at the slowly rotating image of the ship.

"We need our own intel." Derek looked meaningfully at Captain Donovan. "We should be waiting for them on Elista when they go back."

"*If* they go back," Donovan answered, shaking his head. "Commander, we all have more than just a professional concern about that planet, but illegal arms dealing between non-member planets doesn't justify a covert Alliance mission."

Derek could feel the tension building between his shoulders. He exhaled deeply and said, "I know. But I have a really awful feeling about this."

"I do too," the captain conceded. "And I still can't authorize any action right now. We'll stay in communication with our assets on Elista and keep them monitoring the situation.

Lieutenant Rowe, thank you," Donovan said, dismissing her.

She stood and nodded at Derek. "One more interesting piece of info," she added as she headed out the door. "The planet is no longer transmitting the signal."

"I hope that's a good thing. Maybe they've struck a trade agreement and don't want any more attention," Derek answered, but there were alternative reasons for Almagest to go dark, civil war being one of them. Caeli had been part of a resistance movement there, a group set on removing Marcus, the brutal dictator, from power.

"At least the planet isn't a glaring beacon for the Drokarans to lock onto," Kat said.

Derek nodded in agreement.

When Kat left, Donovan turned and said, "Derek, I understand completely your desire to act. We know what's gone on down there, and it's Caeli's home planet." He paused for a moment and then continued. "The situation doesn't warrant action on our part right now. But I promise you, if something changes, we won't stand by and do nothing."

Derek ran a hand through his hair and closed his eyes. "Thank you, sir," he said before getting up to leave.

CHAPTER 3

Derek liked the water in his shower steaming hot, and he stood relaxed for several long moments under the pounding stream. His face was scraped clean and his dark hair cropped short.

When he returned from a covert mission, there was always a period of re-entry, and it wasn't like flipping a switch. Cutting his hair, unpacking his things, putting on his uniform—all helped him make the transition, but it still took him a while to shed his alternate personality.

There was a place he had to go in his head to get the job done in the field, and that other personality, the one he created and held onto, allowed him to do what needed doing. It offered a degree of separation from those actions in his own mind. But sometimes he wondered if he sacrificed a piece of himself each time. Or if maybe that darker side clung to him like a layer of dirt, seeping into the cracks of his skin.

He let the water run over his body until it practically scalded him.

Seated at the work desk in his quarters a few hours later, his finger hovered over the transmit key on his long-range com. *Horizon* was orbiting Telerous, one of the Alliance's research facilities, having just turned over the stealth shield to the waiting scientists there. It seemed like a good time to call home.

He hadn't spoken to Caeli in months, since right before he left for this latest mission on Baishan. A framed photo of her, taken in front of his family home, stood on his desk. In the picture, she smiled at him, but he read the uncertainty and fear in her eyes.

When he had convinced her to leave Almagest, he had no real plan. His only thought at the time was that he couldn't abandon her, that he had to get her somewhere safe. But before he could make any kind of arrangement, *Horizon* had been rerouted to a planet in crisis called Tharsis, and what should have been a diplomatic mission turned into a covert ground operation instead.

Caeli's empathic skills, her resourcefulness, and her previous experience as a resistance fighter on Almagest proved invaluable to the mission on Tharsis. His team ultimately prevented a terrorist attack and saved the planet from a Drokaran invasion force. But Caeli wasn't an Alliance soldier, or even a contracted operative. In his world, she was a civilian.

Sending her to his parents' home on Erithos seemed the best option while he finished his tour on *Horizon*. Captain Donovan gave him leave to fly her there himself, and it killed him to say goodbye a few days later.

Now, he hesitated before connecting the call, worrying over all the decisions he'd made that may have turned out to be wrong. And he couldn't tell her about Almagest, not without more information and not over an open com line. But he needed to see her face and hear her voice, and this need outweighed his apprehension. So, he hit the button.

Seconds later, her image materialized on his screen. She greeted him with a brilliant smile and leaned in toward her monitor.

"Derek," she said.

He couldn't help but smile back at her. "How are you?"

"Busy. I'm working at the military hospital. I'm not sure what your dad told them about me, but I'm on the staff there now."

He could hear the enthusiasm in her voice. "Well, he is the Fleet Admiral."

She laughed. "True. No one asks me any questions."

When Derek was home on Erithos for those few days, he'd told his father everything, from his crash on Almagest to Caeli's ability to read thoughts and heal with her mind. The Admiral understood the need for secrecy around Caeli. Her skills could be used as weapons, her home world exploited for both its pristine natural resources and for its gifted people.

"It's almost like being onboard *Horizon*, with all the technology," she continued. "If I could spend years there, I'd still have more to learn."

He wished she could spend her whole life safely on Erithos. Chaos and brutality plagued much of the galaxy outside the protected Alliance worlds, and he knew her home, Almagest, wouldn't be spared the struggle. He wanted her to have a little more peace, a little more time to heal before she'd have to plunge back into it. But in his gut, he knew it wouldn't be long.

"I'm working on a project . . ." Her voice trailed off and she blinked at him. "What is it?"

She knew something was wrong. If they had been physically closer she would have known exactly what it was; his anxiety would have projected itself straight into her sharp mind.

He shrugged and gave her a weary grin. "I just got back from an away mission, and I'm tired."

She bit her bottom lip. "I know you can't talk, but are you okay?" she asked.

"Yeah," he said and reached a hand up to the screen. It was painful to see her without being able to touch her. "Are you?"

"I miss you," she said, her voice catching. When she squeezed her eyes shut, a tear leaked down one cheek.

"Caeli," he said, swallowing back the lump in his own throat.

"No, I'm okay. Better than okay. I wake up in the morning and I'm not afraid. I go to sleep at night, and I dream. Normal dreams, not nightmares. I go to the hospital, and I take care of people. I come home and I help with meals. I take walks. I laugh." She sniffed and brushed the tear away. "I have a life again."

"I'm glad the nightmares are gone," he said. They'd been fierce, with her terror sometimes invading his mind in the middle of the night before she woke up. "Tell me about your patients."

At that, another smile bloomed across her face. "I'm mostly working in pediatrics, with the kids of the military families. The facility is amazing, and there's always a research project going on."

He stared at her face, trying to memorize the exact blue of her eyes, every tiny line around her lips when she smiled, the way her blond curls framed her cheeks. "I miss you too," he said when she stopped to take a breath.

That night he dreamt about her, but his dreams were fitful and chaotic, filled with fragments not only from his own memories, but from Caeli's as well.

Over the next few days he was on edge, disturbed by the combination of real facts concerning Almagest and the unsettling scenarios he was creating in his own imagination.

It wasn't like him to be this distracted by anything, and he wondered if maybe it was because Caeli's experiences were integrated so deeply in his own mind.

So he kept himself busy, making sure he had very little down time. He ran tactical drills with his entire squadron and worked the remaining kinks out of *Horizon's* newly repaired fighters, many of which had been damaged in the last Drokaran-funded attack.

The flying he enjoyed. *Horizon's* small fighters were sleek, fast, maneuverable, and well-armed. His whole team was in good spirits after the exhausting but exhilarating training sessions, and the sense of unease that plagued him temporarily retreated as he threw himself back into his job.

***

His relief was short-lived. Several days later, *Horizon* received an encrypted transmission from an Alliance agent on Elista. At first his mind couldn't or *wouldn't* make sense of it. The team assembled around him, including Donovan, Kat, Drew, and Reece, watched the video feed silently.

It was Kat who said, in a barely audible voice, "She looks like Caeli."

And she did. Her hair was a lighter shade of blonde than Caeli's, but her face had the familiar bone structure that Derek associated with the Novali, the empathic people of Almagest.

The clarity of the video revealed her pale eyes and the dark, bluish circles underneath them. She couldn't have been more than thirteen years old, but the vacant look on her face worried him far more than if she'd appeared terrified.

It was impossible to tell where she was. The nondescript room could have been on board a ship or in a cell. The surrounding details had clearly been minimized, and when someone leaned down and spoke into the girl's ear, the image of that second individual was blurry and unidentifiable.

A small, domesticated animal skittered on the table in front of the girl. She squeezed her eyes shut when the second individual plunged a scalpel into the animal's chest cavity and then into the back of its skull. It bled and convulsed.

With a sharp prod from her captor, the girl placed her shaking hands on the animal. Everyone in the room watching, save Reece, had directly witnessed Caeli doing the very same thing when she used her gift to heal. Kat and Derek looked at one another in horror.

The animal's seizures and bleeding stopped quickly, and within moments it was eating from a food dish placed before it. The girl reached her hand out to pet the creature's furry head, her gesture innocent and childlike. Derek leaned forward and gripped the side of the conference table so hard his knuckles turned white.

Almost immediately she was given another instruction. At this, the girl shook her head and backed away in panic, but the obscured individual grabbed her arm viciously. Shaking and sobbing, she touched a fingertip to the distracted animal. It stiffened and fell sideways onto the table, dead. A small stream of blood leaked out from its nose and ears, and an amber stain crept across the metallic surface of the table.

Heavy silence blanketed the room, broken when the agent who'd provided them with the video finally spoke. "This is a problem," he said.

Donovan exhaled and nodded. "Tell us what you know."

The agent answered without blinking. "The transmission originates from Alizar Sorin," he began.

While it was the first time Derek had heard the name, he knew this was the captain of the ship that had been back and forth to Almagest.

The operative continued, "I've been keeping a look out for him since Lieutenant Rowe first contacted me. Sorin's communication was encrypted and he clearly wants to keep some level of anonymity, but it wasn't all that hard to intercept and decode the message. He's forwarded this to the Raasvan."

They paused while the implications of this fact resonated throughout the room. The Raasvan were known for human trafficking, among other things. The Alliance attempted to disrupt this illegal enterprise, and felt completely justified in prosecuting anyone for the crime, whether the perpetrators were citizens of Allied worlds or not. But in reality, the Raasvan were careful not to victimize Alliance citizens and shrewdly kept their focus on underdeveloped worlds harboring at-risk populations; thus, there was minimal pressure on the Alliance from within to combat this particular crime. It didn't sit well with anyone who knew how devastating and far reaching the trade network was, but the Alliance had limited resources and simply couldn't police every corner of the galaxy.

"Do you know where he is now, Sean?" Kat asked the agent.

"General vicinity, yes," he answered, "exact location, no. Sorin sent the transmission from orbit and then landed. I can get you those coordinates, but you know how it is down here. There are a million places he could be hiding."

Kat nodded in agreement.

"Are you planning to try and bring him in?" Sean asked bluntly.

All eyes turned to Donovan, who answered, "I think we need to."

Sean nodded and continued, "Okay. I did some research. Sorin works with a crew of four and they've mostly run product for other, bigger organizations. He's stayed under the radar and does just enough to keep his crew busy and well paid, but not enough to be a significant target for any local or Alliance authorities." Sean paused and then added meaningfully, "He's in over his head on Elista."

"Why do you say that?" Kat asked.

"Sorin's clearly found something or someplace new. I'm *not* asking," Sean emphasized. "But if I'm thinking that way, I promise you I'm not the only one. The Raasvan are some of the most dangerous criminals anywhere. If they can cut out the middle man and set up their own operation, they'll do it."

Sean paused again. He rubbed his hands over his face and said, "This girl is more than just a novelty, she's a weapon."

No one in the room denied that fact, so Sean kept talking. "Sorin has already intimated there's more where she came from."

"She could be used as anything from a healer to an assassin," Kat said, shaking her head and pacing around the room.

Derek could tell from the look on Sean's face that he'd already thought of those things, and of all the possibilities in between. "What are the chances we can get to her before Sorin hands her off to the Raasvan?" Derek asked.

"Not great. Most likely the next time Sorin surfaces will be when the transaction is finished and he's on his way out. That's if the Raasvan haven't found a way to grab him before that. We can expend some resources looking for him down here, especially if you send a team. Time is short and the odds aren't good, but once the girl's turned over to the Raasvan, it will be even more difficult to get to her."

"Shit." Derek ran a hand through his hair.

"Yeah," Sean agreed. "Sorin's entrepreneurial; I'll give him that. He sent out this communication ahead of time to spread the word and generate enthusiasm. I'm sure the major players are already positioning themselves and making preliminary bids. He'll have a sense of what they're willing to pay, and this will raise the price he's able to get for her from the Raasvan considerably. They won't like being played like that."

"Sorin doesn't even realize the danger he's put himself in," Derek commented.

"Not likely," Sean agreed.

"Thank you for the intel. We'll be back in touch when we have a plan," Donovan said to Sean.

"Very good, sir," Sean answered.

His image dissolved, and Donovan gestured for everyone to take a seat around the conference table. "Thoughts?" he prompted them.

"We have limited intel and very few assets besides Sean on Elista," Kat said.

"If we can't find Sorin before he hands the girl off to the Raasvan, our odds of getting her back go down," Drew added.

Derek nodded and continued, "And Sorin himself is now most likely being targeted by the Raasvan. We're working with a ticking clock, as usual."

Donovan always sat back and let his team brainstorm, involving himself in the conversation only when necessary. But very early on he said, "The mission will be to extract both Sorin and the girl if possible, but if there's a choice, it has to be Sorin."

It was clear that no one was pleased with that answer, Derek included, but Sorin could lead the Raasvan, or anyone else for that matter, to Almagest. The girl couldn't.

Donovan continued, "It is in the Alliance's best interest for Almagest to remain off the radar, so to speak, for as long as possible. We all know it will become a battleground once non-Alliance organizations know it's there. And the Drokaran threat looms. They can't be allowed to gain more territory. If we can capture Sorin we will have bought a little more time for Almagest, *and* we can gather more intel from him as to what's happening on the planet."

Derek gave a slight nod, but Donovan persisted. "Will this be a problem?"

"No, sir," he answered, but of course it would be. Leaving that little girl behind would not be okay, not with him and not with his team.

Donovan was right about the big picture, though. They needed to get to Sorin. So, what he needed was a plan to recover them both.

CHAPTER 4

They'd been on Elista for three days and were no closer to finding Sorin, who was wisely keeping silent and staying out of sight, than they had been when they'd arrived. Derek was frustrated and working his team hard.

He'd only brought Kat, Drew, and Reece with him, feeling that too many new faces would raise suspicions on a planet where survival often depended on anonymity.

"Kat, I need you and Drew to get some real time surveillance on the Raasvan auction house," Derek said, pacing the room. Since the team was unable to find Sorin's current location, they needed to anticipate where he would go, and this was Sean's best logical guess.

"Got it," she said.

"When Sean gets back, we'll review the interior plans and start thinking strategy."

Derek was still trying to get the measure of the agent. He knew that Sean had been on Elista for over five years, an exceptionally long time to maintain deep cover in such a volatile environment.

"You've worked with him before. What's his deal, Kat?" Derek asked.

She shrugged. "I'm not sure, but he saved my ass when I was

here on mission a couple of years ago. I always felt like he had my back."

Derek nodded. "You guys take off."

He checked in on Reece, who was busy trying to sort through useful decrypted communications, and then, as soon as Sean returned, he joined him at the table.

"All right, here are schematics for the interior," Sean said, opening a tablet and scrolling through the building layouts.

"We need a plan to get in there," Derek said, leaning back in his chair and rubbing his eyes.

"And a plan to get out," Sean added.

"Yeah that would be important," Derek agreed. They sat for a while in exhausted silence.

"Who's Caeli?" Sean asked.

Derek froze for a moment and then looked up at Sean with surprise.

"I heard Kat say over the com that she looks like Caeli," Sean explained; Derek remembered his team's initial shock when they'd first seen the video feed of the Novali girl. "I understand if you can't tell me." Sean shrugged.

Derek paused and then answered, "Caeli's an empath and a healer, just like that little girl."

Sean raised his eyebrows and gave the slightest nod.

Derek wanted to tell Sean *something*. He knew the agent was working very hard on behalf of this mission and that he had top-level clearance, but there was also a tacit agreement in the field that you only shared what was necessary.

If you didn't know something, someone else couldn't get it out of you.

So, Derek was sparing with the details when he continued, "I crash landed on Caeli's planet and she saved my life. The planet is a mess and pretty vulnerable right now. It's in our best interest to keep its location hidden."

"The Raasvan would be brutal if they found it," Sean agreed.

"And Sorin can lead them right to it," Derek said, stating the obvious. He looked pointedly at Sean before adding, "The Drokarans are also still expanding."

"They're the scariest bastards in the galaxy," Sean admitted.

"That they are," Derek said, standing to pace around the table.

"I think I can get your team into the auction as buyers," Sean said.

Derek abruptly stopped pacing. "You're in deep enough to do that?"

"Yes," Sean answered, his expression carefully blank.

Before Derek could form a response, Reece burst in. "Commander, Sorin's communicated with the Raasvan."

He gestured for them to move into the other room where the equipment he'd brought from *Horizon* was scattered.

Reece sat down at a workstation and tapped efficiently on a keypad. Recorded voices detailed arrangements for a handoff at the auction arena in two days' time.

Derek locked eyes with Sean, who responded, "I'm on it."

***

Derek's team was assembled, except for Sean, who was off arranging whatever needed arranging to get them inside the arena. They'd reviewed the interior of the building until they could navigate through it with their eyes closed, and Reece was busy preparing their com devices, trackers, and micro drones to give them as much remote guidance as possible.

Derek was tense but focused. They had a timeline and a target.

When Sean finally returned, Derek tried not to accost him for information right away. He didn't have to wait long, though. Sean pulled up a chair and started speaking. "We're in. My connections are solid and I won't raise suspicion bringing potential buyers with me. He paused and frowned. "It's how we're going to get to Sorin, get to the girl, and get out that concerns me."

Derek had nothing to offer, so he waited. Sean motioned to the three-dimensional schematic of the building that was still projected on the tabletop and continued, "We'll enter here." He pointed at the south side of the building. "We'll check in and be escorted to our suite somewhere along here."

He traced his finger in a semicircle to show where the viewing area was situated. "Each registered buyer has a private room. You can see out, but no one can see in. And we all have an unobstructed view of the merchandise, which is shown here." A small stage was centered below and in front of the viewing suites.

Derek raised his eyebrows at Sean's word choice but didn't comment.

Sean sat back in the chair and rubbed his hands over his face. "Once the auction closes, the winning bidders are escorted individually to this room to complete the transaction."

"So we know where the girl will be at the end of the night," Kat interjected.

Sean nodded and said, "It will be a little more complicated to find Sorin. The Raasvan are supposedly paying him a percentage of the sale price. If they want to string him along for a while, they might make their move after the business transactions are finished. Or they could grab him and stash him as soon as they have the girl." Sean shrugged and sighed. "We know he'll be there. We just have to get eyes on him as soon as we can."

"The micro drones can cover a lot of space," Reese said, opening a metal case. "And these are even smaller than regular Alliance issue. I've been working on modifications."

The tiny device looked like an opaque ball about a millimeter in diameter. When Reece tapped it, miniature propeller wings sprouted from the sides and lifted the drone out of the box. It hovered near the ceiling and was practically invisible.

Derek put a hand on Reece's shoulder. "Impressive job."

Reece glowed under the praise. "Full audio and video feed will come right to me here. And if I have an image of Sorin, I can program facial recognition so the drones will actually be looking for him."

"That's definitely helpful," Sean acknowledged. "We'll have to be flexible with our plan once we're inside." He paused, then added, "And we won't be able to bring any obvious weapons into the complex. The Raasvan are always well armed, but they don't want anyone else to be."

Derek shook his head. "Well, we just have to be creative."

Kat snorted. "Is that what we're calling a suicide mission now, *creative*?"

"On the up side, I do have reliable transportation waiting for us on the outside, as long as we don't raise the alarm too early," Sean said.

"Oh, wonderful." Kat said, smirking.

***

The "reliable transportation" turned out to be an armored vehicle and four very large Elistans carrying enough firepower to take out the entire arena, Derek mused. They arrived in the late afternoon the day of the auction in the sleek vehicle, with plenty of cabin space to fit themselves and Derek's team.

Kat was unusually quiet on the way over. Derek attributed this to her discomfort at having to leave her assault weapons back at Sean's. He had to admit he was pretty tense about this mission too. A lot could go wrong in a short amount of time. And having more than one objective definitely complicated things.

Sean broke the silence just before they arrived at the compound. "This place . . ." he began, then shook his head. "It fucking offends humanity. Just don't react."

Derek caught Kat's gaze. She gave a nearly imperceptible nod. During their years working together in the field, they'd experienced a good bit of humanity's dark side. He knew Kat worked hard to keep her volatile temper in check, especially when her sense of justice was offended. But when she shut it down, she had deadly focus and was one of the best field agents he'd ever worked with.

It was early evening when they stepped out of the vehicle. Sean led them toward an unmarked entranceway and placed his palm on a metallic plate. A red glow illuminated the surface, scanning his palm print, and the door slid open. Upon entering they were greeted by a security team, searched for weapons, and handed off to a beautiful young woman.

As they wandered through the elegant corridors of the arena toward their private suite, Kat nonchalantly toyed with the bracelet on her wrist and released the micro drones secured there earlier by Reece. Without a sound, the tiny machines ascended to the ceiling and scattered.

Derek was so familiar with the layout of the building he could have navigated the hallway without a guide, but when they arrived at their room, he was truly surprised by the decadence of the space. An oversized plush sofa was situated in front of a darkened plate-glass window. A fully stocked bar took up the back wall. Muted overhead lighting cast soft shadows on the thick carpet, and low, pulsing music echoed in the background.

Their escort turned and gave Sean an inviting smile. "I'll be with you tonight until the program begins. Can I offer you drinks?" Her voice was mesmerizing and Derek found himself staring.

Thick curls of ebony hair cascaded to the middle of her back. She had wide, expressive eyes almost as dark as her hair, and dusky, flawless skin. Evocative clothes revealed a lithe body that moved with sultry grace.

"Please," Sean answered.

She poured their drinks. Serving Sean last, she leaned toward him and whispered, "What else can I do for you?" Derek was quite sure she intended them all to hear.

"Nothing tonight, Theia," Sean answered. "We actually need a little privacy before the show starts."

Derek noted Sean's expression and intimate tone. Theia looked disappointed but nodded and left the room.

Drew exhaled loudly and mumbled, "That was interesting," under his breath. Kat glared at him.

Sean sat on the sofa and took a long drink, wincing as he swallowed. "These rooms aren't monitored, so we can speak freely in here," he said.

Derek nodded. "What happens next?" he asked.

Before Sean could answer, a seductive, feminine voice was projected into the room.

"Ladies and gentlemen, bidding will begin in thirty minutes. You will use the panel at the viewing window to enter your bids."

As she spoke, a display panel automatically extended from the wall in front of the plate glass.

"The highest bid will be displayed on the stage monitor," she continued. Through the window, Derek could see a large monitor light up and flash, directing their attention to it.

"Throughout the evening, detailed instructions and prompts will be given to you by the auctioneer. Once bidding has closed, the winner will be notified immediately. When you have finished for the evening, please press the call button on your panel and a guide will escort you to finalize your transaction, or to the exit. Good luck!" she finished.

Sean shrugged at Derek. "That's what happens next."

Derek sat on the edge of the couch, tapping his thumb against his knee while Kat wandered around the room fiddling with the pins holding her long, dark hair back in an elaborate twist at the nape of her neck.

"Don't stick yourself," Drew said.

She rolled her eyes and shot him an obscene hand gesture.

Suddenly Reece's voice echoed through the tiny communication devices they were all wearing. "Commander, I have a location on Sorin. He's alive and under guard."

Derek stood up and motioned to Kat. "Great. I need you to be our eyes." He nodded at Drew and Sean, who would stay behind and wait for a visual on the girl, and then he walked out the door. Kat easily fell into step next to him.

"The halls are mostly empty," Reece reported, "which is a good thing, because you're heading to the other side of the building."

"Of course we are," Kat mumbled.

But they reached the corridor where Sorin was being held with relative ease. They knew they were in the right place even before Reece confirmed it by the large, armed Raasvan guard stationed outside the door.

"Is their security feed scrambled?" Derek asked.

"Yes, sir," Reece replied.

Kat looked at Derek and nodded slightly.

"Be ready with the door on my mark," he ordered Reece as Kat approached the guard.

The guard tensed when he saw Kat walking toward him. "This area is restricted," he said in a clipped voice.

Derek couldn't see Kat's face, but he watched her body language alter slightly. Advancing toward the guard, she reached up to tuck a stray piece of hair behind her ear. "I'm so sorry," she purred. "I'm afraid I'm a little lost. Maybe you could point me in the right direction."

The guard didn't have time to answer. In one quick motion, Kat pulled a pin out of her hair and stabbed it into the side of his neck. His eyes briefly widened in surprise before he crumpled to the floor. Derek relieved him of his gun, stepped in front of Kat, and barked, "Door, Reece."

The door slid open. Another two armed guards stood inside the room. Before they had time to react, Derek fired, and blood and brain matter splattered the walls behind them.

The third occupant in the room was handcuffed to a metal chair. In a panic, he attempted to stand, struggling futilely against the restraints. His dark hair clung to his face with sweat, but otherwise he looked unharmed. *Good*, Derek thought. The Raasvan hadn't questioned him yet.

Derek stepped over the bodies, careful to avoid the spreading pool of blood, and squatted in front of Sorin. Behind him, Kat dragged the third body into the room and, with an unceremonious thump, deposited it next to the others.

Sorin swallowed hard while Derek just stared at him. Finally, Derek said, "They will torture you until you tell them everything you know about Almagest. And then they will kill you." Derek knew by Sorin's expression that he had already worked this out for himself. "I can guarantee your life," he offered. That was all he was willing to promise.

Sorin gave a small nod, so Derek continued, "You will do exactly what I tell you. Otherwise, I'll kill you myself to protect that information." Sorin nodded again.

"Alright, let's get him out of here." Kat searched one of the bodies to find the key code for Sorin's restraints while Derek collected the extra weapons.

"Reece, how's it look out there?" Derek asked.

"Still quiet."

"We won't have long though. Sean, status update," Derek asked, peering into the hallway and motioning for Kat to follow.

"The girl is on next," Sean answered.

"As soon as a winning bid's announced, go."

"Copy that," Sean affirmed.

"Reece, get eyes on her and talk to Sean. We're heading toward the south exit." Derek handed one of the small guns to Kat; they tucked the weapons into the backs of their pants. Sorin stumbled between them. "Just keep walking," Derek coaxed.

The corridors remained relatively empty until they were back to the walkway outside the viewing suites. Here there was more activity as bidding came to a close and buyers went to claim their merchandise.

"We're heading to the exchange," Sean said into the com.

"Oh, shit," Reece broke in. "Commander, facial recognition just identified Taran Sher. He won the bidding for the girl."

Derek caught Kat's eye, his mind already considering what that piece of information might mean. Taran Sher had been working for the Drokarans last on Tharsis. Reece gave Sean a physical description of Sher and in a few moments Sean said, "I see them. This area is well protected by Raasvan security. I can't get close. We'll try to discreetly follow them out."

"Commander." Reece's voice was sounding more panicked by the second. "The Raasvan know something's wrong. I'm monitoring their communications. They just found the dead security guards in Sorin's cell."

Kat and Derek picked up their pace. Derek had a firm grip on Sorin's arm and was practically dragging him along. A crowd had formed at the exit and two Raasvan were eyeing every person as they made their way out of the building.

"We have a problem, Reece," Derek said into the com. "How close can our guys get to this building? Because I think we're going to have to shoot our way out and run."

The Elistan driver broke into the conversation. "We're about a hundred yards away. I'm sending Anton and Costin out to provide cover fire, but you have to move. They're going to lock this place down once the shooting starts."

"Got it," Derek answered.

They were almost to the door. Sorin kept his eyes on his feet while Derek and Kat carefully removed their stolen weapons and held them low and close. Derek thought briefly that they just might walk out of the building, but then he saw one of the guards scan their faces and look back and forth at a small tablet in his hands. The guard froze when he looked at Sorin, and turned to his partner.

Before he could get a word out, Derek shot him in the chest, the body jerking violently backward. Almost instantaneously, Kat took out the other guard. Around them people began to scream.

As Derek started to run, hauling Sorin out with him, he shouted to the crowd, "Get on the ground! Stay down!"

They were about halfway to the vehicle when they heard weapons fire behind them. Anton and Costin fired back, providing enough cover for Derek, Kat, and Sorin to dive into the open doors of the vehicle. The two Elistans quickly followed, and they sped away.

"Sean, Drew, status," Derek shouted into the com, adrenaline still coursing through his body.

"We're almost out of the building. They're increasing security, but I think we can get out quietly."

"Good. Get yourselves somewhere safe."

"I still have eyes on the girl," Sean said, a question in his voice.

"You're unarmed and outnumbered, and we can't help you. Get out," Derek ordered.

"Roger that," Sean answered.

"Damn it," Derek said, slamming his fist into the side of the door.

CHAPTER 5

Derek had Sorin cuffed to a metal chair in an interrogation room on *Horizon*'s lower deck. It didn't escape either of them that his circumstances hadn't changed much.

"I followed directions," Sorin complained when Derek entered the room.

"I promised to keep you alive. You're still breathing," Derek growled.

Sorin clamped his jaw shut.

Derek sat in a chair opposite Sorin and leaned forward, glaring. "I want to know what's happening on Almagest."

Sorin stared back and remained silent.

"You will talk to me, and I won't kill you when I'm finished, but you'll wish I had," Derek threatened in a voice so low it was nearly inaudible.

Sorin blinked and swallowed hard but still didn't speak.

Derek sat back, altering tactics. "Human trafficking. No crime carries a harsher penalty. We've got all the evidence we need." He paused to let his words sink in and then continued, "But your cooperation may entice the sentencing tribunal to be more lenient."

He waited. Finally, Sorin exhaled loudly and looked down at his feet. "What do you want to know?"

Derek ignored the nagging voice in his head that wished this hadn't been so easy.

"Is Marcus, the general, still in power?"

"Yes."

"What's your business arrangement?"

"I broker the ore from his planet in return for weapons and advanced tech, mostly vehicle design specs and energy concepts. I have exclusivity."

Derek stood and began pacing, "What's the political climate? There was a resistance movement. What's happening with that?"

Sorin raised his eyebrows at the line of questioning but answered, "They staged some kind of uprising or whatever. A splinter group escaped and is harassing the military. Marcus downplayed their effectiveness, but I think he's nervous about them. He obviously didn't share much with me, but I was there when one of their bunkers was attacked and it was a pretty violent exchange." Sorin shrugged. "I never stayed on the planet for very long."

Derek nodded. Then he stopped pacing and stood in front of Sorin. "And the girl?"

Sorin didn't meet Derek's gaze. "Marcus wasn't happy with how much he was getting for his metal. Some of it was valuable, but overall it just wasn't as profitable as he'd hoped." Sorin shook his head and continued, "He gave me a little demo of the girl's skill and asked if I knew anyone who'd be willing to pay for it."

Before leaving the room, Derek hovered over Sorin and leaned down to whisper in his ear, "If it was up to me, you'd be out the fucking airlock."

Kat waited for Derek when he emerged from the interrogation. He suspected that the grim expression on her face matched his own.

"You heard everything?" he asked.

"Yeah."

He leaned against the wall and rubbed his eyes. "I hope he rots in prison for the rest of his miserable life."

"That seems too good for him."

Derek nodded his agreement.

"Come on. When was the last time you ate something?" she asked.

He honestly couldn't remember. "Probably the same time you did."

They walked silently to the mess hall. After they'd loaded their trays with food and sat in a quiet corner, Derek said, "We're turning him over to Alliance Command tomorrow. And Donovan will update them on Almagest's status."

Kat just nodded. She picked at the food on her tray but didn't really make an effort to eat it. "I can't stop thinking about that little girl," she finally admitted, sitting back and closing her eyes.

"Me neither," Derek said, pushing his own food around the plate. "Sean said he would keep looking."

"I believe he will," Kat said.

Derek nodded his agreement.

"He had to leave anyway. We blew his cover. He knew it wouldn't take the Raasvan long to connect him with us," she said, shaking her head.

"I hope it was worth it," Derek said. He held on to a small glimmer of hope that Sean could track down the Novali girl, but the fact that Taran Sher now had her made it unlikely.

As if reading his thoughts, Kat asked, "Do you think Sher is still working with the Drokarans?"

"My gut says yes." He exhaled and aggressively stabbed a

vegetable with his fork.

"That must be how Karan escaped custody," Kat speculated, referring to the Drokaran agent their team had captured and interrogated on Tharsis. "And if Sher's still working with him, then it's really the Drokarans who have the girl."

This same horrible thought had been plaguing Derek since Reece first identified Sher at the auction.

Kat shook her head. "I don't even want to imagine what they're doing to her."

"And no doubt Karan will make the connection between this girl and Caeli, and the Drokarans will want to find out where they come from," Derek added.

"The Alliance has to do something," Kat said, tossing a piece of bread back on her plate in frustration.

"You'd think," Derek answered, unconvinced.

***

Donovan, Derek, and the other senior officers waited in full dress uniform on *Horizon*'s flight deck. The Admiral's shuttle had just landed. The moment his feet touched the ground, everyone snapped to attention.

"Permission to come aboard, captain," Admiral Reyes requested.

"It would be an honor, sir," Donovan answered. "At ease," he said to his officers and deck crew as he ushered the Admiral out of the landing bay and to his private meeting room. Derek followed.

Horizon was docked at a space station in the Cor Leonis system, base of operations for the entire Inter-Planetary Alliance, both the civil and military branches. As the seat of the Inter-Allied government, it was the most well protected system in the galaxy.

Sorin had been turned over to the tribunal that morning, and *Horizon* was spending a few days in dry dock to resupply and undergo minor repairs. The crew was offered a brief but much appreciated shore leave.

Shortly after Captain Donovan updated the Alliance's highest-ranking intelligence officer on the latest mission details, he was informed that Admiral Reyes would be paying *Horizon* a personal visit. They'd been told their guest was here to commend the crew for their exemplary performance, both recently on Elista and last year on Tharsis, but Derek suspected it was something else.

The three sat in plush chairs in Donovan's private study. "Captain, I really do want to thank you and your outstanding crew for their work on behalf of the Alliance. Before I leave the ship and they all disperse, I'd like an opportunity to address them."

"Of course, sir. I'll arrange it," Donovan promised.

Reyes turned to Derek. "Commander, our science team is attempting to develop a scanner that will penetrate the stealth shielding technology you acquired. If we're able to deploy it quickly, we'll finally be one step ahead of Drokarans."

"That's excellent, sir," Derek said.

"It is. And we have you to thank. I also read the report from Tharsis. While I understand that it takes a team to carry out a mission, it takes a true leader to plan and execute an operation like the one on Tharsis. Your work has not gone unnoticed."

Uncomfortable, Derek shifted in his seat and then followed the Admiral's eyes to Donovan's expensive collection of liquor at a small bar in the corner.

The captain gestured to the bar. "A drink, sir?"

"I won't refuse."

Derek stood and poured. He handed a tumbler to the Admiral and then Captain Donovan before taking one for himself. They held their glasses up and Reyes offered a toast. "To *Horizon* and her fine crew."

Donovan added, "To staying one step ahead of disaster."

They drank in silence for a few moments until Reyes cleared his throat. "I'm sure you know I have another reason for being here today."

"I suspected as much," Donovan answered, and Derek held his breath.

Reyes placed his cup on the table beside his chair. "The Minister was briefed regarding the situation on Almagest. Commander, you made the right call removing Dr. Crys from that planet. You most likely saved her from an awful fate."

"I wouldn't be alive if not for her skill. It was Caeli who saved me," he said quietly.

"She seems like a remarkable woman," the Admiral said, giving Derek an appraising look. He paused and then continued, "I'm sure you understand that our policy of non-interference cannot be violated. Almagest is a non-member world, with an unstable government, experiencing civil turmoil. Allied assistance is not permitted."

The Admiral glanced at Derek, but directed his next comment to Donovan. "However, the Minister is appalled at the atrocities that have been committed on this world, and at the ongoing criminal activity, namely human trafficking. She is further concerned that Almagest will eventually attract Drokaran attention. So, while the Alliance cannot authorize or sanction any kind of official interference, an *ideal* outcome would be for the resistance movement on Almagest to prevail, and for a legitimate government to be established that could petition the Alliance for membership." He was silent for a moment, then picked up his drink again. "Is my meaning clear?"

Donovan nodded. "Perfectly, sir."

***

A few hours later, Derek sat alone on the recreation deck, drinking a kind of tea Caeli had concocted for them before she left. Donovan found him there and sat down.

"Why don't you take a day off and go down to Cor Leon?"

Derek shook his head. "I'll just get shitfaced drunk, and that wouldn't be a very good idea right now."

Donovan chuckled.

"Want some?" Derek offered. When Donovan nodded, Derek poured another cup. "Caeli made something like this for us when we were on Almagest. She tried to replicate it with the stuff we have here. Not quite the same, but close," he said, taking another sip.

Donovan didn't speak.

"The Amathi were brutal . . ." Derek stopped, swallowing hard. "If they get their hands on her again, they will do worse than kill her." Cradling the warm cup in his hands, he stared into the contents. "I don't want to take her back there." But even as he said the words, he knew he'd made her a promise, and she'd never forgive him if he broke it.

Donovan put a hand on Derek's shoulder. "It's her fight, Derek. More than it is any of ours. She has a right to it."

CAELI

CHAPTER 6

She knew he was there even in her sleep. In Caeli's dream, a hand brushed the hair from her forehead and traced a finger across her cheek.

And then it wasn't a dream. Derek's mouth was on hers, kissing her deeply. She reached up to run her hand over the straining muscles in his back and drew him closer, her heart racing. His hips pressed into hers, and she moved under him, the heat between them already building as her body responded to his. Nuzzling her face into the side of his neck, she tasted his salty skin and inhaled his familiar, male scent.

When he pulled away and took a shaking breath, his dark blue eyes searched her face as if he needed to be sure she was real. Desire rippled off him in waves. But just beneath it she sensed dread. The last fog of sleep cleared away and she opened her mouth to speak.

"Later," he said. She held his gaze for a moment and then nodded.

A slow grin spread across his face, and his eyes wandered from her face to her chest. "Where was I?"

She laughed and put her hand on the back of his neck,

pulling him down for another kiss. "You were right here."

When she touched her mind to his, she felt him exhale sharply. With their thoughts tangled, she could no longer distinguish her frenzied desire from his. The sudden need to have him was so powerful she practically tore his shirt trying to get it off him.

He pulled away briefly to unfasten his belt buckle and kick off his pants. When he climbed back onto the bed, he hovered over her. His gaze locked onto hers and then he was inside her. She heard her own cries echo in his mind, but just as the intensity began to build again, he rolled onto his back and pulled her on top of him.

"I want to see your face," he said, his voice low and hoarse.

The early morning sunshine filtered into the bedroom, along with a gentle summer breeze. Caeli always slept with the windows wide open, the need to smell fresh air an urge she couldn't ignore. In the soft light, a sheen of sweat glistened off Derek's broad chest and she ran her fingers lightly across the sprinkling of dark hair. He groaned and put his hands on her waist, rocking her hips rhythmically.

Soon she was overwhelmed by sensation, her pleasure bordering on desperation. When release finally came, she threw her head back and cried out, then collapsed into his arms.

Later, when she found her voice again, she whispered, "You're really here."

He tightened his arms around her.

"But you shouldn't be," she said, leaning up on an elbow. Derek stared at the ceiling, his face blank. Caeli's chest constricted and she began to shiver under the warm blanket that covered them.

When he told her, his tone was flat and emotionless, but his agitated thoughts competed with his words. *I couldn't save that little girl. I wanted to kill Sorin. Please don't come with us.*

By the time he'd finished speaking, she was shaking violently. She was going home. The words repeated in her mind. She was going home, and she was terrified.

***

Derek's mother, Miriam, smiled when they wandered into the kitchen later that morning. Caeli felt stunned, as if the world around her had somehow changed overnight. She'd been lulled into a sense of normalcy. But now, as she sat down to breakfast, she barely tasted the food.

"How long will you be here?" Miriam asked her son.

"Three days," he answered, catching his mother's eye. "And when I leave, Caeli will be coming."

Miriam nodded slowly. She knew some of Caeli's history. Not as much as Derek's father did, but enough to know that the story they all told about where Caeli came from and how she'd met Derek was a fabrication. Now, Miriam simply placed her hand on top of Caeli's and gave it a squeeze.

"Why don't I invite everyone for dinner tomorrow night so you can have some quiet time together first?"

"Thanks, Mom," Derek answered.

"Dad will get here as soon as he can. Probably later this afternoon," she continued. Derek nodded. He asked about his nieces and nephews and they began chatting animatedly. Derek looked like his mother. He had her thick, dark hair and piercing blue eyes, and when Caeli watched them together a lump formed in her throat.

She loved this family. Sometimes she missed her own so

fiercely that the pain was sharp and physical. But these people had welcomed her and given her a home. She'd had time to heal with them.

Derek caught her brushing a tear away before it fell, and his expression turned somber.

"I think Caeli and I will take a walk," he said, looking back at his mother and finishing a last bite.

"That sounds lovely," Miriam answered.

She shooed them away when they began clearing dishes, and they gratefully stepped outside.

"This must have been a beautiful place to grow up," Caeli said as they walked down a path through the woods holding hands.

"Plenty of room to get into trouble," he answered.

The forest and meadow surrounding the house had become even more familiar to Caeli than her campsite on Almagest. She'd spent countless hours hiking over the hills and sitting by the small, bubbling stream.

She stopped to pluck a blossom, and when she inhaled its sweetness, her eyes filled. "This one smells like home." Absently, she ran her fingers over the smooth yellow petals. "Lia used to make us flower crowns when we were little."

Caeli's childhood friend Lia, by some miracle, had also survived the genocide in Novalis. Once they'd relocated to Alamath, Caeli had joined the resistance and Lia had fallen in love.

"Her baby will be almost a year old. I missed his birth," Caeli said.

Derek led Caeli to a shady patch under an evergreen. He sat and pulled her down next to him. "Lia knows you would have been there if you could," he said.

Caeli nodded.

"What's happening to them?" she asked, her voice an anguished whisper.

She didn't expect an answer. Derek pulled her close and they clung to each other.

***

The following evening the house filled with noise as soon as Derek's siblings arrived with their families. The younger children threw themselves at Derek, tumbling over each other to reach him.

Sitting on a plush sofa in the family room with her legs tucked under her, Caeli listened to the laughter in the room. Derek sat down beside her and handed her a drink. She smiled but had to quickly hand it back when Derek's five-year-old nephew, Will, scrambled onto her lap.

He smelled of grass and dirt and little-boy sweat. When she touched his soft, curling hair, another memory from home washed over her. This time it was Nina's children who filled her thoughts. She'd loved to sing to them in the quiet of the evening, before bedtime, while Nina finished cleaning the dinner dishes.

After the attack on Novalis, Nina had opened her home to Caeli and cared for her when she was too traumatized to care for herself. But months later, to protect the resistance, Caeli had had to leave Nina and the children in the middle of the night, without so much as a goodbye.

But maybe now she would have the chance to explain, to tell Nina the truth, and to thank her for saving her life. Maybe she would get to hold Lia's baby too.

A sharp tug pulled Caeli back to the present. Will twisted a strand of her hair around one finger while he sucked the thumb on his other hand.

"Auntie Caeli is magic," he said, looking pointedly at Derek.

Derek leaned in. "I thought she might be."

Caeli smiled and shook her head. Will continued, "She fixed me when I fell down and hurt my arm."

"She's good at that, isn't she?" Derek nodded. "She fixed me once, too."

"What broke on you?" Will asked, wide-eyed.

"Everything," Derek mumbled under his breath, but then answered, "My leg."

The little boy nodded, satisfied.

A few minutes later he asked, "Why do you have to leave, Auntie Caeli?"

Caeli swallowed the lump in her throat. Realizing she had the attention of more than just Will, she answered, "I have the chance to go home for a while."

"You're going to come back, right?" he asked.

"I want to with all my heart," she said.

Derek put his arm around them both, and Caeli felt his sudden fierce longing for the life they didn't have.

Later, when everyone was gone, Derek found her alone in the bathroom. She was on the floor against the wall with her arms wrapped around her knees.

"Hey," he said, kneeling in front of her.

Her heart raced. The darkness felt like it was closing in around her. "Derek," she said, her voice barely audible, "I'm so scared."

"I know," he said, reaching for her.

"But I have to do this," she said, searching his eyes.

"I know that too." He brushed a lock of hair out of her eyes and touched his forehead to hers.

CHAPTER 7

From her seat next to Derek's in the cockpit, Caeli watched *Horizon* grow larger as they approached the intimidating ship. The triangular shape of the bow tapered into a sloping curve at the nose. Light glittered from the cabin window, and when it seemed they were impossibly close to the ship's hull, the launch bay door slid open. She hadn't realized she was holding her breath until Derek smoothly set the small shuttle down on the flight deck and she exhaled loudly.

As he powered down the ship, her stomach leaped in excitement. Saying goodbye to Derek's family had been awful, but now that she was back on *Horizon*, there were people she couldn't wait to see.

The fear that gripped her whenever she thought about returning to Almagest abated bit by bit the closer she got to *Horizon*. She wouldn't be facing this alone, and knowing that made all the difference.

Kat's wide smile was the first thing she saw when the shuttle door opened. Caeli only hesitated for a moment and then threw her arms around the taller woman. Her embrace was eagerly returned. Drew stood silently next to Kat, but when Caeli turned to him, he pulled her into another enthusiastic hug.

"Nice to see you too," Kat said and winked at Derek.

After she settled her few belongings into Derek's cabin, she wandered to the medical bay. Healing was the only consistent thing in her life, and the infirmary called to her like a homing beacon. She felt centered there, competent, at ease.

Now, standing in *Horizon*'s sickbay, it felt as if no time had passed.

"Caeli!" Dr. Gates drew her into a fierce embrace. "It's so good to see you."

She couldn't help but smile back at the older man's warmth. Last year, he'd allowed her to work with him side by side when she'd been onboard. "I've missed you," she said.

"Tell me all about your work on Erithos," he said, inviting her to sit.

They talked for a while, catching up and sharing interesting cases. When Gates turned the discussion toward the Drokarans, Caeli listened with a mixture of curiosity and anxiety.

"I've made progress working on the DNA samples we acquired," he said.

"I'd like to see that data," she said.

They moved to his workstation and Gates pulled up a file containing numerous reports. When he tapped one open, a three-dimensional image of a brain hovered over the desktop. "Look here, you can see some very subtle structural changes," he said. Caeli leaned forward, intrigued.

On Tharsis, when Caeli questioned the Drokaran agent, Daksha Karan, it was like nothing she'd ever experienced. His mind trapped her consciousness, pulling her into a vortex of numbing isolation. She'd had to fight to find his thoughts, and to find her way back to herself. When she'd recovered from the harrowing interrogation, she'd tried to describe the experience to Derek, but her words were inadequate. The *otherness* of

Karan's mind defied explanation. And there was something else. Something she couldn't put her finger on.

Shivering at the memory, Caeli was anxious to see if Gates' findings pointed toward any kind of biological explanation.

"The tissue samples we have also show enhanced muscle structure, and an increase in the blood cells' oxygen carrying capacity. But there's evidence of cellular degradation happening as well. Here, look at these," he said, accessing more files.

"That supports our theory," Caeli said, looking up from the reports.

Gates nodded. When Derek's team had raided the Drokaran hideout, they'd recovered a supply of therapeutic drugs from the agent's personal affects. From the drugs and biological evidence, a theory began to emerge that the Drokarans' sudden aggression was more than just a grab at territory and resources, but rather an attempt to save themselves from extinction. Their combination of desperation and ruthlessness made them a fearsome enemy.

Caeli immersed herself in Gates' research, and hours slipped by before Derek finally came to find her.

"Hey. Did you two catch up?" Derek asked.

"We did."

"I think he really missed you. No one else enjoys his models and reports quite so much," Derek teased.

Caeli laughed out loud, and then said more soberly, "He showed me his research on the Drokarans."

"Is he making progress?" Derek asked.

"Definitely. The changes to the basal ganglia are what interest me most," she said, and began to chat animatedly. When she glanced at Derek, she could tell by his glazed expression that he had no idea what most of the neurological terms meant, but he didn't interrupt her rambling.

They rounded a corner and Caeli realized she hadn't been paying attention to where they were going. She was mildly surprised when they stopped at a meeting room and Derek touched the sensor panel to open the door. Several people were seated around a table.

"Time to start planning our mission," Derek said, responding to her perplexed look.

***

"What are you thinking about?" Derek asked.

Caeli turned to face him in the small bunk. Even in the dim light she could see lines of worry wrinkling his forehead. Sighing, she put her head on his shoulder and relaxed into his warmth. "I feel responsible for them," she answered.

"Who?" he asked, running his hand down her arm.

"Your team," she answered. "This is my fight, not theirs. It's *my* home."

"It isn't just your fight anymore," he countered gently. "The Alliance may not officially support this mission, but it has to happen. The Drokarans can't gain any more territory." He paused. "And it's the right thing to do."

Caeli nodded reluctantly.

"Everyone in the squadron volunteered," he added. "They all *wanted* to go. I had to choose a team."

She was moved, but not surprised. Still, she fought with the illogical notion that if she hadn't come back to *Horizon* with Derek last year, all these people wouldn't be forced into harm's way. But if she hadn't, then her world could possibly be in even more danger.

Her futile thoughts circled until Derek finally pushed up

onto his elbow and said, "Stop. You are not responsible for this. None of it is your fault. But if we don't act now, while we can, we will be at least partly responsible for what happens next."

She had no answer to give; only the realization that what she understood logically didn't match up with her feelings. Staring at the ceiling, she tried to pull her mind out of its downward spiral.

"This isn't the first time Almagest has had a civil conflict," she said, tucking the blanket around herself and rolling onto her side.

"You found something?" he asked, raising his eyebrows.

Before Derek had left Caeli on Erithos, he'd done some digging about Almagest in the archives. He knew she was desperate to recover her people's history, and his research had given her a place to start.

"Almagest was settled by the first wave of colonists. Initially, all the colonies reported back to Erithos. If you look at a star chart from that era, you'll actually see Almagest noted. But those records are so far outdated no one uses them anymore," she said.

"And by the time the Alliance was established, Almagest had long since gone dark and no one noticed it was missing," Derek said.

Caeli nodded. "Probably because there was so much conflict back then. Most of the early colonies struggled, on their own and with each other. Record keeping and reporting just stopped being a priority."

"Did you learn anything about the war itself?"

"Not too much. Only that it was a civil war, not an outside attack. There isn't mention of Almagest anywhere in the database after the initial report that an internal conflict had escalated." She paused and turned to Derek. "But this is a piece of the puzzle. For generations, we suspected there were other worlds out there, and now we at least know where we come from. That's something." She leaned in and kissed him. "Thank you."

"Glad I could help," he said.

PART 2 - ALMAGEST

Jed looked around the large, ornate office. He scanned the portraits of his predecessors, dispersed artistically around the room. His image would only be the tenth to grace these walls. Almagest was a young colony, the climate in the region volatile, and the work ahead of him daunting. But he'd wanted this job badly, practically tasted it when he was the regional governor. And now the weight of responsibility squeezed his chest like a vice, sometimes rendering him breathless.

He sat down heavily on the oversized chair. The communication with Kev Sarovan had been strained at best. He knew he needed this agreement nailed down, but damn, he didn't trust the Nysari. Not even a little. Squeezing his eyes shut, he leaned back and considered his options. Without this trade deal, he'd lose a large revenue stream and, more importantly, the Nysari presence in the system. Dealing with them cost much more than he wanted to pay, but they provided a measure of protection for his world. Protection that he couldn't guarantee for his people yet.

Sighing, he tapped a panel on his desk and waited. He knew they'd have to take this deal, and he'd probably pissed off Sarovan with his righteous indignation about the terms. He felt a twinge of guilt passing this mess off to Misha, but she'd get it done. Seconds later, a woman appeared on the screen, still speaking to someone off to her left. When she turned, her tight smile didn't reach her eyes. "Sir?" she asked.

"Misha, you need to handle the Nysari. Sarovan's expecting you tomorrow. Get the deal done," he ordered.

"Yes, sir," she answered with a brisk nod.

Some of his top advisors thought Misha was ruthless. He thought so too, but he needed her ruthlessness and her brilliance. And most importantly, he needed her company to continue producing the ships and hardware that were slowly building Almagest's air defense. When the promised fleet was online, he could tell the Nysari to fuck off. And blow them out of the system if necessary. But they weren't there yet.

5523.7.3
ABOARD THE BATTLE CRUISER ZAFER
GENERAL'S PRIVATE QUARTERS

"A toast to our agreement," Sarovan said, holding his glass aloft and smiling.

Misha merely tilted her head and tossed back the burning liquid. She agreed with Jeb's opinion of Sarovan. Being in his physical presence made her skin crawl, but she'd negotiated the deal. Neither side was particularly happy with it, but both needed something from the other, and that made it nearly impossible for either to walk away.

She held his gaze for a long moment and finally spoke. "I wonder if you and I might discuss something else?"

Sarovan's thick eyebrows rose with interest. He motioned with his hand for her to continue.

"I have need of a separate income stream, an untraceable stream, and I think you may be willing to provide it."

"Well, now I'm intrigued. Do tell."

Sarovan's smile was more like a leer, and Misha had to work to keep her face from wrinkling with disgust.

"What I'm working on isn't your concern. What I'm offering is." She reached into her bag and removed a small vial of swirling liquid. "I promise you've never experienced anything like this before."

"I'm not going to drop dead, am I?" Sarovan asked. He tapped his fingers against his leg and squinted at her.

"I wouldn't do that to you, Sarovan."

"You most certainly would." He paused before speaking again. "But you still need me."

He smiled wickedly and held the vial to his carotid, pushing the end lightly against his skin. The dispenser released the drug, and the small rush of liquid entered his bloodstream.

Misha knew the moment he first felt it. His eyes widened and he gasped.

"This little side deal will be our secret," Misha whispered, leaning over him.

"Of course," Sarovan assured her, his head lolling back onto the cushioned chair. He sighed and smiled. "Misha, you've outdone yourself."

Finally, she smiled back. He'd definitely make the deal.

5529.7.9
PRIVATE COMMUNICATION
FROM: UNDERSECRETARY MARISHKA TOROV
TO: SECRETARY GENERAL JED WORTHINGTON
RE: NEGOTIATIONS
FILE ENCRYPTED

Jed,

Signed and delivered. I've uploaded the official document to the General Archive File.

Key points:

He wanted an accelerated delivery scheduled on the titanium. We charged him accordingly.

Three cruisers will remain in the system until this agreement expires. They are authorized to use deadly force to defend our airspace.

See you tomorrow.

Misha

CAELI

CHAPTER 8

"Caeli," Tree called from the cockpit, stirring her from a nap on Derek's shoulder. "You'll want to see this, I think."

Lieutenant Matt Kline, otherwise known as Tree due to his substantial physique, smiled at Caeli and pointed out the cockpit window. Caeli yawned and made her way forward, with Derek following. As soon as she caught sight of the view, she froze. Derek put his hand on her shoulder and Kat turned toward her from the pilot's chair.

"Beautiful from out here, right?"

"It really is," Caeli agreed, gazing at her planet. The landmasses were barely visible; greyish-green shadows blended into sparkling blue oceans. White clouds floated in sharp relief, feathering across most of the northern hemisphere. "You'd never know what was happening," she murmured, and Derek gave her a gentle squeeze.

"Alright kids," Kat said, turning her attention back to the ship. "Off you go. We are ten minutes from high orbital insertion and I'm about to engage stealth mode."

They returned to their seats and pulled the harness straps over their heads. Derek nudged a dozing Drew who, bleary-eyed, fastened himself in.

"Chase, you could fall asleep in the middle of a battlefield," Alaric teased.

"Even when he's awake, you have to take a pulse to make sure he's alive," Kade added, tossing a tiny chunk of uneaten energy bar at Drew's head.

Drew mouthed an obscenity back at them with a lazy grin.

Caeli hadn't known Kai Alaric or Kieran Kade very well before this mission, but as they'd trained and planned together over the last several weeks, she'd come to appreciate their good-natured banter and easy humor.

A quarter-hour later, Kat joined them in the back of the shuttle. "We are in orbit and mapping the planet's surface," she reported.

"Good," Derek answered, unstrapping himself. He moved to an instrument panel at a small workstation and tapped the screen. A three-dimensional image of Almagest appeared hovering in front of him. "We'll orbit several times to collect detailed data. Then we can orient ourselves and update our handhelds."

The rest of the team nodded and chatted casually, but Caeli watched transfixed as mountain ranges, riverbeds, and forests began to populate the spinning globe.

"When it's finished, we'll be able to zoom in on a section almost as close as if we're standing there," Derek said, smiling at her wide-eyed expression. When she didn't move, he added, "But it's going to take a few hours."

Finally, she nodded and sat down. Time seemed to crawl by and she became uncharacteristically edgy. With no real idea of what was happening on Almagest, worry nagged at her, and although she sat physically still, her thoughts darted about. Imagined scenarios, interspersed with her own real memories, futilely played themselves out to deadly conclusions in her mind, until Derek put a hand on hers and said, "One breath at a time."

She closed her eyes. They were her own words, a mantra she'd used to keep herself sane when her life had disintegrated. Derek understood, and he'd reminded her of them on more than one occasion. The last time, her consciousness had been merged with a lethal, arms-dealing terrorist, and the violence of his thoughts had almost pushed her to the breaking point. Derek had been there to pull her back from the darkness, and he was here now, holding her gaze and offering the steadiness of his own disciplined mind. Soon her breathing and heart rate slowed to match his, and her thoughts stopped racing.

She shook her head, frustrated at her own perceived weakness. Derek leaned in and said, "You keep going. That's what matters."

***

The global mapping was complete and the team sat focused on a detailed, hundred-mile section of land surrounding Alamath.

"They're probably somewhere within this radius," Drew speculated. "If they're attacking the town, I'm thinking they can't be too far from their base of operations."

"Agreed," Derek said. "They probably have limited transportation and they need the element of surprise on their side."

"There are cave formations at the base of this mountain range," Kat added. "These are a little further out, but check out these ruins. Great cover there, too."

"Zoom in on those cave formations," Derek ordered, and Kat enhanced that section of the map. "Look at the heat signatures. I think that's their camp."

"Where should we put the ship down?" Kat asked.

"Without actual intel, I don't want to get too close. Everything is guesswork right now," Derek said.

Caeli pointed to a large rock formation adjacent to the Nama River within several miles of the caves. "This was the rendezvous point if and when we had to run," Caeli explained. "If our group was compromised and had to escape, or our leader Jon felt he had enough traction to leave intentionally and go on the offensive, we were to meet here. The plan was to monitor this checkpoint periodically. We could start here, and if no one turns up, we could cautiously approach the caves."

Derek nodded. "That sounds like a plan."

"Let's put the ship down here," Kat said, pointing to a clearing adjacent to a lush forest. "I can get her in right to the tree line."

"Okay, do it," Derek ordered, then stood and stretched. Kat headed back to the cockpit to join Tree, who'd been listening to the conversation while monitoring the ship's flight path. He caught Caeli's eye from his seat and gave her a reassuring wink.

The large man barely fit in his seat, but despite his hulking size, he was one of the gentlest people Caeli knew. For an intelligence agent working in some of the most dangerous regions of the galaxy, it was a puzzling juxtaposition, yet Caeli trusted beyond a doubt that he would do his job and have their backs. She gave him a small smile in return and buckled herself back into the seat.

Her stomach plummeted as the ship began its approach and her fingers turned white from gripping the seat so tightly, but it was also exhilarating to feel such power and speed underneath her. Twenty minutes later they were on the ground, the ship still and silent.

"Caeli, Drew, I need a quick perimeter search," Derek said, nodding his head at the two of them.

It was nearly winter in this part of her world, so she and Drew zipped into lightweight, thermal jackets. Drew checked his weapon.

"Ready?" he asked her.

"No, but let's go anyway," she said, half-serious but trying to sound lighthearted.

Drew nodded knowingly, then touched a sensor panel. A blast of cold air rushed into the cabin when the door slid open, and Caeli inhaled deeply. She looked back at Derek once more, and then stepped out of the ship and onto her planet for the first time in over a year.

Though she and Drew trod lightly, the frozen ground crunched beneath their feet. Early morning frost glittered on dead leaves and a crisp, biting wind nipped Caeli's face. The pale blue sky seemed endless, and sunbeams, delivering little warmth, danced through tree branches and skimmed the browning grasses in the field.

As promised, Kat had tucked the ship into the edge of the encroaching forest. Drew carefully made his way around it with Caeli a few steps behind. She opened her mind and stretched it as far as she was able. She felt Drew's pulsing, dynamic life energy resonate through her entire body, then each of the other team members' in turn. But further out, there was nothing.

"We're alone," she whispered to Drew, not wanting her voice to intrude upon the waking world.

He acknowledged her with a small nod and they returned to the ship.

The rest of the team was busy packing gear and dressing for the weather. Caeli put on a hat and gloves, then double-checked her backpack before securing it in place.

"Caeli will take point. She'll know if anyone's nearby, but be alert anyway," Derek ordered the team.

She and Derek had spoken earlier about the possibility that the resistance group, or even an Amathi army patrol, might be using the Novali to empathically shield themselves. Caeli was relatively certain her ability was strong enough to penetrate any shield, but the team was proceeding cautiously, just in case.

Caeli had thoroughly reviewed the map of this area, but even if she hadn't, she knew she'd be able to find the rendezvous point. All Novali children were taught to track, find food and shelter, and orient themselves anywhere in their world. She wondered bitterly if these skills would be preserved by anyone other than the Amathi army.

They kept to the perimeter of the open field in silence, the brittle grass cushioning their footsteps, until Caeli led them into the forest. She spotted a barely visible game trail and followed its winding path, knowing it would lead them to the river. Inhaling the pungent, earthy smell of decaying leaves and brushing stiff branches away from her face as she walked, Caeli's eyes filled.

Home. She was home on her beautiful, damaged world, breathing the air, feeling the sting of cold wind on her cheeks, sensing the familiar life force of the plants and animals surrounding her. The surge of emotions she'd repressed earlier came rushing to the surface. Grief and loss mixed with longing and hope. Tears spilled down her cheeks, blurring her vision, but her steps didn't falter and she didn't turn around.

***

They reached the Nama River within two hours, and Caeli stopped the group for a short break. Dropping her pack on the riverbank, she took off her gloves and knelt by the flowing stream to refill her water bottle. Derek did the same.

"About another few miles following the river due east," Caeli offered.

Derek nodded. "We can make camp there. I'm willing to wait for a day or so. Hopefully they'll come to us."

"If they're still out here," she said, worried as she sat back on her heels and wrapped her arms around her legs.

"They are. If Marcus launched some kind of large scale offensive to take them out, we would have seen evidence of it." Derek said.

She nodded. "That makes sense."

Derek stood and dusted a layer of dirt off his pants. "Let's move," he said to the group. "We can be at the rendezvous point in another few hours."

When she stopped them for a break in the early afternoon, she sat with the team in a semi-circle, rubbing her aching shoulders and barely tasting the freeze-dried energy bar that passed for lunch. Only Tree was up and pacing the perimeter, on temporary watch.

With part of her mind, she scanned the surroundings, searching for any ripple of noise, any trace of human consciousness beyond the familiar patterns of this small group. The resounding silence was both comforting and worrisome.

"This is a really beautiful planet," Kade commented, staring up at a giant tree trunk. "You must have thought you died and went to paradise," he added, nodding toward Derek and winking at Caeli.

She smiled at Kade's attempt to lighten the mood.

"The thought did cross my addled brain," Derek answered.

A quick flash of Derek's memory appeared in Caeli's mind. They were on the beach under a very similar tree and he was undressing her. She watched Derek try to suppress his laughter while she recalled the details of that encounter and blushed crimson.

He cleared his throat and stood. "Let's get going so we can make camp before the sun sets."

In a few short hours, the air, warmed slightly by the afternoon sun, began to chill again as evening approached. Caeli knew they were nearing the rendezvous point.

"How close do you want to be?" she asked Derek when they were about a quarter mile out.

"This is probably good. Can you find us a spot to make camp? I'd like to be well hidden overnight," he answered.

She nodded. "I'll go look."

An hour later a small fire blazed near a protected outcropping of rocks. While the others finished setting up camp, Caeli scoured the surrounding area for root vegetables and mushrooms. She easily found what she was looking for and, satisfied with her cache, she sat down by the fire to carve skewers. Her knife was sharp and sleek and never seemed to need sharpening. It had been a gift from Derek before he left her on Erithos, an improved version of the one she had always kept with her.

The smell of burning wood and roasting vegetables made her mouth water, and she smiled at the eager expressions worn by the team now all seated around the fire. After passing out the first round, she carried a pile of food to Kat, who'd taken first watch.

Kat smiled at her and motioned for her to sit. It was good to be with Kat again. When Caeli first came onboard *Horizon* after Derek's team had rescued them from Almagest, Kat had been suspicious, and the relationship between them had been tenuous at best. But now, besides Derek, Kat was the one person who knew Caeli's history intimately. The other team members had been briefed on the politics between the Amathi and Novali; they knew their mission details, and they knew the key players in the drama unfolding on Caeli's world, but they didn't understand the magnitude of Caeli's personal losses, or the extent of what she'd endured after her home had been destroyed.

"How are you doing?" Kat asked between mouthfuls.

Caeli considered the question. "I feel disoriented," she admitted. "It's like I never left, and like I've been gone for a lifetime."

"I feel like that every time I go home too. Only these guys really understand my life," Kat answered, gesturing at the team, who were talking quietly around the campfire. "When I see my family, they just don't get what it's like out here. That's good. That's what I want, for them to be protected from it, but it still feels strange to go home." She shrugged. "It's not quite the same thing, but I understand what you mean about feeling disoriented."

Caeli nodded and continued. "I'm afraid too, afraid of what's been happening since I've been gone." She paused for a moment, and then whispered, "And I feel guilty for not being here."

Kat put her hand on Caeli's knee. "You made the best decision you could to keep your friends safe, and to protect the resistance movement."

"I know, but I left them. What if the right decision was to go back and fight? What if . . ."

Kat cut her off. "You will never know the answer to that question. It's pointless to even ask it. But one thing you *do* know is that we're with you now."

"And what if something happens to one of you?" Caeli turned and looked Kat in the eye.

"What if it does?" she countered. "This is our job. None of us want to die, of course, but we're all going to someday."

"Kat," Caeli said, frustrated. "This isn't your fight. Any of you."

"I'm not trying to be callous, but it's our *job*. And we all volunteered to do it."

"I know," Caeli whispered. "I just don't want to lose anyone else."

Kat grinned. "I'm pretty hard to kill, don't worry."

"You better be," Caeli said, and Kat squeezed her hand.

CHAPTER 9

Caeli was awake well before dawn, just as the first hint of pink stained the sky. Her breath puffed in steamy clouds, and she emerged reluctantly from the warmth of the sleeping bag. Her movement woke Derek, who sat up, instantly alert.

"I'm just going to the bathroom," she whispered.

He stretched and nodded, pulling the sleeping bag up around his neck.

She waved to Drew, who had the morning watch, and rounded the backside of the rock formation, temporarily out of sight. A few moments later, she wandered down to the river's edge. After escaping from Marcus's military prison a year ago, she'd made camp along a river similar to this one. Every morning she'd trek to the riverbank to wash and to clear her mind. The rushing water always soothed and comforted her, even when the goal of each day had only been survival.

She knelt on the soft dirt, cupped the frigid water in her hands, and splashed it on her face. The cold shocked her fully awake and she shivered when droplets trickled under her collar and down her neck. Closing her eyes, she stretched her mind out as far as she could, fully expecting that the only life she'd sense would be that of the *Horizon* team.

But there were others. Caeli leapt to her feet and stood still, listening. Their minds fluttered against hers, an indecipherable hum, distant and faint. She rushed back to the camp, treading effortlessly across the hard ground.

"How far?" Derek asked, quickly up and packing his gear.

"Still a few miles away," she answered, her heart thudding in her chest.

He nodded, finished stowing his sleeping bag, and roused the rest of the team.

"We'll break camp and head toward them. Assume they're hostile unless Caeli tells us otherwise," he ordered the team.

Everyone had weapons ready when they left the shelter of the site.

As Caeli trudged forward, listening, one familiar mind resolved above the background noise. "Finn," she whispered, turning to Derek. "It's Finn."

Caeli had to resist the urge to rush forward. Finn was an Amathi soldier turned resistance fighter who had been a close friend. Caeli trusted him with her life, but when she'd fled Alamath, she'd let him think she was dead. The weight of that regret gave her pause.

Derek stopped the group. "Okay, most likely these are friendlies," he explained. "But it's possible he could still be with the Amathi army. Either way we're certainly going to worry them. Caeli, you and I will take point. Everyone else, fall back, out of sight, but within range of us. We'll determine for sure who they are, initiate contact if these are the good guys, or stay hidden and retreat if they aren't. We will not engage unless forced. Everyone clear?"

"Yes, sir," came the unified response.

"Okay, coms on, no chatter," he added.

Caeli took the lead again, with Derek at her heels. The others melted into the woods behind them. She could still feel them nearby even when she couldn't see them at all.

As she and Derek got closer to Finn, Caeli repeated over and over in her mind, "Finn, it's Caeli," and threw the thought at him. She could feel his response, confusion, and doubt transforming into wonder, and finally hope.

"Derek, maybe you should wait here. Let me talk to them first," Caeli suggested.

He frowned and shook his head, but she pressed. "It's okay. He would try to warn me if it wasn't."

Derek hesitated and finally acquiesced. "I'll be right here."

"I know," she said, holding his gaze. Then she turned and continued on.

When Finn's group was crossing a small, open clearing within her sight, Caeli cautiously stepped out from behind the brush. He was close enough already that she could see him, young and handsome, with familiar hazel eyes. But his expression was haunted and his face gaunt. He had a scruffy beard and his hair was long and unkempt, curling out from under a winter hat.

"Caeli?" he called. "Is that really you?"

She swallowed back the lump in her throat and couldn't answer, but she ran toward him and threw her arms around him.

"I thought you were dead," he said, his voice cracking with emotion.

She shook her head, stepping back. "I have so much to tell you," she said, looking around at the faces in Finn's group, all equally as ragged as his. Some were familiar from her time spent with the resistance movement; others were strangers.

He nodded, "We have a lot to catch up on." Caeli could see Finn's face change slightly when he noticed her well-fitting gear, new and in good condition, and the lightweight, dangerous gun she had over her shoulder. He looked at her questioningly.

"I'm not alone," she said.

Feeling the suspicious eyes of the group on her, she shook her head. "They're friends," she assured them, and then she said to Finn, "Please, you have to trust me."

"I do trust you," he answered.

"I'm going to tell my group to come out. They're armed."

Finn nodded. "Stand down," he ordered, making eye contact with the three men and one woman surrounding him. They lowered their weapons but maintained stiff, suspicious postures.

"Derek," Caeli said, knowing he'd heard the entire conversation through the com. He stepped out from the cover of the trees into the small clearing. She was about to make an introduction when Derek spoke.

"Lieutenant Braden," he addressed Finn formally. "I'm Commander Derek Markham, squadron leader from the starship *Horizon* and intelligence agent for the Inter-Allied Forces. It's good to meet you." He extended his hand and Finn took it, looking stunned. Caeli gave Finn a reassuring smile and Derek called the rest of the team out into the open. They materialized from the forest, silent and deadly. Looking at them, Caeli was very pleased they were on the same side.

When the *Horizon* team stood facing Finn and the other worn-looking resistance members, Derek nodded at them and said, "We'd like to join your fight."

Finn looked at Caeli, his eyes wide. "Let's find some better cover," he suggested.

Caeli led them back to the spot where they'd just broken camp and Derek assigned Kat to keep watch from the vantage point. "Caeli's always searching for Amathi patrols, but we can't be too careful," he said to Finn, who nodded in agreement.

The group settled in a circle, some sitting on overturned stumps or boulders, others leaning against the stone outcropping at their backs.

Finn began, "I hope you understand why I'm not bringing you directly back to our hideout."

"I'd have made the same decision," Derek assured him.

Finn nodded then turned to Caeli. "You escaped from Marcus's prison. He was furious, but his search party claimed they found evidence you were dead. I got the message you sent me, but I thought maybe you really had been killed jumping off that damn cliff," he finished, shaking his head.

"I know. I'm sorry," she said.

"Don't be," Finn answered.

"Well, obviously I did survive. I was on the run for about a month. I couldn't make it through a winter, so I headed further south. Derek's ship crashed less than a mile from my camp." She paused and looked at Derek, who continued the explanation.

"My command ship, *Horizon*, heard a signal coming from this system. Our charts didn't even show a habitable planet in this region, so I was sent to investigate. A mercenary ship, which must have also been tracking the signal, fired on me. I tried to land here." He looked down and drummed his left hand against his knee. "My copilot was killed, and I would have been dead within minutes if Caeli hadn't found me."

"We thought we picked up a ship entering the atmosphere. It was about six or eight weeks after Caeli left," Finn acknowledged, as if the piece of a puzzle was falling into place. "We never found evidence of it. Marcus was disappointed, believing it must have crashed into the ocean. But he was sure if there was one ship, there'd be more."

Derek nodded. "He was right about that."

"Yes, he was," Finn answered. "We'll get back to that."

Derek nodded again. The attention of the whole group was riveted on him, so he kept talking. "My team came looking for me. By that time, Caeli had shared what was happening here and I convinced her to leave."

Caeli knew Derek was trying to keep the emotion out of his voice, but he had to pause and clear his throat before continuing. "She was conflicted, but we both knew what Marcus would do to her if he found her. And the Alliance needed to know what was happening here. Caeli could be a voice for Almagest."

"What's the Alliance?" Finn asked, leaning forward.

"When humanity became spacefaring, we colonized every habitable planet we could find. Almagest was one of those original colonies." He stopped a minute to let that fact sink in before continuing, "Early on, during the initial wave of expansion, it was a volatile time. There were conflicts over resources and territory. Newly formed governments failed and whole planets went to war. This is about the time your world went dark. Eventually, though, cooperation and civility re-emerged. The Inter-Planetary Alliance formed as a galaxy-wide body to protect and aid its member worlds. To gain membership, a planet must have a functioning infrastructure and a government that guarantees basic civil rights for its citizens. Most Alliance worlds also have their own standing military. But if they are significantly threatened, or have reached a crisis level internally, the Alliance will assist."

Finn sat back and exhaled loudly. The others looked at one another, speechless.

"You said you were with this Alliance?" Finn asked. Derek nodded. "But Almagest isn't part of that."

Caeli knew where Finn's line of questioning was leading. She knew Derek did too.

"Why are you here then?"

"That's a complicated answer," Derek said. "Caeli is here because I promised her I would take her back into the fight, if and when it looked like the resistance had made a move. And I'm here because I would never let her come back alone."

Derek ran his hands over his face and sat back on his log, blowing out a loud breath before continuing, "But I'm also here with this team to try and keep Almagest from falling into enemy hands. And by enemy, I don't mean Marcus."

Finn just raised his eyebrows and waited.

"It's still dangerous out there," Derek explained, gesturing skyward. "Some worlds are openly hostile toward the Alliance, some groups have no interest in joining us because it's more profitable not to, and one enemy in particular is directly attacking vulnerable Alliance planets. We can't afford to lose more territory to them, or to allow them to expand further."

"So, it's not in the Alliance's best interest for Almagest to fall to your enemy? This is why you're here?" Finn asked, a trace of accusation in his voice.

Derek gave Finn a steady stare. "We aren't even here officially, because you aren't a member world." He looked around at the faces staring back at him. "I know that sounds shitty. The Alliance decision makers know there was a genocide here; they know the resistance has made some kind of move; they know Marcus was working with a mercenary to trade ore, and then Novali kids, for weapons."

At that, Finn dropped his gaze. Caeli could feel anger and guilt radiate out of him, and she put a gentle hand on his arm.

Derek continued speaking. "Politics being what they are, an

official mission here would never be authorized. Almagest is vulnerable to enemies you don't even know exist. But it will never receive protection from the Alliance with Marcus in charge." He paused and then finished, "The intelligence arm of the Alliance is often asked to go off the grid to solve complicated problems."

Finn stared back at Derek, a wary understanding reflected in his expression. Once again Derek looked at everyone on Finn's team before he finished speaking. "Understand this: My team and I are volunteers, every one of us. We all signed up for *this* mission. We've all fought side by side with other soldiers defending worlds that weren't our own. Despite politics, we're here with you, and this is our fight now too, if you want us."

Finn took a long moment before answering, "We can use all the help we can get."

***

The afternoon sun provided some warmth against the chill air. Caeli tucked her hat temporarily into a pocket and kept pace with Finn, who had taken point.

"Every few days we come out here to check the rendezvous spot. We aren't very far from our camp," Finn explained as he led them through the forest. She could feel his unease, but wasn't sure of its cause, and they fell into a tense silence.

She knew Derek had discreetly moved toward the back of the formation to give her a chance to talk privately with Finn, and hopefully reassure him of their intentions. "Finn, they really are here to help us," she began softly, so that only he could hear. "They're some of the best people I've ever known."

"I believe that," he answered, glancing sideways at her.

"What is it, then?" she asked. "Tell me."

He didn't answer for a long time, but when they approached the edge of the rocky hills, at the base of the imposing Orainos mountain range, he stopped. "We're close," he said.

A chill ran up Caeli's spine and a wave of foreboding made her shiver. "Tell me, Finn."

He swallowed hard. "Jon's here. He's still leading us. And Dr. Kellan's here too. But Nina...she didn't make it," he whispered.

Caeli shook her head and backed away from him. "No. No. No," she repeated her denial.

Tears filled his eyes. "Lily's gone too."

She gripped her stomach and doubled over. Finn caught her as she pitched forward onto her knees. Derek was suddenly by her side. *It isn't possible*, she thought. *How could Nina be gone, and her beautiful baby girl with her? But of course it's possible*, she answered herself bitterly. *No one's safe. Anyone could be lost.*

Darkness hovered at her peripheral vision, and her eyes stung with unshed tears. She wanted to scream, but some shred of her conscious mind knew she shouldn't do that. Her heart thudded in her chest and she heaved silent, wracking sobs. Derek pulled her against him.

When the world around her finally came back into focus and she could breathe again, she looked up at Finn. "I'm so sorry," she whispered hoarsely. "Nina was your friend too."

He just nodded silently, his eyes on the ground.

"Who else?" Caeli asked, desperately wishing she could freeze time and never hear his answer.

"Lia," he began, and Caeli gripped Derek's hand. "She's not dead," Finn rushed to add. "But we couldn't get her out. Ben and the baby escaped with us. Lia didn't."

Lia was alive. The baby was alive. Dr. Kellan and Jon and Finn were all alive. Their names played over and over in her mind as Derek helped her back to her feet. The rest of the group had wordlessly passed them, disappearing behind a rock formation, except Kat, who stood with her brow furrowed beside Derek.

She put a hand on Caeli's arm. "I'm sorry."

Caeli shook her head. "I knew things would be bad, but Nina, Lily . . ." she whispered, and then stopped when her voice broke.

Words of comfort would have been empty. Derek took her hand, and Kat touched her shoulder. They walked together into the shelter, and that meant more to Caeli than anything they might have said.

CHAPTER 10

When they turned the corner behind the stone outcropping, the sights, sounds, and smells of humanity assailed them. Wood smoke wafted up from cooking fires; pans rattled; children laughed as they ran over the dirty ground; laundry, hanging from makeshift lines, fluttered in the chill afternoon breeze. Rock over-hangings and small caves provided most of the cover. Tarps, lashed to tree branches, created additional shelter, under which gear was stowed and people congregated.

A young pregnant woman greeted Finn with a warm embrace and a relieved expression. When she turned, Caeli recognized her. "Anya," she said, smiling at the woman.

"Dr. Crys?" Anya let go of Finn and returned Caeli's smile. "I'm so glad you're alright. We all thought the worst."

"I'm glad to be back," Caeli said. And, despite the tenuous condition of the group, despite their uncertain future, despite the fresh, stinging pain of loss, it was true.

Before she could ask Anya and Finn about their baby, another voice shouted her name. She turned to see Jon striding toward her with two young boys in tow. He scooped her into a tight hug, and she buried her head in his shoulder. "Nina and Lily," she whispered.

He nodded silently and held her. Nina had been Jon's sister,

90

and the boys with him were Nina's other children, Micah and Cory. When she felt she could face them she took a breath and stepped away from Jon, squatting on the ground to greet them. Before she could get a word out, they hurled themselves into her arms. "Caeli!" they squealed joyfully.

"You two have grown so much!" she exclaimed, looking over each of them in turn. They were too thin, their clothes threadbare, and their faces streaked with dirt, but in that moment Caeli could only see the echo of their mother and sister. Large brown eyes stared back at her, and she ran her hands through their dark curling hair. "I've missed you so much."

A small group had formed around her, and when she stood, another man stepped out from the crowd. "Ben," she greeted him, voice trembling. Her eyes immediately fell to the squirming toddler in his arms.

"This is Jamie." Caeli reached for the baby. After another chew on the biscuit in his chubby fist, Jamie put his arms out to her.

"Hello," she said, bouncing him on her hip and kissing the wispy dark hair on the top of his head. Startling blue eyes blinked up at her, and his face split into a chubby-cheeked smile. *Lia's son*, she thought. Drool and bits of biscuit trailed over his chin. Caeli laughed and, after giving him another gentle squeeze, reluctantly handed him back to Ben.

Of the people Caeli was most anxious to see, only Dr. Kellan hadn't made an appearance. Caeli searched the faces around her. Anticipating her question, Finn said, "Erik is gone for the day, out with another team looking for food supplies and medicinal plants."

Caeli nodded. "Maybe I'll be able to help with that?" she offered.

Before Finn could respond, Jon touched her arm. "I'm eager to hear your story and meet our guests."

"Of course," Caeli answered.

Jon led Caeli, Finn, and Derek into a larger tent, with a door flap that could be tied shut. Inside, drawings were piled in one corner and mechanical equipment in various stages of repair lay scattered in piles. "Sorry," he mumbled, moving some of the debris out of the way so they could sit.

Finn made the initial introductions, and Derek repeated essentially the same things he had said a few hours earlier.

"So, you are here to assist the resistance," Jon said, addressing Derek. "And if we can remove Marcus from power, your Alliance will consider protecting Almagest from larger threats, threats that you believe are imminent."

"Yes, sir," Derek said.

Jon exhaled loudly and rubbed his eyes. "I'm glad you're here to help. I don't really care why. Right now we have to overthrow Marcus's government and take control of Almagest for the sake of our people, not because of any outside threat." He sat in silence for a moment and then added, "And things aren't looking good."

"There are a lot of children here," Derek said, looking around with concern. "A lot of mouths to feed, and bodies to protect."

Jon nodded. "We took as many Novali children as we could get out of Alamath, along with all our own children, of course. We're running out of food, and winter is only a few weeks away. The kids, and many of the adults, are getting sick."

He sighed, and when he continued speaking, his forehead was lined with worry. "This camp is well hidden, but it's only a matter of time before they find us. Once the aerial craft that was in development gets deployed, we'll be an easy target.

We have to move soon. Finn's team has been scouting for an alternate hideout, but so far we can't find anything that will conceal this many people."

"Do you have anyone still inside Alamath?" Derek asked.

"Jason," Finn answered. "He volunteered. We're able to communicate with him, but it's a short wave signal, and we have to wait for him to initiate contact so we don't blow his cover. He's coordinating the underground network in Alamath, but Marcus is doing everything he can to hunt them down."

Derek glanced at Caeli. His expression was blank, but she could feel his emotions churning. He was worried. So was she.

"What's your next move?" he asked.

"Well, first we have to solve the food and shelter issue," Jon sighed, running his hands over his face.

Derek nodded. "We might be able to help with that." He pulled the handheld device from his pack, set it on the ground, and tapped a sensor. A three-dimensional model of Almagest appeared hovering over it. Jon and Finn stared in awed silence.

"We created this map from orbit, and we can zoom in on any particular spot. When we were looking for potential places the resistance might be hiding, we identified your current camp, and one other place." He touched the spinning globe and a section flattened out into a relief map of the region. "These ruins here, maybe they can provide better cover and shelter for the winter?"

"Definitely worth a shot," Finn said, looking up at Jon, his voice and expression more enthusiastic than Caeli had witnessed so far.

"Get some food and then take a team out," Jon ordered.

Finn stood and dusted off his pants. Derek looked between Finn and Jon. "Do you want anyone from my team to join you? Give some of your guys a break?"

"That's probably a good idea," Jon answered. Finn hesitated, but gave a weary nod.

"Take Alaric and Kade," Derek offered.

"Thank you," Finn said. "I'll go and everyone else can stay and rest."

***

Once Finn left the camp, Caeli busied herself sorting and taking inventory of the medical supplies. They were woefully inadequate for a group this size, and she began a mental list of items they'd need.

Her next stop was the food stockpile. This was even more alarming. Most of the grain looked like it had been stolen from Alamath. Barrels of it lined the back wall of the cave, stacks of wild root vegetables sat piled on the dusty ground, and dried, salted fish and unidentifiable meat hung from wooden racks. But it wasn't enough to sustain this group for much longer.

Caeli needed to do something now. She needed to feel useful. The quiet desperation emanating from the people around her fueled her own sense of urgency. She was heading back to Jon's tent, where he and Derek were still inside talking, when Anya approached her.

"Caeli," she said, her hand protectively over her distended belly.

Anya's face was pale and dark circles rimmed her eyes. Alarmed, Caeli rushed to her side. "Where can you lie down to rest?" she asked.

Anya led her under a rock outcropping, where a pile of blankets and a few personal items made up a surprisingly comfortable and intimate-looking space.

Caeli arranged the blankets and helped Anya onto the pallet. "Tell me what's wrong," Caeli prodded.

"I'm just so tired. I know that's part of being pregnant, but I can't stay on my feet for more than a few minutes. It's getting worse and I don't want to worry Finn." Her eyes filled with tears.

Caeli put her hands on Anya's belly and immediately saw the baby with her inner vision. She was small but healthy, and Caeli couldn't help but smile. Anya's body, on the other hand, was depleted and weak, and as Caeli continued her examination, she felt Anya's belly tighten into a contraction. Her smile faded.

"It's too soon," Anya whispered.

"It is," Caeli acknowledged. "Rest now. That's the most important thing."

Anya closed her eyes and a tear slid down her cheek. Caeli tucked the blanket around her and stood. "I'll be back," she promised.

Standing at the entrance to Jon's tent, she tried to quell her inner panic at the apparent hopelessness of the situation. "Come in, Caeli," Jon said, gesturing to her.

"What's wrong?" Derek asked.

What isn't wrong? she thought. "It's Anya. She's in pre-term labor. I'm pretty confident I can get the contractions to stop, but she has to rest." Caeli paused, then added, "Completely. Until the baby is born."

Jon exhaled loudly and sat back.

"I know you have to move the camp if we can find a better site, but she can't make a trip like that."

"Understood," Jon said. "We'll find a way to deal with it."

"I know Dr. Kellan is still out looking for supplies, but I'd like to go now too. Maybe I could take a few of the older children? Show them what to look for? The extra hands would be helpful."

Jon nodded. "No one leaves unarmed."

"Take Kat," Derek added.

Caeli nodded back at them both and left the tent.

When she returned a few hours later, the sun was just sinking below the horizon and the temperature was noticeably dropping. But she was satisfied with the day's accomplishment. She, Kat, and four teenagers lugged bags stuffed with edible nuts, roots, and various medicinal plants back to the camp.

Her charges, two girls and two boys, had followed her all afternoon, soaking up the information she offered about which things were edible, which poisonous, and prodding her with thoughtful questions about medicinal plants and remedies. Caeli shared her knowledge eagerly.

"The food can be unloaded now, but I'll sort through the medicines in a little while," she instructed, as they dropped their precious burdens inside the camp. The smell of cooking food wafted toward her, and her stomach growled noisily in response. She hadn't eaten anything since the early morning, but she ignored her hunger and went to check on Anya.

She was pleased to see that Anya was sleeping, still tucked under the blanket, as she had been when Caeli left her. Micah sat close by, keeping watch, just as Caeli had instructed him.

"How was she?" Caeli asked, squatting down next to him.

"Mostly she was sleeping. I brought her soup at lunchtime like you said, and I wouldn't let her get up to clean her dishes," the little boy added proudly.

"Good work," she praised. "This was really important. You can take a break now if you'd like, and I can keep an eye on her."

"That's okay," he said. "I'm not tired yet."

Caeli smiled at him. "Great. I'll bring you both some dinner a little later."

Derek was nowhere to be found, but when Caeli returned to the cave and began sorting the medicines, a familiar voice sounded behind her. Turning, she practically threw herself into Dr. Kellan's open arms.

He, like everyone else, looked worn and underfed, but his embrace was strong and his laugh genuine.

Eventually stepping away from each other, they broke into an animated conversation about the general health of the group, Anya's condition, and any notable medicines they'd found during their search for supplies.

"I was just about to start unpacking," Caeli said, reaching for one of the bags.

"I'm glad to have you here, Caeli," Dr. Kellan admitted quietly. "There are so many people to care for."

"Are you the only doctor?" she asked, a knot forming in her stomach when she thought about Dr. Kellan's capable, dedicated team back in Alamath. Her friends.

He nodded. "I've been training Noah and Mia. They're both Novali. Mia's showing the potential to be gifted like you, and Noah is a quick thinker, very good in a crisis. But they're young." He shook his head and continued, "No background in medicine."

"Where's Jana?" Caeli asked. A talented emergency doctor, Jana had helped care for Caeli when she'd first arrived in Alamath.

"She's with us now," he said, referring to the resistance. "But she's still inside the city." A crease of worry lined his brow.

They worked until the last bit of sunlight faded into a purple glow on the horizon. After that, Dr. Kellan lit the lamps dispersed around the space. But Caeli's hands were growing numb from chopping and grinding, and from the biting cold of the evening air. She put the knife down to avoid slicing her own fingers and went to check on Anya before she warmed up by the fire.

***

Derek was back and he joined Caeli by Anya's bedside. Anya, wrapped in layers of blankets, sipped hot soup. She hadn't had any contractions since her enforced bed-rest and Caeli felt temporarily relieved.

"Where's Finn?" Anya asked Derek.

"He's still checking out those ruins. It looks like there's an underground section and they're trying to gain access. The team is going to spend the night there," he answered.

Anya nodded wearily and pulled the blankets around herself.

"I'm here if you need me," Caeli said, standing to stretch.

Derek put a protective arm around Caeli's waist and led her to the fire. "Is she going to be okay?" he asked quietly, tilting his head in Anya's direction.

"I hope so," Caeli answered.

They found a space by one of the cooking fires. Tree and Drew were talking animatedly with each other, and Kat was leaning against a rock with her legs stretched out in front of her.

"What were you doing today?" Caeli asked as Derek handed her a steaming bowl and sat down.

"We were taking an inventory of the weapons stockpile, checking out the communication equipment, and reviewing some of Jon's recent intel from inside Alamath," Derek answered, blowing into the steaming liquid of his own bowl to cool it off.

"Oh, is that all?" Caeli joked.

"And I found us a nice corner in that cave over there," he said, pointing to his left, "where I set up all our gear."

"I do love you," she answered, giving him an exhausted smile.

When Jon joined them a few minutes later, Caeli's mood turned sober again and she couldn't help but ask the question that had been on her mind.

"What happened to Nina and Lily?"

Jon closed his eyes briefly. "After Marcus executed Private Mason and you escaped, his commitment to hunting down resistance members got even more intense. Neighbors began spying on each other; soldiers pulled people from their beds in the middle of the night and interrogated them; a few captured resistance members were publicly shot. His rhetoric got stronger, more divisive."

Jon stopped and looked at Caeli, his eyes alight with anger. "A few of the Novali children disappeared into his bunker and never came out. This was right around the time Marcus made contact with Alizar Sorin and started the trade deals. It was actually Finn who figured out Marcus's plan to sell the kids."

He stopped and took a swallow from the cup he held cradled in his hands. "We had a solid communication network established by then, and a pretty substantial stock of weapons. It was still a challenge to get close to Marcus. Even when he made his public addresses, he was so well guarded. But we knew we needed to take him out, and his inner circle with him. We had a plan."

Caeli leaned forward and wrapped her arms around her knees. She knew Derek and the other *Horizon* team members were listening too.

"Marcus was planning to unveil a new transportation design model and a big crowd turned out for the announcement. We had

four shooters positioned in key locations. They couldn't miss."
He stopped and stared over the fire as if reliving the moment.
"One of our own had to have given up the information, and
Marcus used the opportunity brilliantly. We pieced a lot of it
together later, after we ran." He cleared his throat and blinked.
"Marcus's men killed our guys, probably as soon as they were in
position. He could have left it at that. But he knew the general
public was tense, unsettled, growing more and more outspoken
against his policies. He had his men shoot at the stage, missing
of course, and create just the provocation his guards needed to
fire into the crowd."

Caeli closed her eyes now, imagining it. Imagining Nina
trying to protect her children, rushing them away from the
scene. Scooping Lily into her arms. And then falling. Falling as
the life bled out of her, and her boys screaming as they watched
their mother and sister die.

"In the chaos that followed, this group got out. We already
had a plan if it came to that, you know that part—a rendezvous
point chosen, supplies and weapons hidden, a strategy for
grabbing the Novali children." He stopped once more and
looked at the group around him. "And here we are."

The small group stared silently into the fire until, one by one,
they wandered to their makeshift beds.

.

CHAPTER 11

It took Caeli a long time to fall asleep. She'd always struggled to turn her mind off in the still, dark hours of the night. Although Derek's arm was thrown over her and the steady rhythm of his breathing provided some measure of comfort, she couldn't stop thinking about Anya's tenuous condition, the pervasive hunger and illness plaguing the group, and the atmosphere of fear and desperation that filled the camp. When she woke at dawn, her head felt cloudy and her body ached.

Derek, Jon, and Kat were already seated around a small fire, speaking in hushed tones. Caeli sat beside Derek and helped herself to the warm tea brewing over the flames.

"Finn thinks he's found a new shelter," Derek said, catching Caeli up on the conversation already in progress. "There's some kind of bunker dug right into the side of the mountain that leads to an underground facility. He thinks it's old, but it looks like it remained intact during the Great War because of its location. Jon wants to start breaking camp and move the group."

Jon continued. "We had a communication from Jason, and Marcus's air fleet has been deployed for several days now. He's increased his ability to find us by tenfold. This bunker sounds like it could be just what we need, no footprint at all. He won't see us from the sky, and we'll be able to create a perimeter warning system." His voice was animated and Caeli could feel renewed hope radiate from him. "Derek's offered to transport supplies and some of the weaker members of the group in his ship."

Derek spoke to Kat: "Take Drew and get to the *Eclipse*. Keep stealth mode engaged and find a place to touch down as close to us as you can. We'll start mobilizing on this end."

Kat nodded, swallowing the last of the contents in her cup. "Yes, sir."

"I'll start packing up the medical supplies." Caeli looked to Jon, who nodded.

As the camp woke with the rising sun, Jon announced his plan and began assigning tasks. Soon everyone was engaged in purposeful work, keeping their minds off their empty stomachs and on the tasks at hand.

Within a few hours, Jon was ready to send the first groups out on foot. Some of the older, healthier children and several well-armed adults set off with loaded packs. Jon decided that Dr. Kellan should go and begin setting up camp in preparation to receive the weary and tired groups to follow.

Three different routes to the new bunker had been chosen, all through thick forests and under the protective canopy of the trees. It was Jon's hope that by dividing into smaller groups, they would be able to move quickly and be more easily camouflaged by their surroundings. Their risk of discovery grew as every hour passed.

***

Caeli had dismantled the cooking supplies and was about to start packing them when she heard a low, distant hum. She stopped and looked around, searching for the source, and then she froze in place as the sound became a roar. A shadow darkened the ground under her feet and the aircraft passed directly overhead.

The ship, arching around to make another pass, was wide across, with wings tucked tightly against its body. It was too large to safely maneuver through the valley, and streaked just above the rocky peaks. But when it approached their position, Caeli watched, horrified, as gun turrets dropped from the juncture between wing and body.

Derek's shattered ship had been the first of its type Caeli had ever seen, but now she had a frame of reference for such things. This craft looked every bit as deadly as *Horizon*'s fighters.

Derek was suddenly shouting behind her. Shaking off her paralysis, she dove behind a rock, seconds before the ground where she'd been standing exploded. Derek threw himself down on top of her as chunks of rock became missiles flying through the air. The craft fired a volley into the side walls of the canyon when it passed, bringing piles of stone down to crush everyone below and trapping others behind a mass of rubble. When the wave of attack temporarily ended, Derek got to his knees.

"Kat! Where are you?" he shouted into his com. "Fuck! They're still ten minutes out. Caeli, you have to get to the forest and try to hide. Grab whoever you can and run. They're going to pin us in here. They're not that maneuverable, but they can bring down a lot of mountain on top of us. Disappear. I'll find you."

He pulled her up from the ground and started shouting instructions. "Take cover in the woods. Follow Caeli!"

Anya, she thought, running practically blind and choking on clouds of dust. "Anya!" she screamed.

Anya was on her hands and knees, crawling out of her still-intact shelter. Micah and Cory were next to her.

"We have to get out!" Caeli shouted, helping Anya to her feet and pulling Cory along next to her. Another group converged on her location. The main pass, through which Caeli had entered when they first arrived, was on the other side of the valley. But there was too much open space to cross. The sound of the aircraft's engines grew louder as it returned for another pass.

"Is there a different way out of this canyon?" she asked Anya.

It was Micah who answered, "Over here." He waved them forward.

This time, when the ship attacked, it was met by return fire. While Caeli didn't think Derek's weapon could bring the craft down, it was more powerful than anything carried by the other resistance fighters. At the very least, Derek, Jon, Tree, and some of the others were drawing attention to themselves and luring the craft away from the more vulnerable targets.

Caeli, Anya, and the children pressed themselves against the rock wall and covered their heads as dirt sprayed around them. Caeli felt a warm trickle down the side of her face and when she swiped at it, the back of her hand came away bloody.

During another momentary reprieve, they scrambled through a short, rocky pass and out into a small open field. They crouched and waited until the sound of the aircraft had faded into the distance, and then sprinted for the cover of the forest.

Caeli ran next to Anya, supporting her as much as she could. The brush was thick and tangled, and they tripped as they moved through it, but there was no time to look for a game trail or do anything other than move deeper into the safety of its cover. Caeli kept turning to encourage her followers, and when they could no longer hear the sound of gunfire or the drone of the ship's engines, she allowed them to stop.

Panting, they huddled close, and Caeli surveyed the surroundings. Tall, old growth evergreens shaded them and a newly fallen tree lay sprawled across the moss-covered ground. Caeli helped Anya down to lean against it.

"Are you Mia?" Caeli asked a young woman. When the girl nodded, she continued, "I need you to get everyone, especially the children, settled and check them for injuries."

Mia seemed pleased to have a task and quickly had the younger children seated in a semi-circle on the opposite side of the tree trunk. Caeli could see Dr. Kellan's training at work when Mia began to systematically examine her charges in a gentle but efficient manner.

Caeli turned her attention to Anya, who was pale and gripping her stomach in pain. Placing her hands on Anya's belly, Caeli felt a powerful contraction take hold. It was a different quality than the one she had felt the day before, and Caeli knew Anya's baby was coming. She tried to keep her demeanor calm and comforting, but they both knew the baby was too early.

There was nothing Caeli could do to stop Anya's labor.

When her belly clenched, Anya cried out in pain, and in between the contractions, she begged Caeli to save her baby. An hour later a little girl slipped into Caeli's hands, struggling to breathe with lungs that weren't fully formed. Wrapping the tiny form in her jacket, Caeli handed her to Anya.

"She has perfect fingers," Anya whispered.

"Her hair is the same color as yours," Caeli said, touching the soft downy fuzz on the baby's head.

"We wanted to name her Alina after Finn's mom," Anya said, running her finger along the baby's cheek.

"That's a beautiful name," Caeli said.

And then Anya began to bleed.

Caeli knew immediately that it was too much blood.

"Mia!" she yelled, and the young woman appeared at her side. "Take the baby."

Anya's eyelids fluttered and Mia lifted the tiny burden from Anya's slack grip. Once again, Caeli placed her hands on Anya and, with her inner vision, saw the abruption where the placenta had been violently torn away. She found every leaking vessel, sealing each one off with precision. When she was finished, Anya was unconscious but alive, and Caeli sat back on her heels, drained.

She wiped the blood from her hands onto her pants and leaned back against the log, shivering violently.

"Mia," she spoke, her voice hoarse.

The young woman looked at her, eyes wide and fearful.

"Let me take the baby." Caeli reached out and Mia placed the child in her arms. "Can you start a small fire? Do you remember how to do that?" she asked.

Mia nodded numbly and began to collect pieces of wood. When she squatted down next to the small pile to make the flame, Caeli said, "You have to keep everyone together. Derek will find us."

Mia nodded earnestly.

"Healing makes me very tired," she explained. "I need you to keep us warm, especially Anya and the younger children."

"I will," Mia promised.

Caeli placed her hand inside the warm bundle on her lap and felt the baby's tenuous hold on life slipping away. Her tiny face peeked out from underneath the wrapping of Caeli's coat, and her blue-tinged lips contrasted sharply against her translucent skin.

Allowing her mind to merge with the baby's, Caeli hummed a lullaby she remembered from her own childhood. And then the baby was gone.

Caeli closed her eyes but had no tears left to shed. Stretching her mind out, she found Derek. Right away she knew he was still alive, but she was far from him, and her mind and body were exhausted. She could barely manage to brush her consciousness against his.

DEREK

CHAPTER 12

"Kat!" he shouted into his com.

"Two minutes," she answered in his ear, voice tight. "Hang on."

"Doing my best," he said, crouching behind his boulder as a spray of dirt and rock pelted him.

Earlier, when he'd heard the distant rumbling, he had known what it was. He'd grabbed his gun, and shouted for Tree. Caeli had stood outside staring, her gaze locked onto the sky. He yelled and she moved, tumbling out of the way with only seconds to spare. He was already racing toward her with his heart thudding madly in his chest, and when she dove for cover, he threw himself down on top of her.

Once she was up and running, he fought every instinct to go after her, to make sure she stayed safe. But the best way he could assure that was to disable the Amathi ship if he could, or draw its fire toward himself. He sprinted to the east side of the camp and positioned himself behind a large boulder. Tree and Jon followed and were similarly placed a few yards across from him when the craft flew within range.

He leaned out from the cover of the rock and fired. His gun

was laser guided, and while it was smaller than he would have preferred, its high-energy pulses definitely caused some damage.

The craft roared overhead. Derek tried to aim for one of the large, powerful rear engines. He was rewarded when a burst of flame erupted from it and the craft banked sharply to the left. It corrected itself over the tree line before swinging around again. Derek knew they weren't going to last much longer against its superior firepower, but he had to buy just a little more time.

He'd seen Caeli and the others wedged against the rocky base, squatting low and waiting for the craft to pass before making a run for it.

When the ship was directly overhead, Derek once again leaped out from behind his cover and fired. He chanced a backward look, and exhaled in relief when he saw that Caeli and her group were gone.

Now, as the Amathi ship approached again, another hum rivaled it. Derek grinned and stuck his head out to see Tree give him a happy salute back. He jumped on top of the boulder in time to watch *Eclipse* streak over the tree line and then throttle back to meet the oncoming craft.

"Motherfucker," Kat said, growling over the com as she fired one volley.

The shot took out the Amathi ship's portside wing entirely. It veered hard left and crashed into the side of the mountain. The following explosion was spectacular, shaking the ground beneath Derek's feet. He sat down hard on his rock and wiped the sweat off his face.

"Make sure there's nothing left, then keep circling," he ordered Kat. "I'm sure they've already called in our position. We don't have much time and we need to regroup."

"Roger that. I'll let you know if anyone's coming," she answered.

He jumped off his rock and met Jon and Tree. "They know where we are," he said quickly.

Jon nodded. "We need to look for survivors, and then we need a plan to get out of here."

"Kat will stay up there for as long as possible. We don't need any surprises," Derek said. "But once we've accounted for everyone and salvaged what we can, I'll have her land in the clearing. We can load up and pick a rendezvous point."

A young man and several dust-covered, bloodied adults emerged from hiding. Jon quickly organized some of the survivors into search and recovery teams; others he instructed to salvage what supplies and weapons they could.

"I can find survivors," the young man offered. "I can sense them."

"Thank you, Noah." Jon squeezed the boy's shoulder. "That will be immensely helpful."

"We have to find Caeli," Derek said. "They made it into the forest."

Jon nodded and looked around at the small group, already rushing to complete their tasks. "Liam is a tracker. I'll send him out," he said, waving to get Liam's attention.

Another young man jogged over, and the way he moved suggested to Derek he was military. "Sir?" he addressed Jon.

"You need to find Caeli and the others with her. When you do, lead them along the river south. There's an open field about five miles down. We'll rendezvous with you there. Stay under cover until you see us."

Liam nodded.

"Take Tree," Derek said.

Tree picked up his weapon and said to Derek, "I'll find her."

Derek just stared at him hard, afraid to think of the alternative. Tree gripped Derek's shoulder for a second, and then followed Liam out of the valley and into the woods.

***

Jon estimated that there were fifty people left at the camp when they were attacked. Caeli had escaped with a group of about twenty, and another fifteen were accounted for, most with only minor injuries. But as Noah squatted in front of a pile of rubble sealing off the mouth of a cave, a place that had sheltered people before the airstrike, Derek's stomach turned over thinking about the number still missing.

Noah's eyes were closed and his brow wrinkled in concentration. "People are alive under there," he said, turning to Jon. "Not many, I don't think. Maybe two or three."

"Let's move," Jon ordered, already lifting rocks out of the way and tossing them aside. Derek, Noah, and several others followed, frantically heaving debris and scooping dirt with their bare hands.

They uncovered bodies first. Two adults and two children. Derek moved silently, lifting the tiny corpses and placing them carefully next to one another a few yards away. Then he and Jon removed the adults. Everyone else kept digging.

"Here!" Noah suddenly shouted, scrambling forward on his knees. "I can feel them here."

After several tense moments, three children were uncovered, huddled together inside a cramped cavern that hadn't collapsed but had trapped them in the silent darkness. Their tear-stained faces stared back at Derek, emotionless, and they barely acknowledged the adults who reached for them.

But they were uninjured, and Noah couldn't find any other survivors, so Jon looked to Derek. "We need to get out of here."

Eclipse waited for them, tucked into a tight canyon space. Kat was standing at the top of the lowered ramp. Derek gave her a quick look that let her know he recognized the challenge of her near vertical landing and the skill it took to put the ship down so perfectly.

"Drew's a little green around the edges," Kat said, the corner of her lip twitching. She reached for the collection of weapons Derek handed up to her, and then looked around at the battered group who stumbled forward, carrying as much as they could manage.

Her expression immediately became sober. "Where's Caeli?" she demanded.

"She's hiding out in the forest. Tree went to find her."

Kat relaxed her shoulders. "We can fit most of the gear and all the kids. Should we go straight to the new bunker?"

"Yeah. Unload and I'll contact you if we need you to come back out."

They finished loading the ship in a quarter of an hour. Derek shaded his eyes from the glaring midday sun as he watched *Eclipse* ascend into the blue sky and then disappear. Jon led the remainder of the group quickly out of the open valley and into the surrounding forest.

They were able to make good time and arrived first at the rendezvous point. The group sat hidden near the bank of the river, next to an open field. Wind blew the tall, browning grass, and the afternoon grew chilly as clouds moved in to block out the sun. Derek sat and spoke quietly into his com. "Tree, where are you guys?"

Tree answered, "It's slow going. We're still about a mile out."

"Should I call Kat back here?" Derek asked, picking up the strain in Tree's voice.

"You should," he answered, and Derek's stomach sank.

He got Kat back on the com and told her to meet them at the field. "Kat, stay sharp. The Amathi are looking for us and we've only seen one of their ships."

"Copy that. We'll stay dark and keep an eye out until we have to pick you up. If anyone comes calling, I'll see them first," she assured him.

Derek blew out a breath and drummed his hand against his knee. He'd felt Caeli when she'd touched her mind against his, but it had been a brief and troubling connection. His psyche now echoed with her exhaustion and despair.

When Tree's voice came over the com again to say they were close by, Derek leapt to his feet. Figures emerged from the shadow of the trees, trudging slowly forward. Liam came first, weapon drawn and taking point, behaving every bit the soldier Derek thought him to be. Tree walked behind him, carrying an unconscious Anya. After him, a group of children and a few young adults. Then, finally, Caeli, holding a tiny bundle tight to her chest.

He rushed forward. The closer he got, the more alarmed he became. Caeli's face was ashen, streaked with dried blood, and she wobbled unsteadily on her feet. He was in front of her in seconds, cupping her face in his hands.

"The baby's dead," she whispered.

He closed his eyes and touched his forehead to hers. Fearing the answer, he nodded toward Tree. "And Anya?"

"She's weak but alive. She doesn't know," Caeli said.

He put his arm around her and led her toward the field, where *Eclipse* had just landed.

"Go with her," Tree said, after they loaded Anya, Caeli, and the younger children onboard. "She needs you. I'll make sure the rest of us get there safely."

Derek pulled Tree aside. "I don't want to engage *Eclipse* in another firefight if we can help it. I don't think the ship we took out knew what hit it. I'd like to keep it that way for now. But don't hesitate to radio if you need us."

"Roger that, sir."

Derek boarded his ship and buckled himself next to Caeli, who still held the dead baby in her arms.

CHAPTER 13

Caeli didn't speak for most of the short flight. Her head rested lightly against his shoulder and she seemed lost in her own thoughts. He'd instructed Kat to contact Alaric at the new base and inform him of their situation. Dr. Kellan would be waiting for them.

He pulled Caeli closer and felt her tension ease. He knew she was strong. He knew the horrors she'd already survived. And he knew her resolve. But he also knew that everyone had a breaking point. He'd served with seasoned soldiers who were unable to recover from the trauma and violence they'd witnessed. And sometimes you couldn't predict what trigger would cause them to break.

He briefly wondered about the cumulative effect his own experiences were having on him, and on his ability to function under normal circumstances. He wasn't even sure he could define "normal" anymore. But he was more worried about Caeli.

The plunging of his stomach when the ship began its descent pulled him from his thoughts. He felt Caeli take a deep breath next to him, as if steeling herself to face the next few moments. When the door slid open, Dr. Kellan and Finn were there waiting.

Derek saw Finn look at Caeli, his expression agonized, and then turn to Anya. Finn unbuckled her from the seat where she sat propped up by Derek's jacket and wrapped in a cold weather sleeping bag. Anya's eyes fluttered open. Finn spoke to her gently and then lifted her as if she weighed nothing.

Dr. Kellan put a hand on Caeli's shoulder before herding the children out of the ship. Kat and Drew emerged from the cockpit.

"We're powered down. The ship's secure," Kat said, throwing a worried glance at Caeli.

Derek nodded and helped Caeli to her feet. When he stepped out of the ship, he blinked in surprise at his surroundings. His experience of Almagest was of mostly pristine, natural landscapes—the cave where Caeli had patched him back together after his crash; the ocean, lake, and camp where he'd spent his days recovering; the forests and mountains where he'd hidden with the resistance. His knowledge of Caeli's home, Novalis, and of the Amathi settlement, Alamath, were all from Caeli's memory.

Nothing prepared him for the magnitude of the ruins in which he now stood. Seeing them on a relief map from orbit didn't do them justice. At the height of its earlier civilization, Almagest must have been a very different place.

Caeli's eyes were wide. "My parents spent their adult lives studying ruins, and I never understood their fascination. I even went with them on a dig once," she said, turning to Derek. "But that site was nothing like this one."

Derek suspected they were standing in what had once been a city center. Ruined structures towered among the trees, now strange hybrid beasts, neither wholly artificial nor completely natural. Saplings sprung from between the fallen buildings and twisted into improbable shapes as they reached for sunlight. Mossy growth spread over cracked walls, pillars of metal jutted up from loose dirt, and vines clung opportunistically to jagged surfaces. Nature encroached, reclaiming what humans had abandoned, or destroyed.

They stood and stared, shadowed by the mountains rimming the northern perimeter of the city.

"The bunker is this way," Kat said. "We should move."

She led them to a hollowed out, dome-shaped structure connected to the base of the mountain, built in such a way that, from a distance, it could be mistaken for part of the rock itself. A door panel opened to a damp, dark corridor cut directly into the mountainside. At the end, another door appeared partially open, as if it had been frozen mid-way.

Kat's face was barely visible in the dim light. "Wait until you see this," she said, stepping through the entryway.

Derek's eyes took a minute to adjust. Camp lights had been strung up throughout the room, casting shadows around the space and illuminating the forms and faces of the people that had already arrived.

Looking around, he was convinced he was standing in some kind of laboratory facility.

"Alaric thinks he's found a geothermal generator. If he can figure it out, we might have a power source," Kat said.

"How big is this place?" Derek asked.

"Don't know," Kat answered. "I was only in here for a few minutes before I had to leave again. Alaric and Kade have been exploring. Finn too, until he heard about Anya and the baby."

At that, Derek's attention returned to Caeli. He took her by the elbow and led her to a corner of the room, where Dr. Kellan settled Anya into a makeshift bed and Finn hovered nearby. Caeli approached him and wordlessly handed him the baby.

Finn took the tiny bundle and peered into his daughter's

perfect, still face. Another person approached slowly. Derek recognized her from the camp and knew she was Novali.

In a halting voice the young woman spoke. "I'm Jessa. My parents were followers. I know the songs," she said.

Finn looked at her questioningly, but it was Caeli who answered. "The Novali have people who attend to the dead. They can feel the life force transitioning out of the body, and they have rituals and songs to help with the passage. Jessa is offering to sing to your baby."

Finn swallowed and nodded. "I'd like to bring her to Anya."

Derek and Caeli watched silently as Finn knelt next to Anya, and together they held their baby for the first, and last, time. Jessa's soft, lovely voice chanted in an unfamiliar language. Everyone in the room stopped to listen. A whisper of a smile played over Caeli's lips as she closed her eyes and swayed to the haunting melody.

***

Derek found Alaric and Kade working over a piece of machinery in a cavernous room tucked deeply into the mountainside. Caeli was asleep. He knew she'd need hours to recover and he was anxious to do something useful, so he went searching for the rest of his team.

"It's geothermal," Kade explained. "Brilliant, really. Some of the supporting technology is old, obviously, but we still use the same reactor design wherever geothermal energy is accessible."

"Can you get it online?" Derek asked.

"Yeah," Kade answered. "We've been pilfering for parts and learning the delivery structure. It's pretty intuitive. Give me a couple of hours and we'll have light and heat."

"Fantastic. We could use some good news," Derek said.

Kade had an engineering background that served the team well. Derek's thoughts drifted to Tommy, the pilot who'd died on Almagest last year in the crash. He'd also been able to fix nearly anything he touched. Not their ship, *Equinox*, though. A blown out engine in the cold of space had proved an impossible challenge. Derek had tried to land with no stabilizers, only one engine, and barely any air left. It hadn't gone well. He still missed Tommy's easy laugh.

"Copy that." Kade's voice reverberated around the vast chamber, pulling Derek from his thoughts. Then more quietly, he asked, "How's Caeli?"

"Not good," Derek answered honestly. "And it's only going to get worse."

Kade nodded. "They're in rough shape."

"Heat and lights will be an improvement, though," Derek acknowledged. "Thank you." And he left Kade to finish.

His initial assessment that they had uncovered some kind of laboratory facility was reinforced the more he explored the space. And as he surveyed the dust-covered equipment, he became more and more convinced it had been a medical lab. He really wanted Erik Kellan to have a look.

All the weary groups had intermittently staggered in, with Tree's small band last. Once everyone was accounted for, Derek was able to pull Kellan away for a little while. Caeli, who was awake by then, joined them. They wandered through the still darkened rooms, with Derek's small flashlight cutting through the blackness.

"This looks like a centrifuge," Caeli said, using her sleeve to dust off the transparent cover that shielded the circular device inside.

Kellan nodded his agreement and turned to the tall, metallic units that lined the entire back wall. "I think these are built for cold storage."

"Not sure we should open them," Derek cautioned.

"Agreed," Kellan said, moving toward another piece of equipment. "What's this?" he asked.

Caeli moved next to him and Derek pointed the beam of his flashlight at the countertop. "It looks a little like the gene sequencer in *Horizon*'s med lab," she said studying it. "I wonder . . ." Her words trailed off when the room lit up.

"Thank you, Kade," Derek mumbled under his breath. He flipped off his flashlight, and squinted while his eyes adjusted to the brightness.

Kellan whistled as he surveyed the illuminated room. Derek examined a workstation positioned in the center of the space. A circular tube connected what looked like a processor to the ceiling, integrating it into the power grid. There was a screen flush to the tabletop and a dust-coated sensor panel on one side. Although the power had been restored, the computer system remained silent.

"I bet there's some interesting information in this thing," he said. "I don't see an obvious on/off switch, but that panel looks like a biometric scanner." He carefully blew dust from its surface, and the faint outline of a handprint appeared, etched onto the surface.

Caeli stood at his side. "It's like the access points at the hospital on Erithos," she added, placing her palm lightly on its surface.

Derek fully expected nothing to happen, and he was stunned when the panel beneath Caeli's hand began to glow. She looked up at him, eyes wide. A barely perceptible hum accompanied the light, and Caeli stood frozen with her hand in place.

"It feels warm," she said.

Derek stood poised to pull her away, but she shook her head. The glow stopped suddenly, the noise disappeared, and Caeli shrugged, stepping back.

"I'm sure the security access is programmed to recognize . . ." Derek began. His voice trailed off when the tube lit up and the screen lifted silently from its horizontal position and locked into place on the desktop.

"Did I do that?" Caeli asked incredulously.

"I have no idea," Derek answered. All three stood wordlessly staring at the backlit screen. The luminous tube now threw off a blue-white pulsing light, and icons containing foreign script appeared on the screen.

"Do you recognize the language?" Derek asked.

"It looks familiar," Caeli answered. "We still use these characters."

Kellan stepped closer to the screen, leaned in, and nodded his agreement. "If this facility survived the Great War, there might be a wealth of information about our last civilization stored in there." He paused and looked over at Caeli. "Or it might just be lab records."

"Either way, I think we should put some resources into deciphering it. I'll let Jon know what we've found and see what he says," Derek said.

***

The group was exhausted, Derek included, but he, Jon, and Kellan sat in a quiet corner of the bunker tallying their losses and discussing strategy. Caeli was tending to Anya, and Finn hadn't left her side. The rest of his team were unpacking gear and setting up their own personal spaces, and almost everyone else was asleep.

"We lost most of the food," Jon sighed, rubbing his face with his hands. "Even if Caeli and some of the other Novali can find something tomorrow, we won't last the winter."

"You've raided the Amathi supplies before. Can we do it again?" Derek asked.

"We know there's more security around the warehouses," Jon answered. "But I don't know how to acquire what we need otherwise." He dropped his worry-lined face into his hands. Derek silently put a hand on his shoulder.

"Let's get some rest," Kellan said, and the small group dispersed.

Caeli was sitting on the ground beside Anya, holding the sleeping woman's hand. Finn stood when Derek approached and whispered, "Is there a plan?"

"The beginnings of one," Derek answered. "We can talk tomorrow. Try to sleep."

Finn nodded and started to turn around, but then he looked back at Derek. "We killed their children when we attacked Novalis," he said, his voice barely audible. "We didn't target the kids, but some died. I was there and I didn't do anything to stop it. I deserve this."

"No," Derek said firmly. "No one deserves this."

"I'm not sure I'll ever believe that," Finn answered, and sat back down beside Anya.

From Caeli's expression, Derek knew she'd heard Finn. He reached a hand out to her and she stood.

In the warmth of their sleeping bag, he held her when she buried her face in his chest, too exhausted to cry. Long after she fell asleep, he lay staring up at the ceiling.

5523.7.5
PERSONAL LOG: DR. ELAN JOKAHAR
ENCRYPTED

The entire group is ecstatic. The mutation shows no degradation in five successive generations. The implications are staggering! But of course, we're nearly out of funding. I've uploaded the latest results onto BioCloud, SynGen, and MedShare, and now I'm receiving so many inquiries that I've had to assign someone to answer them full-time. There's so much curiosity and rabid excitement—they won't dare deny us funding now.

5523.7.10
FROM: DR. ELAN JOKAHAR
TO: UNIVERSITY RESEARCH GROUP, DIVISION OF NEUROGENETICS
RE: GRANT PROPOSAL
(3) FILE ATTACHMENTS

Dear Colleagues,

With great enthusiasm, I present to you the results of the Phase 3 trial studies, and request your assistance to bring this project to the next step. Attached please find the completed results from our laboratory trials, a grant proposal, and my testimonial. I eagerly await your reply.

Regards,
Dr. Elan Jokahar
Executive Officer and Chief of Research, Quest Institute

5523.8.9
FROM: DR. SARAI KUPRIK
TO: DR. ELAN JOKAHAR
RE: GRANT PROPOSAL
(1) ATTACHMENT

Dear Dr. Jokahar,

The results of your initial study are impressive and have broad reaching implications. As such, the Ethics Board has convened a special subcommittee to review your full proposal. An invitation will be forthcoming for you and your team to attend any relevant sessions and present your case.

In the meantime, the University is pleased to approve limited funding for your research in the area of endogenous regeneration. Please see the attached letter of award for details on the scope of funding, reporting parameters, and oversight.

Respectfully yours,
Dr. Sarai Kuprik
Chair, Department of Neurogenetics, University Research Group

5523.8.12
PERSONAL LOG: DR. ELAN JOKAHAR
ENCRYPTED

It's not a fortune, but it's enough to keep us going. My team is committed to the vision. We'll press on.

5524.5.5
FROM: DR. SARAI KUPRIK
TO: DR. ELAN JOKAHAR
RE: TERMINATION OF FUNDING

Dr. Jokahar,

It has come to our attention that your team has exceeded the parameters put forth in the grant award with regard to, but not limited to, the human trials of monoamine oxidase A. Your research is now in direct violation of section 61.4 of the Interplanetary Ethics Board ruling on permissible human genetic modifications. Funding for this project by the University Research Group has been terminated immediately.

Yours,
Dr. Sarai Kuprik
Chair, Department of Neurogenetics, University Research Group

5529.10.7
DYNAMICORP
OFFSHORE RESEARCH FACILITY
MALAKA ISLAND, BOREIOS PROVENCE

Misha's transport skimmed to a stop. The magnetic locks engaged and held the small craft tightly to the dock. When the port side door slid open, she exited into the bright sunshine. This was her favorite facility. She loved the site so much that she'd built a modest residence for herself into the leeward side of the mountain. Breathing in the tangy salt air, she felt a rush of satisfaction at the progress she was making here.

After passing through stringent biometric security protocols, all of which she had put into place, Misha headed to the first level. From the observation deck, she watched the engineers and technicians, all fully engaged in whatever project they were tasked with. The best and brightest coveted jobs at DynamiCorp. Access to the finest research facilities on the planet, funding that never seemed to dry up, and a climate that promoted creativity and progress over regulations had scientists and engineers clamoring at her door.

The research on this level was mostly in support of her government contracts, and it was only here that she allowed current and prospective clients to observe her people at work. Most of her visitors had no idea what they were looking at anyway. Misha knew, though. She knew every project currently underway. She tracked which were ahead of schedule and which behind. She knew who in her staff proposed the most revolutionary ideas, who solved the most critical problems, and who had the most tactical minds. So much potential, Misha thought, smiling.

CAELI

CHAPTER 14

Caeli's foraging efforts bought the group only about a week's worth of provisions. There just wasn't much to find at that time of year. When she added her day's meager collection to the small stockpile, it was clear to her they were in trouble.

Jon, Derek, and Finn were in the makeshift command center when she joined them.

"If we don't find another food supply, we're going to starve," she said, leaning against the wall and rubbing her cold hands together.

Jon nodded. "I know. The only plan we've come up with is a raid on the Amathi food stores."

Caeli raised her eyebrows. "That sounds risky."

"We're out of options if we want to feed a group this size," Jon said.

"If we can get a few people inside Alamath, I have an idea," Finn said, and all eyes turned to him. "Marcus has been expanding the monorail line through the mountain range to move ore. What if we could load one of the cars with food, and anything else we can get our hands on, and then ride it out to one of the remote mining camps?" Finn suggested.

"We could have *Eclipse* waiting there to transport the food supply back here," Derek added.

"If we blew the line behind us and had an ambush waiting at the camp, we could unload and be out of there pretty quick," Finn said.

"Timing would be everything," Derek added. "And what do we know about the schedule and route of the trains?"

"Old information," Finn said. "But the mining outposts have to be supplied, so there must be a line for that purpose. We need to figure out which one and where, then we can coordinate the rest."

Caeli sat leaning against the back wall with her arms wrapped around her knees, listening. She made eye contact with Derek before speaking. "We'll need to move around Alamath unseen. I can help with that."

Jon hesitated and then nodded. She felt Derek stiffen next to her, but his expression remained impassive. He had to know she was well suited for this. She could easily find her way around the city proper and the outskirts of town, and she could help keep herself and any other team members hidden with her gift.

"I'll go," Finn volunteered. "I know what I'm looking for."

Jon nodded again. "Let's keep it to you and Caeli."

Derek hesitated before speaking again. "I've asked Kade and Tree to work at enhancing communications. They should be able to amplify an outgoing signal without allowing the Amathi to trace the source. If we can get this technology inside Alamath, to Jason and the other pockets of resistance members, we'll have a reliable channel of communication with them."

Jon sat back and ran a hand over his face. "That could go a long way toward getting us reorganized."

"If Caeli and I are inside, we can use the opportunity to deliver that tech," Finn said.

Derek nodded reluctantly.

"I agree," Jon said.

***

Caeli leaned her head against the seat back as *Eclipse* darted over the tree line. She was surprisingly calm. It actually felt good to be doing something other than searching for food and hiding. Everyone around her seemed to be lost in their own thoughts, preparing for the mission ahead.

She knew every part of the plan had to work. Derek was uncomfortable with the number of moving parts, but no one had a better idea, and the thought of starving children added another level of urgency to their task.

Kat's voice came over the com. "We're two minutes out," she said.

Caeli took a deep breath as the ship descended. When they were on the ground, she quickly unbuckled her harness and reached for her pack and weapon.

Caeli's bag contained two of the transmitters that they would try to deliver to Jason, and Finn's held the third. Light provisions were also divided between them.

"We'll set up camp a few miles outside of the Amathi base and wait to hear from you," Derek said to Finn, who nodded briskly. Chances were slim that a supply train would run to the mining outpost every day. The team might have to wait several days for their opportunity.

"Please be safe," Derek whispered to Caeli while helping her fit the bag securely on her back.

"You too," she answered. He pulled her against him and she could feel his pounding heart. Burying her face in the side of his neck, she took a last, deep breath, inhaling the scent of him, before she turned and walked away with Finn.

They were about a mile outside the westernmost border of the settlement. With Caeli using her gift to hide them, there was no need to begin the operation in the cover of darkness. The early morning sun glittered off the frosty ground and cast golden rays over the drying dirt of recently harvested fields.

In the distance, Caeli could see grain silos, warehouses, and numerous rail tracks converging at the loading docks and then dispersing back out in several directions. This was the central food distribution center in Alamath. Whatever cargo was heading into the mines would likely pass through here.

There was very little sign of human activity as they approached the looming structures. "That's the operation's center," Finn said, pointing to a smaller building set slightly back from the tracks. "If we can get inside, I know there will be a master schedule for the lines."

"How's security?" Caeli asked.

"Not sure. I expect there will be guards posted at the granaries to prevent theft, but I don't think the ops center will be a problem," Finn answered.

They moved quietly toward the entrance of the small office and peered in the window. The space was empty. Finn crept to the side entrance and tried the door. "Locked," he said, and then knelt to open his pack.

Caeli imagined the two of them as only shadows, light and darkness dancing on the frosty ground and against the cinder block wall. She focused on projecting that illusion into the surrounding area while simultaneously scanning for movement in the yard. As Finn worked at the lock, a guard turned the corner at the north side of the silo and paced the perimeter of the building directly across from them.

Caeli placed her hand on Finn's shoulder and he stopped moving. Tense, they crouched together, waiting for the guard to pass. For a harrowing moment, the soldier stopped and stared at the doorway of the building, straight at Caeli and Finn. But then he only flipped his weapon to the other shoulder, rubbed his free hand across his face, and continued on his way.

Finn exhaled loudly and Caeli could see the sheen of sweat now coating his forehead. When the guard turned again at the far corner, disappearing from view, Finn popped the lock and he and Caeli slipped inside.

Finn surveyed the small room and Caeli followed his gaze to the far side, where one section of the wall was covered in graphs and charts.

"This is it. Look. Arrival times, departure times, dates, and destinations," he said, pointing at the various columns.

Eagerly they approached. Finn ran a finger down one column until he found what he was looking for. He tapped the name. "East Orainos Base 1. That's our stop." He traced his finger horizontally to find the relevant dates and times. "The train arrives here tomorrow at 1400 and leaves at 1600."

Finn moved to a desk and began rummaging through files and papers. "What are you looking for?" Caeli asked.

"The cargo manifest," he answered. "Here it is. Number 2110 heading to EOB1. It will already be carrying a good bit of machinery and some weapons. Then it will be loaded here with ten caseloads of grains and produce."

Caeli gave Finn a small smile. "That will get us through the winter," she said.

"Yes, it will," he agreed. "You and I just have to be back here tomorrow afternoon to catch our ride."

***

The neighborhood where they stopped next was closer to the town center. Finn pointed to a small, well-maintained house with a pair of child's boots laying haphazardly at the back door. He paused and stared at the boots with such a look of pain and regret on his face that Caeli reached for his hand.

"You've always believed in me, Caeli," he said, glancing at her.

"Because I know your heart," she answered. He squeezed her hand and then let go.

"This is Anya's sister's house. She's the only person I trust completely besides Jason," Finn explained.

"She's resistance?" Caeli asked.

"She is. I'm sure she was under suspicion when Anya disappeared, so we need to be careful. I don't know how much surveillance Marcus might still have on her."

"Will she be home?" Caeli asked.

"Probably. It's still early, and I don't think she leaves for work until Evie goes to school."

"If we stay hidden for a few minutes, I can tell if there's anyone nearby," Caeli offered.

Finn nodded and led them around the back of the house into the woods that surrounded the yard. They tucked themselves behind a large boulder and Caeli released the shadow image. Stretching her mind out, she first felt the people in the house, and then those in the surrounding neighborhood. She allowed the collective hum of their thoughts to resolve into individual voices.

Her intrusion into these strangers' minds was a gross violation of Novali ethics. There should be no reason to invade someone's privacy. *But the Amathi changed the rules*, Caeli thought, pushing the self-rebuke from her own mind. She continued to sift through the noise, determined to find anyone that might be a threat. There was nothing.

She shook her head at Finn. "Nothing suspicious."

"Good," he answered.

They walked to the back door and knocked. When a woman's voice asked who was there, Finn said, "Cara, it's Finn."

The door creaked open, and a woman who looked very much like Anya peered out, her eyes widening with surprise.

"Finn! Come in," she said, looking cautiously around her back yard before ushering them through the door. She then threw herself into Finn's arms and uttered one word: "Anya?"

"She's okay," he said quickly, and then whispered, "But the baby came too soon. She didn't survive."

"Oh, Finn. Oh, no," Cara said, stepping back to look at his face. "I'm so sorry."

He only nodded. Cara's eyes darted to Caeli, as if just noticing her for the first time, and then back to Finn.

He cleared his throat and introduced them. "Caeli saved Anya's life. Without her, I would have lost them both."

Cara put her hand over her mouth and a tear fell from the corner of her eye. She swiped it away briskly and said, "Sit. I'm making breakfast for Evie. Please have something to eat. You both look like you could use it."

Caeli and Finn sank wearily onto kitchen chairs while Cara spooned hot cereal into bowls.

Caeli held the warm bowl in her hands and inhaled the sweet, nutty aroma. When she picked up a spoon, her hands shook and her empty stomach rumbled. She'd known hunger before, and she knew enough to take food when it was offered.

The thumping of feet marked the noisy appearance of a dark haired little girl, pulling Caeli's thoughts back to the present.

"Finn!" the girl squealed.

Finn scooped Evie onto his lap and hugged her tightly. "Where's Anya?" she asked.

"Not feeling so good right now. This is my friend Caeli," he said, nodding his head in Caeli's direction. "She's a doctor and she's helping Anya feel better."

The girl eyed Caeli with a wariness beyond her years.

"It's very nice to meet you, Evie," Caeli said, smiling.

"Evie," Cara said. "It's really important that you don't tell anyone Finn and Caeli are here, okay?"

Evie nodded, serious. "I won't."

"Good girl," Finn said, plopping her onto her own chair. "But I'm really glad I got to see you."

Caeli swallowed hard, thinking about a world where children had to lie to save themselves, where babies were born and died in the dirt, where they were killed in their mother's arms.

"I have to drop Evie at school and then go to work," Cara said, and Finn nodded.

"We have some communication equipment to set up. I'll put it in the meeting room. Can we stay here tonight?"

"Of course," Cara answered.

"Thank you. Can you reach out to Jason?" he asked.

She nodded.

"We have reliable, long range communications equipment, and I need to get it to him. Find out if there's any way we can meet tonight," Finn said.

"I'll give him the message," she said, helping Evie with her coat. "We have to leave. Help yourselves to anything you need."

"Thank you, Cara," Finn said.

Once Cara and Evie left the house, Finn led Caeli down the basement stairs and through a hidden doorway. They entered what looked like an oversized storage room. A musty smell assailed them as soon as they opened the door, and dust coated the surface of a table wedged against the far wall. Finn lit a few small lamps hanging from metal hooks in the corners of the room. The soft glow bounced off the walls and cast dancing shadows across the dirty floor.

"We used to meet here, but once Anya and I took off, I'm sure it became too risky," Finn said, using his sleeve to brush off the table and set his pack down. Caeli placed hers next to it.

Carefully, he removed the small but powerful com device out of his pack. "Let's get this thing up and running."

He opened the metal casing and lifted the device from its cushioned surroundings. It powered on with a simple tap. Caeli knew it could be used with ear buds for a private communication, or with its tiny speaker engaged for a group conversation. The incoming and outgoing signals were locked and coded, assuring a secure line between users. Finn enabled the speaker and touched a blinking icon. He looked at Caeli and nodded.

"Derek, it's Caeli. Are you there?"

After a moment's silence, Derek's voice echoed back. "I'm here. Are you in a secure location?"

"We are," she answered. "Finn and I have the schedule and cargo information for the next delivery to EOB1."

"We got lucky," Finn said. "The next delivery is carrying food and weapons."

"We could use a little luck," Derek said.

Finn gave Derek the schedule information, and Caeli could hear Derek telling the other team members.

"We'll be ready on this end," Derek assured them. "What's your plan now?"

"I'm trying to catch up with Jason tonight to deliver the other coms in person, and to see if he has any new intel. Then Caeli and I will hide out here with Anya's sister for the night and get back to the station tomorrow to catch our ride."

"Be careful," Derek said, and Caeli could hear the strain in his voice.

"We will," she promised.

CHAPTER 15

The night was pitch black and bitterly cold. Caeli's breath puffed in swirling clouds around her face and she shivered despite several layers of borrowed clothing. Trotting behind Finn, she focused on keeping them hidden and not tripping on her own feet in the dark. They were headed toward a tavern in the city center to meet Jason, the location provided by Cara.

When they came around the corner and onto the main street, Caeli allowed them to be visible. It was nighttime, they were dressed inconspicuously, and they needed to enter the tavern to access the hidden cellar still deemed safe for meetings.

The smell of food and the sound of laughter grew more pronounced as they approached the stone entryway. Finn pulled open a heavy wooden door and a blast of warm air assailed them. The tavern was full and no one paid them any attention when they entered.

Leading Caeli by the arm, Finn steered her toward a small table in front of a roaring fireplace. He glanced behind the bar as they passed by and gave the bartender a small nod. Caeli inadvertently gasped when she realized that the bartender was also a cook from the hospital, a man who had been kind to her when she had first arrived, starving and traumatized, in Alamath. He was also part of the resistance movement and a welcome sight.

She glanced past him but caught the moment of recognition and surprise on his face when he saw her. As quickly as his expression appeared, it evaporated, and he turned away to tend to another customer.

She and Finn sat across from one another at their small table. Although Caeli was rapidly warming up from the fire, she didn't dare remove the hat concealing her blonde hair. Finn, with his scruffy beard and long hair, barely resembled the soldier he had been. They sat undisturbed and unnoticed until the bartender approached.

"What can I get you fine folks this evening?" he asked in a jovial voice. His lightheartedness didn't reach his eyes, however, and Caeli felt tension and worry radiating off him. She opened her mouth, but couldn't speak past the lump in her throat.

"How about a couple bowls of stew?" Finn said, giving Caeli a small, understanding smile.

"Coming right up," the bartender nodded and walked away.

Caeli cleared her throat. "Sorry," she said, shaking her head and leaning forward to speak. "It's just that he was the first friendly face I saw when I got here. It was one moment of kindness, but it gave me hope that maybe I would survive, that maybe not everyone believed the lies about us."

Finn nodded. "Dorian is a good man."

"He is," Caeli agreed. When she had been assigned to work at the hospital a few months after her arrival in Alamath, she'd seen Dorian nearly every day, albeit briefly, when she'd venture down to the cafeteria for a meal. And at her first meeting with the resistance group, she wasn't surprised to find Dorian Bell seated with the group of founding members.

He was back in a few moments with two steaming bowls

of stew, a platter of fragrant, warm bread, and a pitcher. As he served them, he kept a smile plastered on his face and said quietly, "Jason isn't here yet, so you two go ahead and eat. I'll come back." Finn nodded, and ripped off a chunk of bread to dunk in the stew. Caeli did the same.

She had a clear view of the tavern's front entrance and noticed the moment Jason entered. Although he had on civilian clothes, his neat appearance, short cropped hair, and fit body gave away his military affiliation. He looked straight at them, and without acknowledgement sat at the bar.

Out of the corner of her eye, Caeli watched Dorian pour Jason a drink, say a few words to him, and move on to his next customer. Jason sipped his drink for about five minutes, then pulled a coin from his pocket, tossed it on the bar, and walked through the tavern toward the back exit.

Finn and Caeli waited. A little while later, Dorian came back to clear their dishes. "Go to the end of the corridor and turn right. At the second door on the left, head down the stairs. Knock three times. You know the drill."

Finn fished some coins out of his own pocket and stood. Following Dorian's directions, he and Caeli slipped down the narrow corridor, past crates of bottled liquor, storage racks stocked with produce, stacks of clean dishes, and boxes of bread. As instructed, they opened the second door on the left and silently made their way down a dimly lit staircase.

It appeared as if they were in a storage closet, but Finn ran his hand over an empty wall and knocked three times. Caeli heard a click and then the wall opened up in front of them. Jason stood and a grin split his face.

"It's really good to see you still among the living," he said to Finn. "After the airstrike, I had no intel on survivors."

"It was bad, but it could have been much worse," Finn acknowledged.

Jason turned to Caeli. "And I'm looking forward to hearing your story. Marcus was convinced you were dead."

"That was my intent," Caeli answered, moving to embrace Jason.

"It's good to have you back," he said.

Finn was already removing a com device from his pack for a demonstration. "I know we have a lot to talk about, but first I wanted to show you this."

Jason's eyebrows raised and he looked from Caeli to Finn and back again. "That's not Amathi tech. And I'm pretty sure it's not Novali either," he said.

"No, it's not," Finn answered.

They spent the next hour catching Jason up. When they finished, Jason ran a hand over his face. "This changes everything, and it doesn't change anything."

"Well, one thing's changed," Finn said, standing to stretch his legs. "We can talk to each other now."

Jason gave him a brisk nod. "I think we'll keep one set up here, and I'll bring the other with me to the Stefans. They haven't been compromised yet."

Caeli's first meeting with the resistance movement had been at the Stefans' place. She remembered that night vividly, from the cold, star-filled sky to the smell of the hay bales in the barn. Her resolve had almost failed her, but she'd accompanied Jon to the meeting and left with a renewed sense of purpose and some of her faith in humanity restored.

"Good plan," Finn agreed, repacking the equipment and handing the bag off to Jason.

They stood ready to leave.

"Jason, do you know if Lia's okay?" Caeli asked, pausing at the doorway, uncertain she wanted to know the answer.

Jason lowered his eyes and exhaled. "Marcus rounded up all the Novali survivors, adults and children. He's keeping them in a bunker. I don't have access."

"We'll get them out, Caeli," Finn promised. "Somehow, we'll get them out."

***

They spent the next morning laughing with Evie at the breakfast table and stuffing themselves full of Cara's food. When the bustle of the morning ended and they were alone in the house, they sat in tense silence waiting for the hours to pass.

"Come on. Let's send our last communication to the team and go," Finn said, when the sun had crept past noon.

The remaining com device was going to stay right here in Cara's house. While she couldn't host meetings, she was still plugged in to the resistance, and could be a valuable conduit for moving information.

In the dusty basement, Derek's voice once again echoed out of the small speaker as clearly as if he were in the room with them.

"We're in position," he assured them. "How are you guys holding up?"

"We're good," Finn answered. "Ready to move."

"Just get on that train and keep your heads down."

"Will do," Finn said. "See you on the other side."

The afternoon was overcast, the clouds white and full. Caeli had learned to recognize the smell of snow in the air and she was sure it would begin falling soon. They hurried to the depot, their movement shadowed by the power of Caeli's thoughts.

This time when they arrived, the station buzzed with activity. Workers loaded supplies onto waiting trains, crews changed, the stationmaster shouted instructions. Soldiers patrolled the perimeter and inspected the cargo.

"There's our ride," Finn whispered, pointing across the yard to a sleek, silver-gray train gliding to a stop in front of a raised dock. "It looks like they fill the cars and wait for an inspection before closing the doors. We'll jump on when they've finished loading."

"Let's move a little closer," Caeli suggested.

They jogged toward the train and crouched behind a stack of crates. Side doors slid open and immediately the dock laborers began filling empty cars. In less than an hour the train stood ready for inspection.

"It doesn't leave the station for another hour, but we should get on and find a hiding place," Finn whispered.

They crept toward an open door and climbed aboard. When they found a wide crevice between two rows of crates, they tucked themselves out of sight and waited. Finn leaned against a box holding his weapon between his knees, and Caeli did the same. Sweat trickled between her shoulder blades.

She hated waiting. The constant dread she kept in check now saw an opportunity to rear its head. Her clammy hands began to shake, her lungs constricted, and her mind raced.

Finn glanced at her, concerned. "Tell me about the world out there," he asked, lifting his chin upwards.

She exhaled, grateful for his distraction, and grateful that he knew her so well. "Do you want to see it?" she offered.

Finn raised his eyebrows and nodded. Caeli pictured *Horizon*'s bridge, and remembered the endless expanse of space pierced by the glittering of a billion stars. She remembered her first trip to the capital city on Erithos, with towering buildings of glass and metal arching toward the sky. In her mind's eye, she visualized the hospital, the medical equipment, the research, and the healing. Finally, Caeli remembered Derek's beautiful family home, nestled beside a flowering field and gentle stream.

When she broke the connection with Finn, he was staring at her, wide-eyed.

"I know," Caeli smiled. "There's so much more than we ever imagined."

They sat in silence for a few moments before Finn said, "It's complicated out there too, though, isn't it?"

"Epically complicated," Caeli said, laughing.

Voices in the distance were now coming closer and their smiles faded. "The inspection?" Caeli asked.

"Sounds like," Finn said.

Caeli shrouded them in shadows once again as two soldiers boarded the car, looked over the cargo, and checked it against items on their manifest. Satisfied, they hopped back off and the door clanked shut behind them.

Finn fished a flashlight out of his pack, and its tiny bright beam punctured the pitch-blackness of the compartment. The train began to move.

DEREK

CHAPTER 16

He crouched outside the main bunker and peered through the window by the back entrance. Tree was ready to breach the front. Visibility was terrible. White flakes coated his jacket, his gloves, his gun, and every other fucking thing.

"Tree, let's do this," he barked into his com.

"We're ready," Tree answered.

"All teams, move on my mark," he ordered. "Three, two, one . . ."

At once, the bunker erupted. Doors crashed inward, glass shattered, and Derek's team shouted instructions: "Everyone down! Get down!"

They'd already spent hours doing reconnaissance. The outpost ran in shifts for maximum efficiency. Noah and a couple of Amathi resistance soldiers were currently tossing the night shift out of their bunks and rounding them up on the other side of the compound, while Derek, Tree, and the rest of the group secured the operational control room.

The sleeping work force consisted mainly of civilians, but the men in the ops room were military. And they did not all get down. Two, seated at a table, dove out of their seats, flipped the piece of furniture over, and crouched behind it, reaching for their side arms. *Please don't do it,* Derek begged silently.

Once the first gun fired, the room exploded into sound. Voices, cut off mid-scream, echoed around him. Chunks of wall exploded from errant shots. A round whisked by his head and left a burning streak on his temple. But his weapon was better, his training was better, and his team had the tactical advantage. Within moments the firefight ended.

Bodies littered the floor and the metallic tang of blood stung his nostrils. He surveyed the damage. One member of his team was down. The others stood up from their crouched positions and waited in silence for his orders.

"Secure all the weapons. Check for survivors," he ordered.

"Sir," Tree interrupted. "I think we have a problem. We counted ten before we breached. I see nine bodies."

"Shit," Derek cursed and silently reviewed the layout of the entire complex in his mind. The living quarters, including the kitchen area and bunkroom, attached to the operations building by a short corridor. That door was closed and he'd had eyes on it the whole time.

"Noah, is your position secured?" he asked over the com, just to be sure.

"Yes, sir," Noah confirmed.

"Must be that way," he said to Tree, pointing in the opposite direction. They picked their way carefully across the decimated space, boots crunching on glass, bits of wood, and twisted metal. Sensor panels and workstations—those that hadn't been destroyed, and which Derek presumed monitored conditions in the mine itself—blinked.

Next to the workstations, a radio receiver hissed. Derek and Tree exchanged a worried look. They rounded the corner into a wide hallway and Derek pointed at the blood-streaked floor. They followed the trail to a door.

"What do you think? Storage space?" Derek asked.

"Hopefully not a weapons locker," Tree joked halfheartedly.

They stopped and positioned themselves on either side of the doorframe. "Soldier, you are outnumbered and wounded. If you come out now, we can offer you medical attention."

There was no answer and no sound of movement. "I really don't want to go in shooting," Derek said.

Tree nodded his agreement.

Using the butt of his gun, Derek forced the lock and then kicked the door in, hoping his decision wasn't going to get him killed. When the door splintered, he ducked back out of the way, waiting for gunfire that didn't come. Cautiously, he peered around the frame. The room was, in fact, a storage closet, and slumped against the far wall sat a bleeding Amathi soldier, a wireless radio transmitter clutched in his grip.

Derek could see the young man's chest rising and falling rapidly, as if he couldn't take in enough air. A red bloom spread over the front of his shirt, and glassy eyes that still registered fear stared up at Derek as he approached.

Derek glanced at Tree, lowered his gun, and squatted next to the injured soldier. Tree nodded, but kept his gun trained on the young man.

"I'm just going to have a look, okay?" Derek asked. The young man gave him a barely perceptible nod.

Derek removed the device from the soldier's hands and carefully peeled back the tattered shirt. He could hear a wet, sucking sound every time the soldier inhaled and foamy blood trickled from the corner of the young man's mouth.

"Noah," Derek said quietly into his com. "I need you."

"On my way," came the quick response.

The soldier shook uncontrollably. Derek shrugged out of his jacket and wrapped it around the quaking body. When Noah entered the room moments later, his face was ashen. Derek realized he'd had to pass through the carnage in the control room to reach them. But, to the boy's credit, he kept his expression neutral as he knelt on the floor and laid his steady hands on the soldier's ravaged chest.

After a few seconds, he stood and stepped away, motioning for Derek to join him. All Noah's careful composure crumpled when he turned away from his patient. "I can't," he whispered. "If Caeli were here, she might be able to manage it. But there are bone fragments in his lungs and blood in the space around his heart. I don't . . . I can't."

Derek put a hand on his arm, "Can you make him comfortable?" he asked.

Noah nodded. He took a deep breath and wiped his eyes, then knelt back beside the soldier. Derek joined him.

"Have you ever seen the ocean?" Noah asked, his voice soft.

The soldier's eyes widened slightly and he shook his head.

"Would you like to?"

The young man swallowed and tried to answer, but a rasping cough was all he could manage. Noah put his hands back on the soldier's bloody chest and closed his eyes. "The smell is fresh and salty," he said. "The sand feels soft on your feet, and the sun is warm. It's so warm. The waves make a crashing sound when they hit the beach."

Noah's thoughts were so powerful and vivid that Derek was standing with him on the beach. The tangy scent of seawater clung to his nostrils. Sand sifted between his toes, and his body warmed from the sun's rays. Powerful waves lapped against the shore, a heartbeat, rhythmic at first. But the cadence slowed to a gentle pulse, until finally the water was still.

When Derek opened his eyes again, the soldier was dead, staring peacefully at some distant horizon.

Silence filled the room. Noah sat back on his heels, tears streaked down his pale face. Derek didn't have any real words of comfort to offer, but he'd seen that same stunned expression on the faces of both soldiers and civilians after a fight, and he knew he needed to get Noah moving.

He put a gentle hand on the boy's shoulder and said softly but firmly, "We have a train to meet. Let's finish this."

Noah stared back at him for a long moment and finally gave a small nod, pulling himself to his feet.

"Have the civilians gear up and escort them to the mine entrance. We'll meet your team there," he ordered and Noah disappeared around the corner.

Tree hadn't moved far from his position just inside the doorway, but he'd slung his weapon over his shoulder and was leaning against the wall, rubbing his hands over his face.

Derek carefully removed his jacket from the body and stood. "What a fucking waste," he said, looking at the still face of the young man.

***

A thick metal door sealed the mine entrance. This part of the compound connected to the main buildings through an underground tunnel access. The end of the tunnel opened into a large storage area filled with sealed metal crates, presumably full of ore ready for transport.

A small room, partitioned off from the main holding area,

stood at the right side of the door. To the right of that, an elevator shaft, large enough to hold several of the storage crates, led up to the loading docks.

Derek entered the room and gestured for one of the Amathi workers to join him. "How many are down there?" he asked.

The man swallowed hard and cleared his throat before answering. "Fifteen. We work in groups of fifteen."

Derek nodded. "We are going to lock everyone down there for a while. You'll stay out here with Liam." He nodded his head at the former Amathi soldier turned resistance fighter. "Once we're finished, you can let them all back out. But not before." He paused to give the man a moment to process the instructions, and the implied threat, before continuing. "It may be a while before you're resupplied. How long can you last?"

"We, uh, we have enough food for another couple of weeks," the man answered.

"Good. Now open the door."

With shaking hands, the man pressed a few buttons. A hum vibrated up through Derek's legs and he leaned out of the room in time to see the metal doors rumble open.

"Tree, get them all in," he ordered.

Tree herded the group of workers into the hole that had been carved into the side of the mountain. When the last one crossed inside the yawning cavern, Derek turned back around. "Shut it," he said, and the door slid closed, locking into place.

Once the base was secured and Liam left in charge of the control room with the lone worker, there was nothing to do but wait. Derek set up a perimeter watch, but the visibility was now so poor that an entire Amathi patrol could be on top of them before they had much of a warning. He thought it unlikely though, considering the rail was the only pathway in or out of the remote camp.

Nearly the whole team had moved back to the ground level, and all were avoiding the carnage in the ops room. Derek paced near the exit waiting to hear from Drew, becoming more anxious by the moment. When Drew finally did make contact, Derek could hear the worry in his voice.

"The train is almost an hour overdue. The weather might slow them down, but the rail line is designed to run in this."

"Whatever happened, let's give them a chance. They'll get here," Derek said, with more confidence than he felt.

"Roger that. We'll wait," Drew answered.

Derek leaned back against the wall and closed his eyes. He couldn't feel her. When Caeli was close by, he always felt her. The constant brush of her mind against his had become a familiar, welcome sensation, and he keenly felt its absence now.

He thought about what his plan would be if the train didn't show up. They couldn't stay there and wait indefinitely. He'd have to get everyone back to the hideout, and then he'd go into Alamath himself. *Some plan*, he thought.

CAELI

CHAPTER 17

The ride to the camp should have taken about four hours. When the train stopped after two, they knew something was wrong. Finn stood, flashlight in one hand, gun in the other. "I'm going to open the door between the cars and see if I can find out what's happening."

They moved out from their hiding place to the front of the car, weaving between crates. Finn found the door panel and punched a key. The door slid open. Snowflakes and icy wind whipped through the compartment, stinging Caeli's face. She blinked against the white glare.

Finn stepped out onto the cable that connected their car with the one in front of it. Shoving the flashlight into a pocket and swinging his weapon over his shoulder, he grabbed a handrail and leaned precariously around the edge of the car.

Caeli held her breath. But within a minute, Finn stepped back into the car unseen, dusting a layer of snow off his jacket.

"Nothing wrong with the train, as far as I can tell. The weather's bad, but that won't stop the rail line. The magnetic coils heat up to melt the snow and ice," he explained. "Let's sit tight for a few minutes and see if it starts up again."

Finn slammed the compartment door shut and the car was enveloped in silence. He slid back down against the wall, holding his gun between his knees.

In the darkened space, Finn shut his eyes and leaned his head back. Caeli felt his exhaustion, and just underneath that, his carefully walled off anguish.

"Finn," she whispered.

He looked up.

"I'm so sorry about the baby," she said. And just when she thought she had no tears left to shed, her eyes filled.

"She was so small and perfect," he said, his eyes meeting Caeli's.

"Finn, I made sure the only thing she felt was peace and love. I . . ." she stopped and choked back a sob. "I'm sorry."

Finn reached out to Caeli and took her hand. "I'm grateful that you were there to hold her. For the few moments she was alive, if it couldn't be Anya or me, then I'm grateful it was you." She squeezed his hand and they sat quietly together.

In the stillness of the car, Caeli felt the whispering of different minds. She stiffened and stretched her own mind out. There were dozens, coming closer.

"What is it?" Finn asked, gripping his gun and standing up.

"People are coming. Troops, I think," she said, scrambling to her feet. "We have to get this train moving again."

Finn nodded. "We need to get up to the control car." He heaved the door open and gestured at the cable he'd been standing on earlier. "The cars all connect like this. Let's go this way. We're already close."

Finn stepped back onto the cable, reached to the outside panel of the next car, and opened the door. He stepped inside and held a hand out to help Caeli jump through. They made it through three more cars this way and then stopped at the last one.

"We have to take them by surprise," Finn said. "We'll only have a few seconds to control the compartment. Can't be more than two or three of them. It's a small space."

Caeli focused on the car in front of them. "Two," she confirmed.

"Ready?"

She dropped her pack onto the floor, shifted her weapon back into her hand, and gave him a brisk nod.

As soon as Finn touched the panel and the door slid open, he burst into the compartment shouting, "Don't move! Hands up!"

Caeli dashed in behind him to see two stunned conductors stumble out from behind their seats, hands raised. The space was tight, with only two chairs for the crew and a small galley space where she and Finn now stood.

"Over there!" Finn gestured at the two men. "On your knees! Hands on your head!"

They did as they were told. Caeli could feel the fear rippling off them.

"Why did you stop?" Finn asked.

The two men exchanged a brief glance before the one man answered, "EOB1 is under attack. We're to hold here and wait for a regiment to board before moving out."

"The only way to reach the base is by rail, so they want to get troops on this train," Finn explained to Caeli.

"Someone was able to get a message out of that camp," she said.

"It sounds like things got complicated during the raid," Finn said.

"I hope they're okay," Caeli whispered, stretching her mind out. But Derek was too far. She couldn't feel him, but she could feel the growing panic from the men kneeling in front of her and the frenetic energy of the rapidly approaching troops.

"Hurry, Finn. They're getting close," she warned.

Finn moved toward the train's control panel and shifted his attention to a dozen blinking lights. "If they move, shoot them," he ordered.

Caeli nodded. She stood stone faced and unblinking, her hand steady and her mind clear. She knew they weren't going to move as long as she didn't give them an opening.

Finn was muttering to himself, "Throttle. Brake. System shutdown. Com." He turned back to her. "Okay, I got this."

"What about them?" she asked.

"Please," the younger man began, his eyes filling.

"Shut up," Finn barked. "Caeli, behind you in that locker," he said, nodding his head at a metal closet to her right. "There should be some foul weather gear. Take it out. Open the main door and toss it."

Thermal jackets and overalls hung from a hook inside the locker. Caeli shouldered her weapon and removed two sets of the clothing. When she opened the main cabin door and threw the bundle into a white dome of snow, cold air rushed inside.

"Get up," Finn ordered the men. They stood on shaking legs. "Get out, gear up, and wait near the line. The patrol will be here soon and they'll find you."

Caeli felt the weight of their relief crash over her like a wave. Before Finn shoved them out the door, Caeli heard him say, "We aren't killers."

DEREK

CHAPTER 18

Just as he was about to find Tree and give some new orders, Drew's voice broke the com silence. "The train just passed us," he said, clearly relieved. "We're going to blow the charges and head your way."

Derek breathed his own sigh of relief and let the rest of the group know.

"Stay sharp. We don't know why they were delayed. It's possible there are still hostiles on that train," he warned.

The cold wind and whipping snow prevented Derek from seeing more than a few feet in front of him. He waited with his team on the loading docks, apprehensive, until a familiar voice said in his ear, "Derek, is the base secured? We are incoming."

"Base is secured. Good to hear your voice."

When the train glided to a silent stop on the platform and the front compartment door slid open, Caeli jumped out first. Even through the blinding white, he could see her wide smile. With his gloved hands, he cupped her face and kissed her hard. She leaned into him and returned his kiss with enthusiasm.

"You okay?" he asked, and she nodded.

"There's enough food on this train to get us through the winter."

He smiled back at her. "Then let's move it onto *Eclipse* and get out of here."

When she stepped back, her eyes found the bloodstains on his jacket and she looked back up at him, alarmed. "It's not mine," he said.

She tilted her head and asked, "Are *you* okay?"

"They didn't go quietly," he answered, swallowing back the lump in his throat.

Caeli nodded at him with silent understanding.

Before they departed East Orainos base for good, Derek ordered one case of food left behind for the miners.

***

Over the next few weeks, palpable relief filled the resistance camp. *A good meal and a safe place to sleep will do that,* Derek thought as he stretched out on his sleeping pallet. Caeli lay next to him on her side, blonde curls framing her sleeping face.

He rolled toward her and touched his thumb to her cheek. He wanted to wake her up. They had a modest amount of privacy in the little alcove Caeli had staked out for them. She'd tucked their sleeping gear behind some shelves, hung their outerwear from the corner, and lined their boots up off to one side. When they woke in the mornings, she'd tidy the small space, and he noticed that if he moved a boot, knocked over a bag, or messed with the blanket, she would wordlessly fix it.

It was such a small thing to know about her, but details like that were in short supply. He'd never actually lived with her. The closest he'd come was when he'd been recovering from his injuries in her hidden cave, and then when they shared a cabin on *Horizon*. Hiding in an underground bunker for the winter didn't count as living with her either, but witnessing her little quirks made him smile.

When her eyes fluttered open, his mouth was on hers before she could say a word. He pulled his pants down past his hips, and then frantically tried to wrestle hers off while she gripped his shoulders. She trailed her tongue over the soft spot between his ear and throat, and her hot breath on his neck made him groan.

He buried his head in her neck, and then buried himself inside her. He paused for a moment at her sharp intake of breath, but she rocked her hips and opened her mind completely. Her urgency built inside his body, and when the wave of release crashed over him, he couldn't distinguish her feelings from his own.

Sprawled on top of her and sweating, he didn't move until she gave him a light shove in the chest. "I can't breathe."

Reluctantly, he rolled to the side, pulling her close.

"Good morning to you too," she said, laughing.

He squeezed her shoulders. "This is the first time since we've been here that I feel like we can catch our breath. Make a plan."

"Get these people healthy," Caeli added.

She stared silently at the ceiling, and when she spoke again, the ease of the moment had shifted. "I asked Jason about Lia."

Derek stiffened.

"Marcus rounded up all the Novali. He's got them locked away in a bunker. What is he doing to them?" She turned toward him, searching for answers he couldn't give.

He shook his head wordlessly and she continued, "We're in no condition to attack Alamath, I know that, but every day we do nothing is another day Lia has to suffer at his hands."

She turned toward him, her eyes staring past his into the nightmare of her own memories. Her breathing became ragged and the force of her thoughts assailed him.

Sitting up, he pulled her against his chest. "Don't go there, Caeli," he said gently. "Stay right here with me." She shuddered in his arms, and he touched his forehead to hers.

"Stay here with me," he repeated.

Her mind was open to him, and he knew she was fighting to regain control of her thoughts. He felt powerless when she sank into the terror of her past. Sometimes he could help by offering her another thought, by linking his breathing to hers, by talking her through it. But sometimes she would sink so deeply inside herself, all he could do was hold her until she came back to him.

No more than a few minutes passed when she fell limply against him, sighing with exhaustion, her hair clinging damply to her forehead.

"Think you can rest a little more?" he asked.

She nodded, her eyes already closed.

When he was sure she'd fallen asleep, he moved carefully out of the sleeping bag, pulled the blanket back over her, and brushed a kiss across her forehead.

***

Derek joined Jon at a makeshift table in the area designated as the command center. One of the radios Kade had rigged rested silently in the corner. Jason should have checked in by now, and his lack of communication was becoming more alarming by the day.

The Amathi resistance fighters on the inside had to feel like they were in limbo. There weren't enough of them to launch a meaningful attack, and they already lived with the constant fear that even their limited clandestine work would flush them out of hiding and place them in the crosshairs of Marcus's firing squad.

Derek held a steaming cup of tea in his hands, warming himself against the constant chill of the underground bunker. It was worse in the mornings, before moving bodies and their bustling activity had a chance to heat the space. But he and Jon had a routine of meeting early and talking strategy, or sometimes just sitting together before the day began.

This morning, Derek was silently worrying over the Novali trapped in Alamath when Jason's voice jolted him from his thoughts.

"Marcus executed the train crew you ambushed during the raid. He said they should have fought harder before sacrificing government property. He acted like they were sympathizers with the resistance, and he used the opportunity to make an example of them." The strain in Jason's voice carried over the airwaves. "He questioned the civilian dock crew too but let them go. It's bad in here. There's a curfew, and Marcus has renewed his efforts searching for you."

Derek cursed under his breath, and Jon hung his head.

"I don't have a lot of time," Jason continued, sounding harried. "Alizar Sorin should have returned by now and Marcus is getting anxious."

"Do you think he'll start transmitting again?" Derek asked.

"He's not ready to do that yet. But we all know Sorin isn't coming back, and the General won't wait forever."

Derek tapped his thumb against his leg. A new clock was ticking.

"I have to go, but Cara wants to know how Anya's doing?"

Jason asked.

"Getting stronger," Jon answered.

"Good to hear. I'll make contact again as soon as possible."

Once Jason signed off, Derek and Jon sat in tense silence.

"We have to make a move," Jon finally said. "We can't stay hidden underground forever. Our food supply won't last indefinitely, and I doubt we'll be able to pull off another raid. Not that I'd be willing to risk it again anyway." He paused and closed his eyes. "And they have the most vulnerable members of our population locked in prison camps."

Derek nodded, thinking about his earlier conversation with Caeli. "I can't have Marcus looking for another trade partner either. He's going find someone no one will be able to deal with."

"We have to try to put something in motion. Marcus knows we're out here. The longer we wait, the more I feel like the net will close around us," Jon said.

A kernel of an idea began to form in Derek's mind. He stood and paced around the small space. "Maybe I could get inside Alamath," he finally said.

***

"I don't like this," Caeli said, her forehead creased with worry. She'd listened without comment when he presented his idea to the *Horizon* team, Jon, Erik, and Finn. But now, in the privacy of their own space, she gave voice to her anxiety. "You don't have much of a plan beyond getting inside."

"I'll figure it out as I go along," he assured her. "It's what I do."

She sat down at the edge of the sleeping pallet and wrapped

her arms around her knees. He sat next to her.

"I need to find out what's happening with the Novali. And we have to plan a coordinated effort. I might be able to access Marcus and his inner circle without suspicion that I'm with the resistance, and that's worth something right now. I'll be more useful inside," he finished.

Truthfully, he didn't know what would happen once he got into Alamath, but something had to give. And he had to make sure Marcus didn't resume recklessly transmitting his beacon into the surrounding systems again.

He was silent for a minute, then turned to her and added, "We have to force a solution soon. Time is going to run out for Almagest if we don't."

Caeli leaned her head back against the wall and closed her eyes. "I know," she whispered. "I just can't see how we win this."

"We have to win it," he said.

"Or die trying," she added.

"Or die trying," he repeated.

She opened her eyes and looked at him. "I don't want to die." She paused, swallowing hard, and he waited for her to continue. "Not anymore. I did for a long time."

He knew this. He'd felt her dark, self-destructive thoughts when she first empathically shared her story with him. But for some reason she needed to speak aloud, so he listened.

"I want a life now. I want a life for us all," she said fiercely. "And I want a life with you."

She'd never said those words to him before. He knew she loved him, but he also knew she held back, and he'd never been sure whether it was because she was uncertain of him, or of her own precarious future. But now the unabashed longing in her voice gave him an answer.

He'd already said as much to her. And when he couldn't communicate with words, he'd communicate with his thoughts and with his raw emotions. Now, he felt as helpless as he ever had in his life when he couldn't promise her a future, but he wouldn't insult her with false assurances. He reached for her, and she leaned into him.

"Please be careful," she pleaded.

She frantically undressed him, and they made love with an urgency that left him breathless.

***

The sun blazed against the cold blue sky, melting the snow pack into wet slush. Derek trudged through the mess toward the town border and the Amathi military checkpoint, unarmed. It was a choice he and Drew had discussed at length. Bottom line, the Amathi were going to take his weapons before allowing him into the city anyway, so better not give them a reason to shoot him before then.

Drew and Alaric waited with the ship. They'd disengaged the stealth tech after tucking her into a secluded glade a few miles from the checkpoint while Derek hopefully gained an audience with Marcus. It was a risky plan, but Derek couldn't afford to second-guess himself now.

He spotted a guard tower in the distance and strode confidently in that direction until a sharp voice demanded he stop. He complied, and waited as a small company of soldiers emerged from the base of the tower and headed in his direction.

Six guns trained on his chest. He kept his arms slightly raised and his movements to a minimum. One soldier stepped forward. "State your business," he demanded.

"I'd like to meet with your General," Derek answered, intentionally vague.

The soldier's expression remained neutral, but Derek knew his off-world accent, foreign clothing, and bold request gave the young man pause.

"Where are you from?" the soldier asked.

"Not this backward planet. No insult intended," Derek answered, grinning.

To his credit, the soldier didn't blink at Derek's impertinent tone. He merely narrowed his eyes, raised his weapon, and hit Derek across the temple with the butt of his gun.

CHAPTER 19

Something felt sticky along the side of his face. And his head itched. Derek tried to lift his arm to scratch it, but he couldn't move. Confused, he blinked and attempted to bring the world back into focus.

As his blurry vision cleared, he realized he couldn't move because he was cuffed to a metal chair. Momentary panic surged through him and he jerked on the restraints. The abrupt movement shot a blinding jolt of pain through his head. Blinking, he relaxed back into the chair, took a deep breath, and tried to remember where he was and what he was supposed to be doing.

The windowless room was sparse and empty, save for a dingy light bulb swinging over his head and a metal table pushed into the corner. It looked like a cell. He must have been in Marcus's bunker.

The metallic smell of his own blood stung his nostrils, his head pulsed painfully in time with his heartbeat, and his clothes were damp from having been dragged along the wet ground. *Well, this is nice*, he thought as his teeth began to chatter.

As uncomfortable as he was, he was pretty sure Marcus wouldn't leave him to rot for too long in this musty room, and he wasn't disappointed. In a few moments, the door slid open and the General himself entered the room.

Derek sat frozen. Caeli's memory of being locked in a cell with this man while he tortured and killed a young soldier flashed through Derek's mind, as real as if it were his own. He fought to keep his expression blank.

Marcus wasn't a large man, but his energy and presence filled the room. Flanked by an armed guard, he closed the space between the door and Derek in two strides. His smile, although broad and disarming, didn't reach his eyes.

"I must apologize for your rather rough treatment, but we can't be too careful," Marcus began.

Derek remained silent.

"My sentry tells me you aren't from Almagest. What can I do for you?" he continued, spreading his arms in a magnanimous gesture.

"You can un-cuff me," Derek said in a low voice.

"Not just yet," Marcus said, his face contorting into a sneer. "I'll ask again, what can I do for you?"

Derek stared at him, then shrugged and said, "I thought I might be able to do something for you."

Marcus raised his eyebrows and nodded for Derek to continue.

"You had a trade agreement with Alistar Sorin?" Derek asked, though his tone suggested he knew the answer.

Marcus narrowed his eyes. "I expect him back anytime now."

"He's not coming back," Derek said bluntly.

"And why is that?"

"He met with an unfortunate accident." Derek answered, throwing Marcus his own cold smile. "But I may be able to step in and continue with your arrangement."

Marcus squatted down directly in front of Derek and stared at him. "Where's your ship?"

"It's here," Derek answered vaguely.

Marcus nodded and then stood. "Bring her in," he said to his guard.

The door slid open again and a young woman entered the room. Another guard followed, with his gun solidly planted between the girl's shoulder blades. Dark blond hair clung to her dirty face, and worn clothing hung from her painfully thin body. Derek knew her instantly. It was Lia, Caeli's childhood friend. He clenched his jaw.

"My dear, I need to get some information out of our guest," Marcus said, turning to Lia. Lia didn't even try to fight the order. She merely looked at Derek with resignation and knelt in front of him, placing a trembling hand on his knee.

"I'm told this doesn't hurt a bit," Marcus said, cheerfully clapping his hands together and stepping out of the way.

Derek drew in a sharp breath at Lia's touch. A tingling sensation prickled his nerve endings and a dull humming throbbed in the back of his head. Suddenly he felt her presence in his mind, a gentle brush against his consciousness. And while the sensation was familiar, Lia's mind felt altogether different from Caeli's.

Her myriad thoughts played in his mind like background noise, eventually resolving into silence. But he could feel her waiting.

"Find out who he is and where he comes from," Marcus ordered.

The tingling returned as Lia pushed urgently into his mind, asking Marcus's questions and searching for answers. Instinctively he tried to resist, but her consciousness sifted through his thoughts as easily as a breeze parting the blades of grass in a field. He fought the violation, struggling against the intrusion. His pulse raced and sweat beaded on his forehead.

"*Please forgive me,*" Lia's plaintive voice begged in his mind.

He caught her gaze and forced his breathing to slow. "*Lia,*" he said in his mind.

Her eyes widened and she gasped.

"*Don't react,*" he warned. "*I'm with Caeli. She's alive.*"

Lia's eyes filled and she began to shake.

"*Just answer the way I tell you,*" he coaxed.

She made no outward move, but a glimmer of hope spread its warmth throughout his brain.

"His name is Derek," she began in a halting, shaky voice. "He works mostly out of a system called Elista. He flies a ship called *Eclipse* with a small mercenary crew. They're nearby." Lia stopped and looked at Marcus.

"What happened to Sorin?" Marcus demanded.

"He killed him and stole his cargo," Lia said.

Derek smirked and shrugged at Marcus. "I have bigger guns."

"Why is he here?" Marcus asked, speaking to Lia but staring at Derek.

Before Lia could answer, Derek jumped in. "I want to resume trading. I sold most of Sorin's cargo, and I'll keep that profit as a good faith deposit. But you have some very valuable merchandise here." He paused and looked appraisingly at Lia. "I know where to find competitive bidders."

Marcus narrowed his eyes and held Derek's stare for several heartbeats. Then he turned to Lia, who gave a small nod. "He's telling the truth."

"I'm mainly interested in acquiring information and technology." Marcus said, now addressing Derek directly.

"Hard for me to acquire anything handcuffed to a chair," Derek said.

Marcus inclined his head slightly and motioned to one of the guards, who knelt and unlocked Derek's cuffs. Derek rubbed his wrists but didn't move, uncertain if he could actually stand without falling over. The pounding in his head was making him nauseous. He tried to ignore it, but he must have looked as shitty as he felt.

"Take our guest to the infirmary and have his head tended to, and then show him to Sorin's old quarters," Marcus said, addressing the guard again, and then he turned back to Derek. "We'll speak again very soon."

The guard gripped Derek under the arm and hauled him to his feet. The room spun and he nearly blacked out, managing to grab the edge of the chair in time to steady himself. He saw Marcus nod to the other guard before exiting the room. The other soldier shoved Lia toward the door, but she turned quickly to look at Derek and a question appeared in his mind. "My son?"

Derek focused on his memory of Caeli holding Lia's son and kissing the soft curls on the top of his head. Lia closed her eyes and exhaled before turning to leave.

***

He recognized the infirmary from Caeli's memories. It felt like he'd awoken from a dream to find he was still in the dream. Or it could just be the concussion. They'd used some kind of tissue glue to patch his torn scalp back together, and then shot him up with a powerful painkiller. He was pleasantly high, but not as clear-headed as he'd like.

The guard escorted him from the hospital to another bunker that looked to Derek like military housing.

"You can clean up and rest in here," the guard said, opening the door to a small, efficient room.

Derek nodded, surveying the space. A tidy bunk, a small storage bin, and a bathroom tucked into one corner were about the extent of it.

As soon as he was left alone, he sank down onto the bed and closed his eyes. Between the drugs and the stress of the day, mindless sleep pulled him under in minutes. When a sharp rapping on the door woke him, he had no idea how long he'd been out.

Disoriented and sore, he splashed some water from the tap onto his face before joining his escort. They left the bunker area and met Marcus in his personal quarters, a functional but comfortable space, with a spread of food laid out on a large table.

Marcus, seated at the head of the table, motioned for Derek to sit. "You must be hungry," he said.

At the suggestion, Derek's stomach rumbled. Wordlessly, he sat and loaded a plate with food. While he wouldn't describe the atmosphere in the room as relaxed, Marcus spoke to him conversationally and without any threat or artifice in his voice.

"We're just now establishing an air fleet with six well-tested ships and three new prototypes. Once we work out all the bugs, I'd like to turn our attention to reaching low orbit."

"So, are you looking to purchase designs for launch systems and satellites?" Derek asked.

Marcus nodded. "We have the facilities for construction, but not the know-how. Any schematic data I've been able to recover from our archives is incomplete. My engineers work with partial designs and their own imaginations. Not that they aren't talented, but it's been a challenge. And besides, the world out there kept making progress, even when Almagest was tossed backward in time by a millennium." Marcus took a long drink.

"What happened here?" Derek asked. "This planet's a pretty well-kept secret. You have to go back to some of the original colonization records to find mention of it."

"We nearly blew ourselves into oblivion," Marcus answered, shrugging. "Most of our history went with the infrastructure."

Derek sat back in his chair, suspecting that Marcus knew more than he was letting on, but he pushed the conversation in a different direction. "What about that girl today? The one who mind-fucked me? How many of you are like that?"

Marcus narrowed his eyes. "*We* are not like that. *They* are a dangerous group of genetically modified humans, who have been a threat since they came into existence."

Derek raised his eyebrows and Marcus continued, "The Novali were manipulative and powerful. Their threat needed to be eradicated, and I did so. The remainder of their kind are under control."

Marcus's smile chilled Derek to the bone, and once again he glimpsed the brutal dictator lingering just under the man's surface.

"Well, thank you for this outstanding meal, but if I don't get to my ship soon, my crew will become alarmed and do something rash. That won't be healthy for our future business together," Derek said, now also smiling as he stood.

Marcus nodded to his armed guard, standing stone still at the door. "Take a unit to his ship and give him the coordinates for Kavala field," he ordered. And then to Derek, "You can bring your ship into the city proper. There's a landing strip at the west end of town, and a hangar. You and your crew are most welcome here as we work out our negotiations."

***

Derek sat in *Eclipse*'s cockpit and entered the coordinates for the landing field into the navigation system. He ran a hand through his hair and winced when he touched his healing scalp.

"You okay, sir?" Alaric asked, brow furrowed.

"This planet keeps trying to kill me," Derek joked. He turned to face his team and continued more seriously, "Let's get *Eclipse* into the hangar. Stick with the story that we need a few days for repairs. We can start gathering intel and I'll try to connect with Jason."

"How closely do you think we'll be watched?" Drew asked.

Derek shook his head. "Not sure. Marcus believes our cover story. But he also thinks I'm an unscrupulous killer, so there's that. He's got a lot on his mind and we aren't an immediate threat, but we still need to be careful."

5524.8.6
PRIVATE RESIDENCE OF THE SECRETARY GENERAL
CAPITAL CITY: AL AMAR PROVENCE

The launch had gone off without a hitch. Jed poured himself a drink and sat in the quiet of his personal library. The house was empty, and rather than appreciate the solitude, he missed his family. His wife had taken the children to the shore for several days to escape the heat of the city. They'd called to tell him they'd watched one of the launches from the beach.

Many of the smaller ships, which would eventually make up the bulk of Almagest's fleet, could be constructed in ground-based facilities, but the large cruisers required space docks. The final pieces of equipment necessary to complete that infrastructure had just entered orbit.

Jed stretched contentedly and stood, intending to raid the kitchen and prepare himself a meal, when he noticed the tablet on his desktop flashing with an incoming message request. Only a select few people had access to this private line, and he had just spoken to his family. Sitting back in the chair, he enabled the encryption code and tapped the blinking icon.

"Owen. This is a surprise."

"Sir, I'm sending you a file." Owen's voice was clipped. "She's embedded an override code deep into the networked systems. Your engineers will never find it without the data I'm transmitting."

"Are you compromised, Owen?" Jed asked, his brow knitting with tension.

"No, sir. She has no idea," Owen answered. Jed thought, No, she certainly doesn't.

"I've got it. I'll send it to Reeves now. Thank you, Owen. Stay safe." At that, he disconnected the call and stared stone-faced at the blank screen.

When he'd been elected to the highest office on the planet, Jed had inherited a team of covert, elite, highly skilled intelligence operatives, dedicated to assuring the security and continuity of Almagest's fragile government. Over the years, he'd made personal appointments and added select, trusted individuals to the clandestine group. Owen was one of them. It had been Jed's call to plant him inside DynamiCorp, a move that had been received with skepticism. There was no evidence to cast suspicion on the company, nothing to suggest they were anything more than a research and development facility with the government as their largest client. Nothing, that is, but Jed's gut instinct.

5524.8.6
OFFICE OF THE UNDERSECRETARY
CAPITAL CITY: AL AMAR PROVENCE

She'd watched one of the launches from her office window and stared transfixed as the unmanned rocket hurled upward. It was one of her rockets. They were an old design, one she'd repurposed for this kind of cargo mission, but they were reliable, and Misha needed reliable. Over the course of the next few launches, she had some cargo of her own to lift into orbit.

Dear Dr. Jokahar,

I have been following the results of your work with great interest, particularly those demonstrating heritability of engineered modifications. I understand that you are currently self-funding this research. I wonder if we might come to some mutually satisfactory working relationship? The visionary thinking behind your work is quite in line with my own, and my resources would certainly expedite forward progress. Should you wish to pursue a partnership, I will arrange a meeting in person. I await your reply.

Respectfully,
Marishka Torov
Founder, DynamiCorp

5525.3.6
PERSONAL LOG: DR. ELAN JOKAHAR
ENCRYPTED

Misha Torov is brilliant. She understands my work and she supports the vision behind it. No, she more than supports it, she believes in it. She's sending me a fresh supply of volunteers, of which I am in desperate need. We've decided that I'll continue to work here, in my facility, until she completes construction on the new bio-laboratory on *Valera Island. We toured Malaka and she's promised me Valera will be just as well appointed. This confluence of positive events fuels my belief that we are creating a new vision, the right vision, for the future.*

_5525.9.9_
TO: MARISHKA TOROV
FROM: DR. ELAN JOKAHAR
RE: REPORT ON PHASE III
FILES ATTACHED (6)
ENCRYPTED

Misha,

The results thus far are spectacular! We are seeing major increases in cognitive function, as well as neuronal and systemic cell regeneration and repair. The attached data includes quantitative analyses of all affected alleles and full panel results on all measurable changes. These mutations are all confirmed to be germinal.

Regards,
Elan

5526.2.3
TO: DR. ELAN JOKAHAR
FROM: MARISHKA TOROV
RE: FACILITY COMPLETE

Elan,

Make preparations to transfer operations to Valera. I look forward to seeing you there.

Misha

5527.4.3
TO: SECRETARY GENERAL JED WORTHINGTON
FROM: AGENT OWEN GARETH
ENCRYPTED

DynamiCorp is transferring significant assets, equipment, and personnel to a new facility. The location coordinates are: 3.0758° S, 37.3533° E. The fact that the existence and purpose of this facility have been so well guarded is most alarming.

CAELI

CHAPTER 20

"These are medical logs," Caeli mumbled under her breath.

Kat looked up from the piece of equipment she had disassembled on the work desk in front of her. "Did you say something?" she asked.

Caeli nodded. "The amount of data here is staggering. It's like they were running an enormous experiment."

Kat stood up and moved to look over Caeli's shoulder.

"I wish Dr. Gates were here," Caeli said, pointing at the screen. "These look like genetic markers, and this column looks like the individual test subjects."

"Can you read the notes?" Kat asked.

"I can make out bits and pieces. If my history lessons were right, this information is from our founding civilization, which imploded over a thousand years ago. The written language has definitely evolved some."

Kat nodded. "Let me run a translation program. Our database contains all the current and obsolete languages from the colonies, dating back to the first migration wave."

Caeli moved over and Kat sat in front of the screen. "Maybe I can get this to load."

After a minute, Kat sat back and drummed her fingers on the console. "Well, something's happening, but it might take a little while. Let's go check in with Noah and get some lunch."

Caeli stretched and nodded. Noah was on shift manning the communication radio. Caeli had already stopped by once today, eager to hear from anyone inside Almagest. And Kat's non-stop motion told Caeli that she was just as anxious.

They found Noah seated on the ground, leaning against a wall. He held a small knife in one hand and chunk of wood in the other. A cup, an intricate pattern carved on its surface, was emerging from the amorphous block.

"No news," he said before they could ask.

"Damn," Kat mumbled under her breath. Noah nodded and kept working.

"That's beautiful," Caeli said, squatting down next to him.

He gave her a small smile. "My sister was a much better artist."

At the sadness in his voice, Caeli glanced at Kat, who tilted her head and said, "I'll go grab us some food."

Caeli let herself sag against the wall next to Noah. "Do you want to tell me what happened to her?" she asked.

He was silent for so long that she didn't think he was going to answer, but suddenly he stopped carving. His anger hit Caeli with the force of a tidal wave. She blinked and he exhaled loudly, the effort of reining in his emotions evident on his face.

"I tried to find her when the soldiers shot into the crowd, but it was chaos. People were running and screaming and stepping on each other to get away. I made it back to our house but no one was there." He paused and swiped a hand across his cheek, brushing away a stray tear. "Through the resistance network, Jon and Erik had been quietly tracking the whereabouts of all the Novali. You know this part already?"

Caeli nodded. "It was part of the plan when I was still here."

Noah nodded and continued, "We had the same instructions as the resistance members. Have some basic provisions ready if we needed to run. Meet at a rendezvous point. So, I grabbed my bag, and went out looking for her. There were soldiers in the streets already, raiding houses and dragging people out." He paused again and turned the knife over in his hand. "I knew how to stay hidden, though. I liked to explore, be alone. I learned my way around Alamath early on."

As he spoke, a knot of dread built in Caeli's chest, the feeling now as familiar as her own heartbeat.

"The closer I got to the city center, the more difficult it was for me to stay out of sight. I tried to stretch out my mind and find her that way, but there was so much noise. Before I knew it, I was back where I started, just outside the barracks. They hadn't cleared the bodies off the ground yet . . ."

He stopped talking, his eyes fixed on his hands. Caeli put a gentle hand on his shoulder.

"It was Jon who found me. He told me the Novali were being rounded up and taken to a bunker. We had to leave. I argued with him. I didn't want to leave without my sister. But he convinced me that I wouldn't be any help to her if I were captured. He promised we would go back for them all once we had a chance to regroup and make a plan."

The tears Noah had been fighting finally fell unchecked. "It's been months. We haven't gone back. What's happening to her?"

Caeli had no answer to give, at least not one that would be a comfort to him. When Kat returned with their lunch, they ate in heavy silence.

***

She couldn't breathe. A rough hand held her by the throat. Rocks dug into her back, their sharp edges piercing her skin. His smell made her gag.

"Caeli, wake up."

She gave up the struggle, but still he hurt her. Because he wanted to. Because he could.

"Caeli!" A familiar voice called to her, pulling her from the darkness.

Gasping for breath, she finally opened her eyes to see Kat's concerned face hovering over hers.

The nightmare receded, but its lingering aftermath left Caeli shaking, her sweat-soaked hair plastered to her forehead and her legs tangled in the blanket.

Kat reached for her hand.

"Sorry I woke you again," Caeli whispered.

With Derek and Drew gone, Kat had wordlessly moved her things next to Caeli's and had been witness to the nightly terrors that plagued her companion's sleep.

Keeping hold of Caeli's hand, Kat lay back down on her own pallet. "Don't apologize. I'm sorry you had to live through the shit that's giving you nightmares."

Caeli couldn't help but smile. Kat's brash and forthright nature contrasted sharply with her own gentler demeanor, but now it was one of the things she loved most about the woman.

"It's being back here, I think," she said. "When I was living with Derek's parents, I reinvented myself. I just pushed everything out of my head and pretended none of it ever happened. This world felt so far away, it was almost like it didn't exist. Like it was part of my imagination and not my reality."

"And now you're living with a heightened sense of anxiety and fear again. You're back in it and it's triggering your stress," Kat said.

"I didn't want to come back," Caeli confessed. "I wanted that other life. I wanted it so badly."

"No one who really understands war wants to come back to it," Kat answered. "We do what we have to."

"Do you miss home?" Caeli asked, curious.

"*Horizon* feels more like home than my home ever did," Kat said. "I grew up on a mining colony. Most people worked there for a few months at a time and then lived somewhere else, but there were some families. It was a backward place though. Not much opportunity. I couldn't wait to leave, and I joined the Alliance as soon as they'd let me."

"Looking for adventure?" Caeli joked.

"Looking for anything meaningful," Kat answered earnestly. "But yeah, I do love to fly." And Caeli could hear her smiling.

"If I haven't said it already, thank you for being here. I know you didn't have to take this mission."

"That's the meaningful part," Kat answered.

Caeli sighed. Sleep finally felt like a possibility. She squeezed Kat's hand as her eyelids fluttered shut.

In the morning, Jon greeted them with the news that Jason had made contact. *Eclipse* was in an Amathi hanger, Derek and the team were safe, at least for the moment, and it seemed as if Marcus believed their cover story.

"Jason is going to try and make direct contact with Derek soon, so we can begin to form a plan," Jon finished.

"Progress," Kat said. Jon nodded in agreement.

Caeli breathed a sigh of relief. At least for the moment, she could focus on something other than her worry. "I'm going back to the lab to see if that translation's completed."

"I'll catch you later for breakfast," Kat said.

When Caeli sat at the workstation, the language scrolling across the screen was perfectly legible. The disparate bits of information riveted her attention, and hours passed before she even thought to look up.

5527.2.1
DYNAMICORP
OFFSHORE RESEARCH FACILITY
MALAKA ISLAND, BOREIOS PROVENCE

Misha was linked into the simulation. It felt as real as if she were seated in the cockpit of the fighter, but she was merely a voyeur. Cassian Vahn handled the ship with inhuman speed and agility, even when she accounted for the biomechanical interface. There was also ruthlessness to his decision-making. His kill rate was one hundred percent, with the loss to his own squadron minimal. And those losses had been clearly sacrificial, calculated to maximize damage to his virtual enemy. Misha allowed herself a small smile.

When the mock battle ended, she waited for Vahn in the locker room.

"Captain, I want you to design a continent-wide assault simulation and run the operation from an orbital command module," she said the moment he entered the room.

"Yes, ma'am," he answered, shrugging out of his IVA suit. Misha tilted her head as she surveyed him appreciatively. Always a fit and well-muscled man, he possessed a physique now chiseled to perfection. He ignored her stare, understanding that it was clinical in nature.

"Your performance continues to improve," she commented.

He nodded. "Response time, speed, and agility for the entire group have increased."

"How do you feel?" she asked.

"Never better," Vahn answered.

5529.9.5
PERSONAL LOG: DR. ELAN JOKAHAR
ENCRYPTED

As with any revolutionary scientific breakthrough, ours is not without its unexpected results. I am careful not to impose judgment, yet I find these outlying traits disconcerting. Misha sees limitless possibilities for the Beta group; however, their empathy seems to engender in them a moral rigidity. They are most reluctant to explore the limits of their skill if they believe an action contradicts their perceived ethics, and they are surprisingly resistant to any form of coercion.

5530.2.2
ABOARD THE STARSHIP DEFENDER, FLAGSHIP OF THE
ALMAGEST FLEET

The ceremony was being transmitted planet-wide, live from the bridge of the ship. Jed stood at a podium, awaiting the signal from his media director. At her cue, he began to speak. "People of Almagest, it is with great pride that I speak to you today from aboard the Starship Defender. She is aptly named." He paused while the camera panned across the array of uniformed soldiers, standing in formation and at attention on the deck. "While we strive for peace in our region and in our time, the galaxy remains a dangerous place. It has been my mission, as your leader, to assure our safety amidst the chaos around us. Today marks the day when our security no longer depends on outside, contracted forces, but rather is provided for by our own proud fleet and networked defense infrastructure."

Jed stepped out from behind the podium and nodded at Misha, who stood behind him and to his left. She presented him with a small, polished wooden box. When she opened the lid, he carefully removed a medallion from the velvet interior.

"Captain Reeves," Jed said, and the ranking officer stepped forward. "You are hereby promoted to Admiral of the Fleet." He pinned the medal to Reeves' uniform lapel. "The bridge is yours."

Reeves saluted him, "Thank you, sir."

5530.5.5
DYNAMICORP
OFFSHORE RESEARCH FACILITY
VALERA ISLAND

The Beta group was becoming problematic. While initially they had been willing participants in the trials, their new abilities had altered their sensibilities. Many now voiced strong opposition to the scope and nature of the project. Some requested to be withdrawn altogether.

Misha and Jokahar began quietly and methodically removing the Betas from the general population, sequestering them in an isolated section of the facility. The island was practically an impenetrable fortress. Valera, nearly twice the size of the Malaka compound, had been designed not only to keep unwanted visitors out, but also to keep resources, information, and even people in.

5530.7.9
TO: THE HONORABLE ANA RIVEN, CHIEF JUSTICE,
ALMAGEST TRIBUNAL
FROM: SECRETARY GENERAL JED WORTHINGTON
RE: SEARCH AND SEIZURE REQUEST
(3) ATTACHMENTS
ENCRYPTED

Your Honor,

Attached please find forensic data forwarded by the Defense Intelligence Agency. DIA analysts have determined that the embedded algorithm is an override code for the planet-wide networked defense system. They believe this malware was installed by DynamiCorp before delivery of the contracted hardware. If deployed, this malware would enable third-party control of Almagest's starship fleet, including but not limited to navigation, weapons systems, and communication.

DIA has determined that DynamiCorp is an imminent threat to the security of the planet. I am requesting an immediate search and seizure warrant for all DynamiCorp property and assets, and subsequent arrest warrants for senior management and staff.

Respectfully,
Jed Worthington
Secretary General

5530.7.9
OFFICE OF THE SECRETARY GENERAL

"The Fleet is on alert and ground troops are ready to move once we get the all clear from the judge," Jed said, pacing the room.

The Director of the DIA was silent on the other end of the line.

"We have to get into that new facility," he continued. "I don't know what the hell she's up to over there."

At that the Director asked, "What's her endgame, Jed?"

Jed stopped and stared into the screen at the Director. "My job," he answered with certainty. "She'll never get elected without my backing, and she knows that I know her too well to endorse her. She's a sociopath, Ethan. She's brilliant and powerful, and her corporation has infused more capital into the planet's economy than any other private enterprise. But she can't ever be allowed control of this government."

"So, you think she's encrypted remote access tech into the system? To do what?"

"Flex her muscles. Threaten me. Coerce me into assuring she'll be my successor." Jed shrugged. "Once she activates the malware, she knows we'll have to take the whole fleet offline while we purge the system. She's making a point."

DEREK

CHAPTER 21

"What if we could at least get the Novali out?" Derek suggested.

He'd been in Alamath for three days before Jason knocked on his door in the middle of the night. Their meeting was brief and Jason's instructions clear: meet at the tavern the following evening.

Now, in the hidden back room, a group of Amathi resistance fighters gathered with Derek and his small team to share intel and try to form an action plan.

"They're well-guarded," Jason cautioned.

"What about a distraction? Something big enough to pull the guards away?" Drew offered.

Jason nodded. "But let's not waste the opportunity. We need to hit something that will work to our advantage."

"The air fleet?" suggested one of the younger soldiers.

"We can't risk damaging *Eclipse*," Derek answered.

"The experimental planes are in a different hangar," Jason said. "We could try to take out that facility."

"Okay," Derek agreed. "Let's think this through. If we can blow the building, that'll make a hell of a distraction. How do we get our hands on enough explosive material?"

"We have one significant stockpile of stolen weapons that Marcus never found. There are some explosives in the mix," Jason said.

That was good news. At least they wouldn't have to steal it first. "We'll need another team ready to move the Novali. And we can't assume all the guards will leave. We need to get to those weapons."

Jason nodded at Derek. "Everything is at the Stefans."

Derek knew that name. He could even picture the place from Caeli's memories. Sometimes it still felt strange to have an image in his mind that he knew didn't belong to him. "I want Drew to get a look at the hangar and then assess your supply. Once we have an inventory, we can work out the details."

"I can take him to the Stefans now, and tomorrow he can check out the hangar," Jason said.

Derek nodded at Drew. "Be careful."

"Always," Drew answered.

The small group disbanded, and Derek and Alaric headed back to their quarters to try to catch a few hours of sleep.

***

In the morning, Derek sent Alaric to collect com devices from *Eclipse* while he went to inspect the compound where the Novali were being held. The large, cinderblock building was all one level. Ragged children played in a dirt yard just off the back door, while a few listless adults sat against the wall watching. Morning sunlight glistened off the barbed wire surrounding them, and Derek momentarily froze in his tracks. He glanced once at a stone-faced guard and forced himself not to look back at the tiny figures. Worried that he would draw unwanted attention to himself, he only made one pass by the building.

When he took a seat at the tavern bar a few hours later, he had a cursory idea of the number of guards on duty at the compound, and he had a good sense of the surrounding terrain, but not much else.

Dorian Bell greeted him from behind the counter, serving him a large cup of ale and a steaming plate of food. When Drew and Alaric walked in a few minutes later, engaged in a seemingly casual conversation with one another, the bartender placed the same items in front of them.

A modest crowd inside the tavern enjoyed their midday meal, and conversation buzzed throughout the small space. Derek's small group didn't draw a second glance. "We can make some noise with the stockpiled ordnance, but it isn't enough to do serious damage. Do you want me to try and take a few thermal charges from *Eclipse*?" Drew asked, between bites of food.

"No," Derek said, shaking his head. "They're watching the ship. We can't do anything to arouse suspicion."

"Okay. Then I'll place what we have for maximum effect. It will definitely be a diversion. That's all I can promise."

Derek took a healthy swallow of ale. "This will be risky," he said, knowing he stated the obvious.

"The Novali are being treated like animals. We came here to help," Drew said with his typical matter-of-fact perspective.

Derek looked to Alaric. "There's never going to be a good time. For their sake, I think we have to take the chance."

"Jason's on board," Drew added.

Derek caught Dorian's eye and gave him a quick nod. The older man came over to refill their glasses. "We'll do it tomorrow night. First I need to get a message to Jon and Finn," Derek said to his comrade.

Leaving Alaric and Drew to finish their meal, Derek followed Dorian through a storage room and down a dimly lit hall. Dorian paused at a nondescript door with boxes of dry goods stacked along either side and fished a key out of his pocket. They entered the small space, which looked to Derek like a closet, and pulled the door shut behind them.

The long-range communication radio sat silently on a table. Derek knew that Caeli and Finn had been here to set it up, and he briefly allowed an image of Caeli to drift through his mind. He hoped he'd hear her voice on the other end of the com, but when he put the receiver in his ear, adjusted the transmitter, and turned the device on, it was Noah's voice that echoed back at him.

"How's everyone doing?" Derek asked.

"Better," Noah answered. "Anya's getting stronger, and all the kids are looking a little healthier."

"Good to hear. I need you to get a message to Jon and Finn immediately," Derek said, his tone turning brisk.

"Go ahead," Noah acknowledged.

"Tomorrow night at approximately 2100, we are going to attempt to break the Novali out of the prison camp. I'll give them rendezvous coordinates. Finn will need to take a team and meet them at the position I'm going to relay to you now."

Derek gave Noah the coordinates. The Novali would have to trek about five miles away from Alamath into the surrounding forest. He didn't think they'd be able to travel too much further without some assistance, but he had to get them under cover and out of sight.

"Got it," Noah said. Then, after a brief pause, he added quietly, "Good luck."

Derek knew that Noah's sister was most likely in the camp.

He wanted to promise the boy that he would get her out, that she would be safe, but it would be a hollow promise. He could only try to execute their plan flawlessly. And hope that nothing went terribly wrong.

***

While Drew and Jason, both dressed in Amathi military uniforms, carefully packed their bags, Derek handed out coms and weapons and reviewed the strategy out loud one more time.

"Drew and Jason will plant the devices. My team will set up a perimeter around the prison camp. Hopefully, the explosion will draw some of the guards away. Regardless, that's when we move in." He paused and looked around. The faces staring back at him wore tense expressions, except for Drew, who kept the ghost of a smile in check. He always looked like that right before he was going to blow something up.

Alaric rolled his eyes, and Derek shook his head before he continued, "Gregor's team will be waiting for us to release the Novali. They'll provide cover fire, if needed, while the Novali get clear and into the woods."

Gregor Stefan, the burly farmer in whose barn they stood, nodded his head and shouldered his weapon. "We'll see them safe," he promised.

"Once we know they're away, everyone needs to disperse quickly. I don't know how long it will be before they notice our handiwork, and you have to be well clear before then," he finished.

A chorus of acknowledgements filled the room, and the group was ready. Derek did a quick com check before moving out. They had six of the long-range types that the *Horizon* team preferred for undercover missions. A favorite of Reece's, the small devices practically disappeared when they touched skin.

Derek had handed one each to Drew and Jason, who would be on opposite ends of the hangar setting charges, then distributed the others to Gregor as well as Alaric and Dorian Bell, both of whom would be leading groups to clear the prison camp.

Once outside, the three groups moved silently in different directions. A chill wind bit into Derek's face and his breath condensed into a cloudy mist. While temperatures warmed during the daytime hours with spring approaching, puddles still froze overnight.

Derek's feet crunched on icy dead leaves. He worried over the condition of the Novali, and hoped he wasn't freeing them only so they could die of exposure in the forest. *Finn will get to them in time*, he told himself.

Within a half hour, Derek and his small group were positioned near the south entrance of the prison, with Dorian at the north and Alaric west. The east face had no entry point, only a series of rectangular, barred windows running just below the roof.

A few minutes later, Gregor checked in from his position at the tree line. "All teams, stay down and out of sight until I give the order," Derek said. He didn't ask for a report from Drew or Jason. Their coms were open but they risked easy exposure with one wrong move. He knew they would check in if and when they could.

For now, he waited. Derek tried to be still, but he couldn't help lightly tapping his thumb against his thigh as he knelt on the cold ground. He had a clear view of the guard at the south gate. A stadium light affixed to the building bathed a ten-foot circle in bright light, and the soldier's figure cast an elongated shadow on the ground where he stood.

Minutes ticked by. Patience was never his strength, and yet so much of his job required it. The temptation to let his mind drift was strong, but years of training and the knowledge that everything could change in an instant kept him firmly grounded in the present moment.

As Derek shifted positions to relieve a cramp in his leg, several quick, sharp cracks sounded in his ear, followed by a scuffling sound. The hairs on his arms stood up, but then Drew's voice said in his ear, "Guards are down. Entering the building on the north side."

"Approaching south side entry," Jason reported. Another series of cracks echoed through the com and then Jason said, "I'm in."

Derek listened as Drew calmly talked Jason through setting up the explosives. Drew could arm or disarm just about anything, but Jason had almost no experience in this area, and there hadn't been much time for training. He'd volunteered for this part of the mission because he was familiar with the facility.

"Charge one set," Jason said, his voice a little shakier than Derek had ever heard it.

Just then a muffled shouting started over the com. Derek could make out broken pieces of the conversation.

"What the hell? Jason, is that you?"

"Back off, Jonah."

"Did you shoot them?"

"Stand down."

"What the fuck? No. You stand down."

There was a thud that didn't sound like a gunshot, and then

a sharp cry of pain. Derek stiffened. A few seconds later Jason said, "I'm okay. I need to set the last charge."

Drew calmly talked him through it and then instructed him to get clear of the building.

"I can't leave Jonah here. He's unconscious and in the blast zone."

Derek heard Jason's labored breathing over the com. Drew announced that he was clear, and then another commotion broke out.

"What's going on here?" a sharp voice asked.

Jason didn't answer the question. Instead, he said clearly, "Blow the charges."

CHAPTER 22

Derek heard the explosion over his com at nearly the same time he felt the ground tremble beneath his feet. His stomach clenched.

"Drew, report," he demanded.

"All charges have been detonated. I'm going to circle around and see about Jason." Derek could hear the urgency in Drew's voice.

"Be careful," he warned. Dressed in an Amathi uniform, and with years of covert training experience, Drew would be able to slip right into the action unnoticed. But Derek felt like he had to say the words anyway. Even the best-trained soldiers could make a mistake under pressure.

"Will do, sir," Drew answered.

Derek watched the guards begin to nervously congregate at the main entrance of the prison camp. He turned briefly to the group behind him. They waited with anxious faces and tightly gripped weapons. "Let's give it a second and see if some of the soldiers are drawn away."

As he spoke, several guards broke from the group, hurried into armored vehicles, and sped away toward the chaos at the center of town.

"All teams, prepare to take out the guards on my mark," he said calmly. Then, "Three, two, one, now."

Aiming his weapon carefully at the stadium lights, he pulled the trigger, and the entryway plunged into darkness. Still crouching, he slid his night vision goggles over his eyes and motioned his team forward.

They jogged toward the south entrance, and before the guards could make sense of what was happening, Derek pulled his trigger again. Bodies crumpled silently to the ground, and he let out the breath he was holding. A trickle of sweat dripped down his temple as he stepped between the fallen soldiers.

Through the strange greenish light of his night vision goggles, he could see their faces, frozen in death. The weight of regret threatened to settle heavily on his shoulders. If he allowed it to grab hold now, he'd be mired in it.

"South entry clear," he reported. His team circled around him, tight to the door, and waited to hear from Alaric and Bell. A few elongated seconds passed. Finally, both teams reported that their positions were clear.

"Breach now!" he ordered, and then blew the locks off the door.

***

This part of the operation concerned Derek. The only information he had about the bunker's interior layout had come from one of the resistance soldiers who'd made a supply run here a few weeks earlier.

He hoped he'd sent Dorian Bell through the service entrance, which, at this time of night, should be empty. And he hoped he was going to find only a small operational control center, minimally staffed, on the other side of this doorway.

When he kicked the door open, he found two startled soldiers, who threw their hands in the air as soon as they saw him.

"On the ground! Now!" he shouted. They complied.

The small room they'd entered looked like a cross between an office space and a lounge. It provided a buffer between the outside exit and the Novali living quarters. Derek ordered one of his team to stand guard and motioned for the others to follow. He made quick work of the lock, and when the door slid open, he entered the dimly lit space.

He passed a kitchen area to his right and, further in, approached a bunkroom. The smell of sweat and sickness assailed him. Frightened eyes peered out. "It's alright. We're here to help you."

Bodies cautiously rustled out of bed. The children looked half starved, and the adults, mostly young women, stared at him, terrified. He searched the faces around him and found a familiar one. "Lia," he called to her. "It's Derek."

She gasped and rushed forward. "Derek, what are you doing here?"

"We can get you out. Jon is sending a group to meet you and lead you to the resistance camp. Dress warmly."

Lia turned back to the group. "Let's get the kids dressed," she said, rushing to one little boy. The other adults followed suit, and within moments a ragged band of about fifty people stood before him.

Derek looked them over, concerned. Worn clothing, threadbare and torn, hung off emaciated bodies. A baby coughed and the child holding him patted his back. "Take the blankets off the bed. It's cold. Lia, you're going to have to keep them moving. We've got to get you all a good distance away from here to the rendezvous point."

She feverishly tugged blankets off the bed. Derek shouldered his weapon and helped her, wrapping small bodies, tucking and tying in the ends so the material wouldn't drag on the ground and trip them.

Once again, he had a sick feeling that he was rescuing them only to send them out into the elements, weak and alone. Lia must have sensed his reticence. She turned to him, and in a shaking but fierce voice said, "I would rather die out there than stay here for one more minute."

He gave her a slow nod. "Gregor Stefan is waiting. He'll escort you to the town perimeter and then give you directions to the meeting point."

Lia touched him lightly on the arm. "Thank you."

"When you see Caeli," he hesitated, his throat tightening, "tell her . . ."

"I will," Lia said, smiling. Derek caught a flicker of the young woman from Caeli's memories, bright-eyed and full of life, not this broken, waiflike girl that stood before him.

He led the group to the back exit and handed them off to Gregor. "Be safe," he whispered to Lia as she hurried through the door.

Heading back to the south entry, he pointed at the guards who were still face down on the ground and snapped at his team, "Lock those two in a supply closet and let's get out of here."

In moments, they were back outside.

"Everyone, move out, quickly," he ordered. Silent figures disappeared into the darkness. Alaric appeared at his side and they crouched behind a large, bare tree trunk.

"Drew, report," he asked, wiping the sweat off his forehead with the back of his hand.

"Jason's injured but alive. They have him, Derek. And they know he blew up the building," Drew said.

"Fuck."

"Yeah," Drew agreed.

"Meet back at our quarters. We'll figure something out," Derek said, his mind already racing.

***

"I need to see the General now," Derek demanded.

"He's dealing with some issues," a young soldier answered, barring the entryway into the military command center.

"I can see that. I can also see that you're under attack. I don't give a shit what civil unrest you have brewing here, I need to get to my ship and make sure it isn't damaged. I can't get past the roadblocks and security, and I need the General to fix that for me." He said the last through gritted teeth.

"The situation is under control. The General is concerned for everyone's safety. I'll give him your message, and I'm sure he'll attend to you as soon as he's able."

Derek had to give the young man credit for maintaining his composure. Moving uncomfortably close to the guard's face, he said, "That's not good enough."

In one quick motion Derek swept his leg behind the soldier's, knocking the other man's feet out from under him. At the same time, he grabbed the weapon out of guard's hands and hit him across the chin with it.

Blood splattered Derek's shirt and the other man went down hard, his breath knocked out of him in a rush. Before he could recover, the gun was pointed at his head. "Maybe you'd like to reconsider and open that door for me?"

The General looked up, startled, as Derek shoved the young soldier through the door ahead of him. The other people in the room all reached for weapons.

Quickly, Derek held up the gun in a position of surrender. "No need for that. I only want a moment of your time." He handed the weapon back to the bleeding soldier. A glimmer of anger passed over the General's face, quickly masked.

"You must understand my concern for my ship?" Derek added, removing all artifice from his tone.

"Of course," Marcus answered curtly. "I'm still assessing the situation, but the hanger housing your ship was undamaged."

"That's good to know."

"I'll have you escorted there as soon as we can assure your safety."

"Mind if I wait?" Derek asked, but he knew it didn't sound like a question. Marcus must have decided it wasn't worth the energy of an argument and nodded once.

"Sorry for my less than diplomatic tactics."

"I'd be concerned as well," Marcus said in a conciliatory tone. Then, distracted, he turned his back on Derek and continued the briefing with his inner command.

Derek nonchalantly sat in an empty chair at the far corner of the room and tapped his fingers on his leg. The soldier he'd disarmed and assaulted gave him a nasty glare as he left the room to take up his guard post again. Derek ignored him and tried to listen to Marcus's conversation.

"Give me a full damage report," Marcus barked at one of his men.

"Some of the prototypes sustained damage, and the hangar is unstable. We have crews trying to repair the structure."

Marcus slammed a fist on the table and then swept his arm across the top, sending the contents crashing to the ground. Even Derek jumped at the sudden violence. "We clearly haven't flushed them all out." Marcus began pacing. "You have one in custody?" he asked.

"We do, sir. Captain Jason Logan. He was caught detonating the bombs, but was injured in the explosion."

"I want him brought here now," Marcus demanded. After a moment's pause, his voice became tight and deadly.

Palpable tension filled the room. Eyes shifted downward. No one answered.

Derek waited, his stomach churning. Within a quarter hour, the door opened again and two soldiers dragged a bloody, barely conscious body into the room. Before the soldiers let him go and he crumpled to the ground, Derek caught a glimpse of Jason's face, etched with pain.

Marcus hovered over Jason. "Put him in the chair and restrain him. I'm not going to waste any time here. Bring Lia," he ordered.

Derek froze. It hadn't been two hours since their raid on the prison camp, and he knew the Novali would be slow moving.

Two soldiers gripped Jason under his arms and hauled him into a chair, binding his wrists with metal cuffs. Derek remembered being in that position all too well and inwardly winced.

Jason noticed Derek almost immediately, but the flicker of surprise in his expression was fleeting and went unnoticed by everyone else in the room.

Marcus squatted before Jason. His menacing smile chilled Derek to the bone, and his words even more so. "I am going to make an example of you, but not before you give up all your traitorous friends."

Jason stared straight ahead, but Derek saw the sweat bead on his forehead and his chest heave with quick breaths. Powerless, Derek kept his expression carefully neutral.

Everyone turned when two soldiers burst into the room. "The Novali are gone," one said, barely containing the panic in his voice.

"What?" Marcus bellowed. "The guards?"

"The perimeter guards are all dead, but half the garrison was pulled away when the hangar was attacked. The two night watchmen were locked in a supply closet. They have no idea who attacked them. The intruders all wore masks."

"This was a coordinated attack," Marcus said, his voice now low and deadly. He took a threatening step toward Jason.

At this, Derek stood. "Are you telling me that not only was my ship nearly destroyed, but my cargo is gone?"

"Your ship is undamaged. And we'll get the Novali back," Marcus answered.

"At first look, the Novali seem to have gone off into the forest," one soldier offered, with slightly less hesitancy in his voice.

Derek kept silent.

"Send out our tracking teams," Marcus ordered. "Tell them not to engage the Novali if they find a trail, but follow at a distance and see where they end up. We may have an opportunity to end this once and for all."

Derek chanced a quick look at Jason, who closed his eyes and hung his head. The Novali were skilled at blending seamlessly into their surroundings and disappearing when necessary, but he wasn't sure a group of sick children and traumatized young women would be able to evade the Amathi soldiers.

5530.8.1
DYNAMICORP
OFFSHORE RESEARCH FACILITY
VALERA ISLAND, BOREINOS PROVENCE

Elan sat quietly at his desk reviewing the latest batch of data. His chest swelled with pride when he thought about how far they had come, how much progress they had made. They were reshaping humanity! He allowed the tears to fall from his eyes and splash onto the smooth, reflective surface of his desk. This would be his legacy.

A loud, intrusive alarm startled him from his musings and he leaped to his feet. A human-sounding voice began delivering instructions over the intercom system. "All personnel, this is not a drill. Initiate the Omega protocol." The message continued to repeat as Elan, confused and agitated, punched in the code for Misha's direct emergency line.

"Elan," she said in a tight, controlled voice. "We need to evacuate Valera and move all the test subjects to the Infinity."

"What's happening?" he asked.

"My source inside DIA tells me that the government is preparing to confiscate our research. Although Valera's location has been kept secret, I'm ordering the evacuation as a precaution. We have less than 72 hours . . ."

"Our data?" he interrupted, his voice rising in panic.

"Is already being transferred to Infinity," she assured him. "Get yourself onto the transport. Commander Issin has taken charge of the facility."

Elan left his private quarters and made his way through the medical lab and out into the common area. Misha's minions, as he had mockingly named her mercenary army, directed the crowd with self-assured authority. They had been the first and largest group to submit to the testing. Elan appreciated their innate strength and physical prowess even as he preferred the superior intellect of the scientists and engineers.

Most of the military unit had been reassigned as soon as their therapy was complete, but a contingency remained to assure the security of the facility. Elan stood amidst the rushing bodies, searching for Issin. He found her easily. Taller than him by a head, she had dusky skin and sharp, high cheekbones. Her black hair was pulled severely back from her face and she wore a stony expression. He was both viscerally attracted to her and terribly intimidated at the same time.

"Commander," he began in a halting, almost reverent voice. "The Betas will need a good deal of assistance. I think I'll head to that section of the compound and help."

"They aren't being evacuated," Issin said, freezing Elan in his tracks.

"What?"

"Please make your way to the transport, Doctor," Issin ordered politely before turning her back on him.

He blinked once and tried to process this piece of information. The Betas were all locked in the isolated wing of the facility. Their failure to embrace the project now posed an unacceptable security risk. Elan and his staff had given up trying to convince them that they were part of the greatest human endeavor ever conceived and simply continued to run their experiments.

Some part of him recognized that he had crossed a line by imprisoning the Betas, but he easily justified this as a necessary means to a glorious end. To abandon them, though, that was monstrous. They would be dead in a matter of days.

5530.8.2
TO: JED
FROM: OWEN
ENCRYPTED

They know you're coming. Malaka is being evacuated and all data scrubbed.

5530.8.2
OFFICE OF THE SECRETARY GENERAL

"Fuck!" Jed yelled, slamming a fist against his desk. His senior staff didn't blink. "I wanted to get in and shut her down quietly." He'd hoped to avoid any destabilization of his government. If they had taken her into custody, he could have demanded her public resignation, compelled her to say it was due to personal issues, and kept this whole mutinous mess out of the public's eye. Now whatever she did, he'd have to react instead of call the shots.

But he was certain of one thing: she'd attempt to use those override codes. When she did that, she'd have to expose herself, and he'd be waiting.

5530.8.4
ABOARD THE INFINITY
BOREIOS SEA

"The timeline for implementation has been accelerated." Misha said, standing on the inner deck of the vessel. "Prepare to take command of the orbiter and assign troops to all ships."

Vahn nodded.

"As soon as everyone's onboard, you'll launch."

"Very good, ma'am," Vahn said, and turned to carry out Misha's orders.

She watched while a small transport ship magnetically locked against Infinity's hull and the equipment and people were offloaded. Infinity was her greatest engineering triumph to date. Seaworthy and massive, its vertical thrusters could nonetheless lift it into orbit. From land or sea Misha could deploy and command her small, private, and very deadly, army.

5530.8.5
OFFICE OF THE SECRETARY GENERAL

Jed sat at the head of the table in the operational command center. On a large screen, he watched and listened to the raid on Malaka. The team had breached the island's perimeter and entered the compound. As suspected, the space was abandoned, but there were still protocols to follow in order to secure the facility, and it would be a while longer before DIA could send in their tech teams. Knowing Misha as he did, Jed didn't think they'd find much, but they had to try.

The Valera team was still on approach. This mission made him nervous. He had no intel on what was happening there, but the team was prepared for a full engagement. Tapping his fingers nervously on the tabletop, he waited for the unit commander to check in.

It was near dawn when the video feed began to stream. "Sir, we have surrounded the island and are coming ashore." The audio and video were so clear that Jed felt as if he were there with them. The team fanned out and cautiously approached the main entrance.

"There's no perimeter security," Captain Alana Darcy reported, although Jed was forming that conclusion himself anyway. "We're entering the main facility."

Jed met Captain Darcy during their required service year in the military after general studies. Both she and Jed stayed on for several more years, but where Darcy saw her future as part of the growing military force, Jed set his sights on the civilian path of leadership. In Jed's opinion, there were few people more capable than Alana Darcy.

"Main entryway is deserted," she said.

Blue emergency lighting cast an eerie glow inside the building, and the team was met with silence.

"Alpha team, through that corridor. Delta that wing."

Jed's frustration grew as he listened to Darcy order her unit to search the premises. If Misha had evacuated this facility, they were no more likely to find useful information here than they would at Malaka. Jed found himself muttering expletives under his breath as he paced circles around the large conference table.

Each team leader had a camera fixed to their gear, and a split screen view captured all perspectives while they searched their assigned areas.

"This level is clear," the Alpha team leader announced.

"Copy that," Darcy answered. "Delta?"

"We've got a locked wing down here, Captain," another voice reported.

"Let's see what they're hiding," Darcy answered. "I'm on my way to you."

Jed's eyes were riveted to the screen as Darcy made her way through the staff living quarters to the opposite end of the compound. A member of Delta team was attempting to break the security codes on the double doors.

Darcy's patience for that quickly wore thin. "Enough. Let's blow the door," she ordered.

5530.8.5
OFFICE OF THE SECRETARY GENERAL

Jed could hear the sounds over Darcy's com as soon as she and Delta team stepped through the wreckage of the door—a low, persistent moaning interspersed with weak cries for help.

"What the bloody hell?" Darcy murmured.

The same dull blue emergency lighting cast shadows on the walls, illuminating the bodies that were huddled together in corners, some weak and alive, some dead.

"We need medical here, stat!" Darcy barked.

"Captain, transport and medical teams are on route to your location."

"Roger that. Alpha team, assure me the premises are secured. Delta, let's start caring for these people."

Jed sank down into his chair at the head of the conference table, his breakfast threatening to reappear.

5530.8.7
CRITICAL CARE UNIT, BRASOV HOSPITAL
BRASOV MILITARY BASE, AL AMAR PROVENCE

"The human body can last quite a long time without food, but water, as you know, is another matter," Dr. Mel Regis explained, scowling at Jed. "These victims were without food or water for about four days. Obviously, some didn't survive. The rest are being treated for dehydration and the resulting complications. I'm optimistic that all will recover."

Sighing, Jed ran a tired hand over his face. "It's imperative that I speak to some of them soon. I need answers quickly."

The doctor nodded his head. *"They've been the subject of genetic testing and modification. We all need more information."*

Regis picked up a tablet and scrolled through some data. *"We have a few patients who are now alert and conscious. I can allow you a few minutes with each."*

Jed stood and followed the doctor.

5530.9.6
OPERATIONAL COMMAND CENTER
ALMAGEST JOINT MILITARY FORCES
BRASOV MILITARY BASE, AL AMAR PROVENCE

Jed had called the emergency meeting to brief his military command and the four regional governors. Though the information about Misha was still highly classified, he knew it was only a matter of time before something leaked, and he could only imagine the panic that might ensue should certain information become public before he'd worked out a containment plan.

Next to him sat a young man, thin with gaunt skin and haunted eyes. Jed nodded at him and he began to speak, *"My name is Rory Aylen. I was a bioengineer for DynamiCorp for five years."*

All eyes focused intently on Rory, who cleared his throat and swallowed several times before continuing. *"Director Torov was always interested in genetic engineering, in improving the human condition. When Dr. Jokahar joined the company, the rate of progress multiplied exponentially."*

"Who's Dr. Jokahar?" one of the governors asked.

Rory turned to her. *"He's a medical doctor and biochemist by training, and a pioneer in the field of cell regeneration and gene therapy. His research project was defunded because he ventured outside the regulatory limits set forth in his grant. Director Torov recruited him."*

Rory paused and held his hands out beseechingly. "You have to understand. Most of us were idealists, researchers and doctors who thought we were making great strides on behalf of humanity. The culture at DynamiCorp allowed us to pursue our research without a lot of bureaucracy and, for better or worse, without independent oversight." He shook his head and looked down. "We volunteered for our own experiments."

Heavy silence filled the room. Jed handed Rory a cup of water. "Please continue," he said.

"The therapy increased computing speed; improved our reflexes, physical health, and strength; and tapped into parts of our brain that were currently dormant. She named us all the Populi Novi, meaning the 'new people' in the old language. The next generation of human evolution."

Rory paused again before continuing, "And what makes all this even more unprecedented is that it's germinal. The changes are passed along to our children."

"Rory, tell us why you were left behind for dead," Jed prodded.

Rory exhaled loudly and closed his eyes. "They called us the Beta Nova group. We're a statistically significant anomaly. Instead of, or sometimes in addition to, the predictable results of the therapy, some of us experienced different changes. Right now I can feel your fear, your confusion, your horror. If I focus on one of you, I'd be able to hear your thoughts even more clearly. The Betas are empathic, telepathic, and some things we don't even really understand. We were a wonderful and terrible unforeseen consequence." He was silent for a moment, and then, looking around the room, he continued, "Misha saw obvious potential. But we were changed. I mean in more ways than just the obvious. Because we could feel more, perceive more, we understood Misha's intentions, we saw through her idealized plans and into her ruthlessness, her darkness. We felt Dr. Jokahar's weak character. We knew he turned an intentional blind eye. But by then it was too late. She sequestered us in a locked wing and continued to run her experiments. I assume that when she had to evacuate, we were too much of a liability. So, she left us to starve."

Quiet horror registered on the faces of everyone in the room.

CAELI

CHAPTER 23

Caeli handed Erik a steaming cup of tea. They both needed a break. The infirmary space was as well stocked and prepared as they could make it, and now all they could do was wait. A nervous excitement filled the entire encampment. Ben trotted in and around Caeli, chasing a wide-awake Jamie, who sensed the energy of the grown-ups and wouldn't settle down to sleep.

The team sent to meet the Novali, led by Finn, had been gone since the previous morning, but the trek to the rendezvous point was at least a full day's walk by foot. They weren't overdue yet. Still, with every hour that ticked away, tension crept into Caeli's body. She rubbed her neck and stretched her aching back.

Erik put a gentle hand on her shoulder. "Why don't you try to rest for a little while?"

"My mind will just race if I sit still. I hope they're okay," she added.

Erik didn't offer her empty platitudes. Even if the Novali made it safely to the hideout, they were most assuredly not going to be okay.

Caeli sat, trying to push another disturbing thought from her mind.

Erik sat beside her. "Caeli, what is it? I know you're worried, but is there something else?"

She glanced at him and then let her eyes drop. "I need to show you something," she said finally, and led him to the lab. Seated at the terminal, she was slightly nauseous when she pulled up the files she wanted Erik to look at.

Trading spots with him, she waited.

When he finally sat back, his stricken expression told her he'd come to the same conclusion she had.

"The Novali were the undesirable side effect of a terrible experiment," she said, her voice laced with both horror and despair. "We were a mistake."

"Caeli, no," he said, turning and gently touching her shoulder. "It doesn't matter how your people came to be. You have as much a right to existence as anyone else."

"Maybe we don't," she whispered.

"You can't really believe that," Erik said, now gripping both her hands in his. "Whatever intentions our ancestors had, it doesn't matter now. I'm here. You're here. And we want the same thing. We want a world with room for us all."

"How did we lose our way like this?" she asked in a whisper, knowing that even a full factual account of the last war wouldn't really answer her fundamental question.

Erik could only shake his head.

When they left the lab, Caeli wrapped herself in a blanket and dozed on her pallet, only to be startled awake a few hours later when a blast of cold air followed the disheveled group of Novali into the bunker.

Caeli stumbled forward to greet them. Trembling bodies stood wide-eyed and shivering. Erik took the lead, ushering them inside.

Family members found one another with cries of relief. Caeli saw Lia just as Lia found her own husband and son and rushed toward them. Covering her mouth with her hand, Caeli held back a sob as Lia fell to her knees and cradled her son.

Erik's words echoed back at Caeli. However they had come to be, the Novali were here now, and they deserved to live without fear. They deserved to have homes, find love, and raise children. They deserved it as much as the Amathi.

Erik touched her arm. "I'm seeing some hypothermia. We need to get the little ones warmed up."

Caeli nodded and, wiping her cheek with the back of her hand, forced herself into motion. Instinct and training took over, and together she and Erik moved among the Novali, assessing their wounds and treating illnesses and injuries.

Once all the urgent medical needs had been attended to, everyone had been fed, and the children were warmly settled and sleeping, Caeli finally sat down with Kat, Jon, and Erik around the remains of the cooking fire, picking at her own meal. The adrenaline had worn off and she sagged against the wall, exhausted.

When a shadow passed over her, she looked up to find Noah standing in front of them with a stricken expression on his face.

"Noah, what's wrong?" she asked, alarmed.

"My sister isn't here," he said.

Jon blew out a breath and handed Noah a steaming cup, motioning with his hand for the boy to sit next to him.

"Does anyone have information about her?" Jon asked.

Noah nodded. "She was captured, but Marcus took a special interest in her. She has skills like yours, Caeli."

Caeli looked first at Kat, then at Jon. Her stomach knotted and an icy finger of dread crept up her spine. Kat leaned forward and asked, "How old is your sister, Noah?"

"Thirteen. Why? What do you know?" he asked, his voice rising in panic as he looked back and forth between them all.

It was Jon who answered first. "There's no easy way to say this, Noah. We think Marcus may have been trading some of the Novali to off world mercenaries in exchange for technology and weapons."

Caeli watched the implications of this settle on Noah's face, and his expression went from horror to fury to utter misery in a matter of seconds.

"He traded my sister?"

Kat opened her mouth to speak and then closed it again, looking to Caeli for silent guidance. Caeli gave her a slight nod.

"We looked for her, Noah. There are people still looking for her. We won't give up," Kat promised.

Tears streamed down his face. "She was all I had left."

Later, when Caeli and Kat lay near one another on their sleeping pallets, Kat spoke in an anguished voice. "We couldn't get her out. We had to leave her behind."

Caeli knew that mission had been only partially successful in Derek's mind as well. It was one more choice he'd had to make in a long line of impossible choices. And Caeli understood as well as Kat that Noah's sister was as good as lost.

***

A day passed after the arrival of the Novali with no word from Derek or Jason. An uneasy feeling plagued Caeli. She tried to ignore it as she sat with Lia and told her friend about her last days in Alamath, her escape from the military prison, and how she'd later watched Derek's ship fall out of the sky near her hidden camp.

"And you saved his life even though you didn't know where he was from or why he was here?" Lia asked, the trace of a smile tugging at the corner of her mouth. Jamie was draped across her lap, asleep. "Always trying to fix what's broken."

"You would have done the same," Caeli answered, shaking her head.

"I'm not sure anymore," Lia said, more soberly. "I don't have as much faith in people's intentions. I might have run in the other direction. You don't run from anything."

Caeli looked down. "I did run."

"Caeli, you had to leave. Marcus would have gotten the information he wanted out of you. Eventually, he would have found a way. You know it. That's not running away." Lia paused and shook her head emphatically. "You protected your friends. You protected the resistance movement."

"But I left with Derek. I left you all behind. And when it was time to come back . . ." she paused when her voice broke. "When it was time to come back, I didn't want to."

"It's not wrong to want a life. We all deserve to have a life."

Caeli acknowledged the comment with a resigned sigh. "I know. But I can't shake this guilt. Guilt that I'm still alive, guilt that I got to leave here, even for a little while, guilt that Derek's team is fighting our battle."

"Every wrong in the world isn't your fault, you know," Lia said, narrowing her eyes at Caeli. "Enough of this. Talk to me about Derek."

At the mention of his name, Caeli's face broke into an unintentional smile.

"There's the hopeless romantic I know and love." Lia laughed.

"Was he okay? When you saw him?" Caeli asked.

"The first time he was handcuffed to a chair and had a concussion. And the last time he was breaking us out of the prison camp. He wanted me to tell you he loved you."

"He said that to you, out loud?"

"Well, not in so many words, but I do read minds, you know." Lia laughed, and Caeli with her.

"Do you love him?"

"Yes. But it isn't always easy, and we haven't exactly had a normal relationship."

"What's normal anyway?" Lia asked jokingly.

Caeli smiled back at Lia, but a lump formed in her throat and her eyes filled when she answered, "Waking up without thinking it may be your last day together, because either he's not going to come back or you aren't."

Lia took her hand. "I know," she said.

"Sorry." Caeli wiped her eyes with the back of her hand.

"You don't have to hold it together with me. You know that," Lia said.

Caeli nodded. "How about you? Are you okay?"

"I'm with Ben and Jamie now. I'll be fine," Lia assured her, stroking the little boy's silky dark hair.

"He's the most beautiful baby. Now give him here," Caeli said, holding her arms out to take the sleeping boy.

Lia stood to stretch. "Take a nap with him," she said. "You look exhausted."

Caeli eased herself down onto the pallet and tucked the baby's warm body against her side. In moments, she fell into a deep and dreamless sleep.

***

The following night, Tree manned the silent radio, while Caeli hovered over more decrypted files in the laboratory room. Kat paced around them silently, but her nervous energy vibrated through Caeli's body, making her edgier than she already felt. There was still no word from anyone inside Alamath. Caeli knew Derek would have communicated with them by now if he'd been able to. With most of her attention focused on the radio, practically willing it to come to life, she could barely focus on the data that was scrolling across the screen in front of her.

Finn and Kade wandered into the room, back from attempting repairs on the water filtration system, which had been periodically breaking down and filling the pipes with residue.

"How'd it go?" Tree asked.

"Think we found the problem," Finn answered. Then, looking around at the tense faces, he added, "Nothing yet?"

Tree shook his head.

"Damn," Kade muttered.

"We should be thinking about a plan to get in there," Kat said.

"Caeli and I can do some recon inside. She can keep me hidden," Finn suggested.

"I think we should bring that idea to Jon," Kat agreed.

A distant, muffled scream pierced through the room, interrupting their conversation and freezing them into stunned silence. Indistinct shouts and crashes followed. Everyone stood and rushed to the door.

It was Kat who put her hand up. "Wait! We don't know what we're running into."

Just then, Noah charged around the corner into the lab. "The Amathi found us," he said, his face stricken.

"There's no other way out of here," Kade said.

"And we've only got side arms," Kat added. "We won't be able to do much damage."

"Anya," Finn whispered.

Caeli put a hand on his arm. "I can hide us."

Kat paused and then nodded. "I think it's our best shot. They're going to search the place. Shut down the computer. Hit the lights," she ordered.

Caeli stood frozen. She could feel the terror from all the people on the other side of the building. Their screams melded with the waves of panic that crashed into her mind.

"Where do you want us, Caeli?" Tree asked. When she didn't answer, he touched her shoulder. "Caeli?"

She shook her head. "How about under the lab tables? They won't accidentally run into us that way."

Everyone hurried to find a place out of sight and out of the way. Caeli huddled between Finn and Tree. She tried desperately to block out the noise in her head. Finn put his head on his knees, and she could feel his anguish as clearly as she could feel the fear from the captured resistance members in the other room.

"Caeli, if we fight, we're dead. If they take us, we can't do any good," Tree said, putting his arm around her shoulder and pulling her in next to him.

She swallowed and nodded. "I know, but I can feel them."

"If you hide us, maybe we can get out alive and save them," he said.

She squeezed her eyes shut and imagined their figures blending seamlessly into their surroundings. Picturing the entire room, silent and empty, she held that image in her mind, and then exhaled the vision into the space around her.

Her heart raced as voices came closer, and panic tugged at the corners of her mind. She shook with the effort to keep it at bay.

Soldiers entered the room, cautiously at first, then, thinking they were alone, searching with interest.

"What is this?" one asked, pointing at the computer-processing unit.

"No idea," answered another. "This place is massive. I've never seen anything like it."

"I'll recommend a science team come back and assess. Let's go. We need to get these people loaded and out of here," another said. Caeli's stomach churned and the air around her felt thin. She couldn't take a deep enough breath. Past and present began to blur.

They'd been marching for hours. Her ribs throbbed from being kicked awake by a soldier. Her head hurt so badly she was nauseous, and the blazing heat of the sun made her dizzy. When they stopped, the commander of the unit told them that if anyone went missing, another from the group would be shot. They were herded like animals into the makeshift camp, trapped and helpless.

Her vision began to darken at the edges. She struggled to hold the shadow picture in her mind's eye and keep the team hidden, but her surroundings fell away and she tipped into blackness.

DEREK

CHAPTER 24

Fear was a palpable resident of Alamath now, with soldiers patrolling the streets and watching homes and businesses. Derek hadn't been able to get near the radio transmitter at the tavern, and he didn't dare approach Cara.

Whenever he thought about Jason, his stomach clenched. His mind raced to make a plan, but anything he came up with seemed like it would land them in a worse situation, if a worse situation were even possible.

Marcus did allow Alaric to inspect *Eclipse*, and Derek ordered him to make sure all the ship's systems were online, just in case.

After three days of tense waiting, Marcus summoned Derek to his command center.

"We've found them," Marcus said without preamble.

Derek kept his face composed, but his heart slammed in his chest and a cold sweat broke out on his forehead. "Good to hear."

"They may be damaged, but I ordered that they be kept alive. I should have something of value for you," Marcus added with a tight grin on his face.

Derek didn't trust himself to speak. Caeli's memory of the torturous trek from Novalis to Alamath after her home was destroyed played through his mind. Her terror mixed with his simmering rage, and with his growing sense of futility.

"I'll finally be able to root out the rest of the traitors and contain the Novali threat once and for all," Marcus said.

Derek cleared his throat, attempting to sound casually curious. "Obviously, I'm not from here, but it's my understanding that the Novali lived separately from the Amathi and didn't have much contact with you. When did they become a threat?"

"The Novali have always been a threat. They were created to improve the human condition, designed to be the next step in evolution, but instead they turned on the rest of the planet and nearly destroyed it. A thousand years ago, the war they started almost annihilated us," Marcus said, now pacing the room.

Derek tried to reconcile that idea with what he knew of the peaceful, intuitive Novali. "How do you know all this?" he asked.

"We've found fragments of old records and pieced together the story from ruins and rumors. There's always some truth behind rumors passed down over the generations," Marcus said wryly.

"That war was a long time ago."

A muscle twitched in Marcus's jaw. "Even after it was over, when we were crawling out of the wreckage, we couldn't find a way to live together. The Novali can't be trusted."

Derek didn't dare ask Marcus to explain himself, but he didn't have to.

"They spied on us for years. My father was too trusting, and my brother after that," Marcus said, staring past Derek into some distant memory. Derek stayed silent, not wanting to interrupt. He might never have the opportunity to get inside Marcus's head like this again.

"I once thought as they did, that the Novali were pure in their intentions. I even allowed myself to get close to one, back when we still had trade arrangements and diplomatic relations with them. I was young, naïve. She was beautiful and alluring in the way the Novali are." He stopped and turned to Derek, his face hard. "But she wasn't here for me. She was here to keep track of our inner circle, to feed information back to their Council, to make sure we hadn't figured out a way to communicate beyond our limited airspace."

Marcus circled back to the table and leaned forward, placing his hands on the glossy, dark surface. "My father made excuses for the Novali, and my brother was weak. And both of them lacked vision, imagination." He waved his hand through the air expansively as he spoke. "They couldn't fathom a bigger picture. Once, we were a vibrant, technologically advanced society. We built things, we explored, and we covered this entire planet with our civilization. We were part of your world too," he said, nodding pointedly at Derek. "I will return us to that."

When Marcus straightened, the distant look had faded completely from his face, replaced by the chilling smile Derek now recognized.

"My crew tells me *Eclipse* is almost ready to fly," Derek said, knowing the time for sharing had ended. "When will you have cargo for me?"

"My battalion will return within the hour, and then we'll find you something suitable."

***

Drew's anxiety rivaled Derek's, and Alaric was uncharacteristically silent as the three waited near the empty prison camp. Vibrations from the approaching armored vehicles hummed up through Derek's feet before he saw the convoy in the distance. His small group tried to look only casually interested as they wandered through the growing crowd of spectators.

Stone-faced soldiers jumped out as the vehicles came to a stop at the front entrance. They threw open the back doors of the trucks and motioned to the occupants. Worn, dirty bodies stumbled out.

Derek searched the ragged group, locking eyes with a bruised and bloody Jon, who tried to hide the desperation from his face. Novali children, too exhausted and traumatized for tears, clung to adults. He caught sight of Lia, her arms wrapped tightly around her son, and Anya, with Nina's two little boys holding on to her.

Weary resistance fighters surveyed the surrounding crowd. Derek watched them straighten and stare down the soldiers. He knew that look. He'd worn it himself once when he and his team had been caught behind enemy lines, in a different place, during a different battle. Their stance had been the same. If they were going down, at least they were going down fighting on the right side of history.

He, Drew, and Alaric wordlessly wandered apart, searching for the same faces. He didn't see Caeli, and he didn't feel her. Either she wasn't here or she wasn't able to reach out to him with her mind. Both options scared the shit out of him.

Soldiers separated the Novali from the Amathi resistance fighters and herded them toward the prison building. Derek suspected Marcus would want to interrogate his own rebellious people back in the barracks, and when soldiers began shoving the Amathi in that direction, he was pretty certain that's where they were all going to end up.

As he made his way back to Drew, a commotion broke out. Soldiers shouted at the resistance fighters, who pushed back against their captors. Movement from the center of the group caught his eye, and suddenly Jon was through the perimeter soldiers. While his group threw their bodies in front of soldiers to buy him time, he climbed on top of the hood of an armored vehicle.

When Jon's voice rang out over the chaos, the crowd fell into a stunned silence. Even Marcus's soldiers stood momentarily frozen.

"This is not who we are!" he shouted. "We do not imprison our neighbors! We do not turn on each other! We do not blindly follow orders out of fear!"

From the periphery, Derek saw Marcus emerge from a vehicle on the opposite side of the roadway.

"Together we can create a better world. But we have to take a stand! You have to take a stand!" Jon gestured to the crowd.

Marcus jerked the weapon from the hands of his startled bodyguard as Derek pushed his way through the crowd toward him. Time seemed to slow. Marcus lifted the gun and steadied it. "*No,*" Derek whispered, knowing he wouldn't get to Marcus. Knowing even if he did, he couldn't stop what was about to happen.

He turned toward Jon in time to see the older man look directly at Marcus, lower his arms, and close his eyes. A small pop punctured the silence and Jon's chest exploded in a red burst. He tumbled backward onto the dirt.

***

Derek paced the room while Drew sat still and ashen-faced on the bed and Alaric leaned silently against the wall. All three were shaken by Jon's death, and no one had a clue where Caeli, Kat, and the rest of their team could be. Derek knew they couldn't get close to any of the imprisoned Novali or resistance fighters to find an answer.

"They have to be alive," Drew finally said, a note of desperation in his voice. "No way they all got taken out. I didn't see Finn or Noah either."

"Maybe they escaped somehow," Derek agreed, appreciating that their own wishful thinking might be blinding them to the most likely outcome.

But he wasn't willing to entertain that possibility or give up on them. "We need to get *Eclipse* in the air. If they're out there, we'll find them," he said with more confidence than he felt.

His words had the desired effect on Drew and Alaric. They nodded and started packing up their few belongings in preparation, a renewed sense of purpose to their movements.

"I'm going to push Marcus to give us our cargo sooner than later. Plan to meet at the tavern in a couple of hours."

When he arrived at Marcus's command center, one of the guards nodded at him and said, "The General was about to send for you."

He entered the bustling space and found Marcus studying some documents on a large table.

"Ah, there you are. Damage reports on the ships and hangar deck," Marcus said, gesturing to the piles in front of him.

"How bad?" Derek asked.

"It will take us months to rebuild the hangar, but the ships only suffered minimal damage. They've been moved to a temporary structure," Marcus answered, his lips pressed into a thin line.

Derek took little satisfaction from the results, considering the operation had cost them Jason, and in the end, hadn't even saved the Novali. "Good to hear about the ships," he said, managing to sound sincere.

Marcus gave him a brisk nod and a cold smile. "I'm going to wipe out this treasonous scourge once and for all. I have my best interrogator back."

Derek swallowed hard, knowing Marcus must be referring to Lia.

"And that brings me to you."

Derek's heart skipped a beat, but Marcus motioned for him to follow. "I have what you came here for."

Derek trailed behind Marcus, through the facility, and into a lift. His stomach plunged when the car dropped and then came to a smooth stop several floors underground. He'd been held somewhere down here when Marcus first questioned him, but he was unconscious when they'd brought him in, and barely functioning when they'd brought him out. Now he looked around curiously.

He doubted Marcus had constructed the bunker himself. Most likely he'd stumbled upon it the same way the resistance fighters had discovered their hideout. Derek thought it must be another remnant from the planet's founding civilization.

From Caeli's memories and from his work with the resistance group, Derek knew that Marcus used this extensive underground space for weapons storage and holding prisoners. With only limited egress, it was easily secured. Derek took note of every detail.

They stopped in front of a guarded door.

"Open it," Marcus ordered. One of the guards hurried to comply and then followed them into the room.

Inside, Lia sat holding her baby. Three other young Novali women huddled next to her.

"These three are for you," Marcus said.

Derek's stomach rebelled, even as he kept his expression impassive. "What can they do?" he asked.

"This one is another mind-reader," Marcus said, pointing to the young woman on the end, who wrapped her arms protectively around her legs and began to visibly shake.

"Useful," Derek said, raising his eyebrows.

"And those two can heal, and therefore injure or kill," Marcus continued. "They're still relatively untrained, but I'm sure with proper motivation they'll learn quickly."

"Excellent," Derek said.

"Let's have a little demonstration." Marcus clapped his hands, startling the baby awake.

Bile rose in Derek's throat and his heart raced.

"You two stand up," Marcus ordered the young women he'd identified as healers. Gripping each other's hands and trembling violently, they stood.

Marcus pulled out his sidearm and unflinchingly shot one of the girls in the shoulder. She cried out and crumpled to the ground, blood trickling from the wound. The other girls shrieked and the baby wailed. Derek involuntarily took a step forward before he clenched his hands into fists and stopped himself. Lia held the baby tightly to her chest while silent tears streaked down her dirty cheeks.

"Heal her," Marcus demanded, pointing the gun at the other young woman.

Sobbing, the girl knelt by her friend and put her hand over the wound. Blood seeped between her fingers. Derek watched her close her eyes and take a breath. Rivulets of sweat dripped down her temple, but her quaking hand steadied. After several moments, the injured girl's ragged breathing smoothed out and she opened her eyes, nodding slightly.

Marcus smiled at Derek. "Go see for yourself."

Derek hesitantly walked over and knelt in front of the girls. He kept his face a frozen mask, not daring to let so much as slip of emotion show through. The wounded girl looked at him with a combination of fear and revulsion.

"Let me see," he said quietly, sitting back on his heels and keeping his hands on his thighs.

She peeled back the threadbare material from her shoulder, just enough so he could see her injury. The skin was an angry red, but the entrance wound had sealed, and a tidy white line of scar tissue was the only remaining evidence that she'd been wounded at all—that and the bullet neatly embedded in the wall behind her.

Derek chanced a surreptitious glance at Lia, whose gaze was fixed steadily on his face.

"*Caeli?*" he asked in his mind, both needing and dreading Lia's answer.

"*I don't know,*" she replied.

If Lia hadn't seen Caeli injured or killed when the hideout had been raided, and she hadn't been captured and brought to Alamath, then she could have escaped. The rest of his team *could* have escaped.

Derek stood and slowly stepped back. "*Marcus is going to use you to interrogate Jason. Give him something, but as little as possible. Tell Jason that we haven't given up. And Lia, hang in there,*" he said, hurrying to finish his thoughts.

Marcus interrupted Derek's silent conversation. "Remarkable, aren't they?" he asked gleefully.

Derek turned to him. "They are. So why are you willing to give them away?"

Marcus motioned to the guard, and he ushered them out of the room. As they made their way down the corridor and back into the lift, Marcus continued the conversation. "I'm not giving them away. I expect quite a lot in return," he said. "And besides, there are more. Even the children with only one Novali parent show some signs of this mutation. I have plenty to work with."

Above ground, back in Marcus's command center, cold afternoon light streamed in through the windows. "I'd like to get going as soon as possible," Derek said.

Marcus faced him. "You're not going anywhere."

"Excuse me?" Derek's voice held the hint of challenge.

"I've learned my lesson, and I'm not willing to risk losing this much cargo. Your team can go, but you'll stay." Marcus clapped a hand on Derek's shoulder. "You seem close with your crew. I'm betting they'll come back, and thereafter we'll have a long, mutually beneficial relationship."

Derek was stunned into silence.

"Your ship is under close guard, so don't even think about taking off ahead of schedule," Marcus warned. "I'll have the young ladies escorted to the hangar after dark." He then turned his back on Derek and strode away.

***

"No way," Drew protested. "We aren't leaving you behind."

Derek sighed and took a long drink. Drew and Alaric sat to his left at the tavern bar, with Dorian Bell wiping glassware behind the counter in front of them.

"You have to go. Find the others. We can stay in touch over the long-range com," Derek said.

"I don't like this," Drew said, and Alaric nodded his agreement.

"I don't either, but if I'm still in here, I might be able to help Jason."

"How?" Drew asked.

"I have no idea yet," Derek admitted, shaking his head.

They drank in silence for a few minutes, and then he said, "Just find our people."

CAELI

CHAPTER 25

Caeli awoke to find Tree hovering over her, his brows furrowed in concern. She blinked in confusion and tried to sit up.

"Take it easy," Tree warned. He put an arm around her back and effortlessly lifted her to a seated position.

Kat crouched next to her with a water bottle in hand. "Have a little," she offered.

Caeli took a sip, trying to clear her addled brain. "What happened?" she asked.

"What do you remember?" Kat prompted.

Suddenly, her memory flooded back, like a wave slamming into her brain. "The soldiers. They were here. I tried to hide us. I couldn't do it."

"It's okay. We're okay," Kat hurried to reassure her.

"Why didn't they find us?"

Kat smiled and nodded at Noah. "This guy has some skills that even he didn't know he had."

Caeli looked at Noah, who shrugged sheepishly. "Are you feeling better?" he asked.

"I'll be fine," she assured him.

Kat leaned in and asked, "Caeli, what happened?"

She opened her mouth and then closed it again, unable to force the words out. Kat put a gentle hand on her arm.

"It was like I was there again. It was so real," Caeli finally whispered.

"Oh, Caeli," she said.

Caeli shook her head vigorously. "They're gone now. We have to make a plan. Where are Finn and Kade?" She slowly stood on swaying feet. Tree held onto her until he was certain she wouldn't fall over.

"We're right here," came Finn's voice from behind.

Caeli turned and locked eyes with him. She wasn't the only one in the room who was suffering. The Amathi soldiers had Anya. "What do you want to do?" Caeli asked.

"We head toward Alamath," Finn said.

Kat nodded. "We stay hidden, then try to get inside and link up with Derek."

"That sounds like our best bet. There aren't enough of us to launch an effective assault from the outside," Finn agreed.

***

Caeli's mind cleared in the brisk late winter air, and she tilted her face to catch a few dazzling rays of sunlight that snuck between the branches. She marveled that the sun rose and set, unimpressed by the mess human beings had made of her world, and that the seasons marched on, indifferent to any cause.

The small group kept to concealed game trails, relatively certain no one was looking for them, but cautious nonetheless. Caeli swept her mind out, listening for the whisper of an unfamiliar mind, and hearing nothing. When the temperature dropped dramatically with the setting sun, they stopped to make camp.

"I'll take first watch," Finn offered, and, without waiting for a reply, walked off.

Kat and Caeli sat huddled next to one another around the fire. "He's never been able to shake off the guilt," Caeli said to Kat. "He blames himself for not trying to stop the attack on Novalis. And now, if anything happens to Anya . . ."

Finn's anguish was so powerful it seeped into Caeli's psyche despite her best efforts to filter it out. "I'm going to go sit with him," she said.

She got up and carefully wandered to a rock outcropping where Finn's silhouette cast a dark shadow against an even darker sky. "Hey," she whispered, climbing up to sit next to him.

He glanced her way but stayed silent.

"We'll get Anya back. We'll keep going until we do," Caeli said.

"It's my fault she's even out here with us. I convinced her to join the resistance. If she dies, I . . ." he stopped and rubbed his hands over his face. "I'm tired, Caeli. I don't have anything left to give. No matter what I do, what decisions I make, we end up here again, with the people we love dying around us."

"None of this is your fault," Caeli said, placing her hand on his arm. "And we can't give up. Aside from Jon and Erik, no one has done more for the resistance movement, more to save all our people, than you."

Finn was silent for a long moment. Finally, he looked at her. Even in the dark, she could see the worry on his face. "I've had those kinds of flashbacks before too. They're terrifying. Are you okay?"

She let out a slow breath and shrugged. "I don't know. But I'm more worried that I almost got us captured."

"You're human, Caeli," Finn said.

"I could say the same to you," she countered.

Finn let out a short, genuine laugh, and they sat in companionable silence watching the stars drift across the sky.

For the entire next day, they trekked slowly but steadily toward Alamath, stopping only for short snack breaks. When it was time to go to bed in the evening, Caeli fell gratefully into an exhausted, dreamless sleep.

In the still of night, Kat shook Caeli and the rest of the team awake. "It's *Eclipse*," she announced excitedly. "They're setting down in the adjacent field."

All traces of sleep evaporated as Caeli rushed to disentangle her body from the sleeping bag. "Derek?" she asked Kat.

"I don't know. It was Alaric who reached me over the com," Kat answered.

They quickly broke camp and hurried to the landing sight. As they approached, the ship's cargo door slid open and the walkway extended. The soft glow of the interior cabin lights pierced the surrounded darkness, a warm beacon in the cold night.

Drew's tall figure appeared first in the entryway. Kat unabashedly ran to him and threw her arms around him. When he lifted her off her feet in a tight embrace, Caeli couldn't help but smile. They parted and Kat stepped back.

"Derek's still in Alamath. Come onboard," Drew said, waving them up.

Caeli hurried toward him. "Is he okay?"

"Yeah. He's trying to figure out a way to get Jason out, but I'm not going to lie, things are pretty rough."

While *Eclipse* was designed mainly for reconnaissance and short-range missions, it could accommodate its crew for several days. Inside, Caeli noticed that the jump seats in the main cabin had been converted to bunks. Three forms lay on them, bundled under blankets and unconscious. She stopped short and looked to Drew.

"Our cargo," he explained. "Marcus drugged them. They were out cold before we put them on the ship."

Once everyone was onboard and settled, Drew updated them on the situation inside Alamath. While Drew spoke, Caeli hovered over the three sleeping girls, giving them a quick check up.

"We need to get back inside," Finn said when Drew finished his report.

"I agree," Drew answered. "But Derek said he was going to try and contact us. I think we should give him a little time to do that. We'll have a better shot at being useful if we can talk to him first."

Finn reluctantly agreed and tossed his heavy pack onto the ground.

Drew shifted uncomfortably on his feet, looking from Finn to Caeli.

"What is it?" Caeli asked. She stood, her stomach now churning.

"Jon," Drew answered.

She closed her eyes, willing him not to finish his sentence. Shaking her head, she backed away and stumbled against the wall.

"I'm sorry," he said.

Caeli turned toward Finn, sure that his stricken expression mirrored her own. Tears spilled down her cheeks as she moved into his arms and buried her head in his chest.

Finn's tight embrace didn't waver and he didn't lift his head from Caeli's shoulder. She felt the waves of grief ripple off him, just as surely as she could feel his chest heave against hers.

"I don't think I can do this without him," he whispered so only she could hear.

"But you will," Caeli answered, just as softly. "We all will."

The rest of the crew stood in stunned silence. It was Kat who put a gentle hand on Finn's arm and said, "We're going to finish this fight. His life, and his death, will mean something." She paused and walked toward the cockpit. "I'm going to engage stealth mode and alarm the long-range sensors. We all need sleep. Get some rest."

Caeli pillowed her jacket underneath her head and lay down tucked against the wall. When she squeezed her eyes shut, her body shook with silent tears. She couldn't fathom that Jon was dead, and she wanted Derek. She wanted him safe and next to her, but even as she stretched her mind out to reach him, she knew he was too far away.

***

Panic coursed through her body. Caeli sat up with a start and looked at the sleeping bodies strewn around her. Drew and Kat were curled together in the far corner, Tree lay stretched on his back snoring lightly, and Finn slept propped against the wall. Kade and Alaric had opted to sleep in the cockpit.

Caeli's heart thumped rapidly in her chest while the adrenaline coursed through her body. Although it must have been a bad one, she couldn't remember anything about her dream. When the last remnants of sleep faded, the panic still didn't subside. Then, from across the cabin, she heard a soft sobbing. Still wrapped in a blanket, one of the young Novali women lay wide-eyed and frightened.

"Oh," Caeli said with a start, realizing that the torrent of emotion hadn't, in fact, been her own.

She crept around Tree's large figure and knelt beside the shivering girl. "It's alright. You're safe. No one here is going to hurt you."

Caeli grabbed her water bottle from her pack, and then helped the girl to sit up. "Sip slowly," she cautioned. "Marcus gave you a powerful sedative. Your stomach might be upset."

With shaking hands, the girl took the bottle and drank cautiously.

"What's your name?" Caeli asked.

"Mariel," she whispered.

"I'm Caeli," she offered.

Mariel's eyes widened. "Caeli Crys?" she asked.

"Yes," Caeli answered confused. "Do I know you?"

"No, but you knew my mother." Mariel raised her eyebrows in astonishment. "I'd just entered the Academy of Medicine before Novalis was attacked. She said I should look for you, that you were the daughter of her old friend, and that you were a healer too."

"Mari is your mother!" Caeli said, covering her mouth.

The younger woman nodded. "I'm named after her and my grandmother."

"I first met her when I was six or seven. We were visiting the clinic, and I was wandering around and exploring. You weren't even born yet. Your mother was there for an exam. She asked me if I wanted to feel you move, and I did. But I didn't just feel you, I saw your perfect little body inside of hers. It was the first time I recognized my gift." Caeli sat back on her heels, staring past Mariel into the shadow of her own childhood memories. "But after my parents died, I lost touch with your mom. You were still a little girl."

"Where are we?" Mariel asked, her voice still hoarse and rasping, and Caeli drew her thoughts back to the present.

"On a ship. It's a long story. When the other girls wake up, I'll tell you everything."

"Marcus shot Isa," Mariel whispered, gesturing to the young woman next to her. "I did my best to heal her, but it was a deep wound, and I don't know if I repaired it fully."

Caeli shuddered. "I'll take a look."

She reached past Mariel and put her hand on Isa's shoulder. With her mind's eye, she traced the blood as it flowed smoothly through its vessels. Scar tissue marred muscle, but otherwise there was little evidence of injury.

Caeli gave Mariel a small smile. "She's healing nicely. Excellent work. Can you rest for a little while longer? I'll stay right here in case they wake up," she promised.

"I'm still so tired," Mari admitted, her eyes already fluttering closed.

Despite her bone deep exhaustion, worry and a dark, simmering anger in Caeli's belly kept her awake while the rest of the ship slept.

5591.1.9
PERSONAL LOG: DR. ELAN JOKAHAR
ENCRYPTED

There's a storm raging outside. Infinity's stabilizers keep the pitching to a minimum, but I've always hated the sea. Misha assures us that the Alamath Defense Force won't be able to locate us, even with their newly deployed orbital fleet. Something about Infinity's hull material.

While I prefer to work on dry land, I have no complaints about the laboratory facilities onboard. With all Phase IV trials complete, I'm now synthesizing the compound for mass distribution.

Misha and I discussed a protocol for managing the anomalous Beta results. If the initial trial numbers trend, approximately ten percent of the population will exhibit these traits. I am still troubled by the loss of the first Beta group, but I've come to accept that they were an unfortunate but necessary sacrifice for the greater good.

5591.2.1
ABOARD THE DYNAMICORP ORBITAL COMMAND VESSEL
LOW ALMAGEST ORBIT

"We have a lock on Defender, and all ships are in position," Vahn said, looking over his shoulder at Misha.

"Good. Keep them out of sight until I make contact with the Secretary General," Misha ordered.

"Yes, ma'am. Initiating a communication request now." Vahn tapped the panel in front of him, and in moments a flashing icon indicated an open line. He nodded at Misha.

She stood, straightened her jacket, and cleared her throat as Jed's image appeared on the screen in front of her. He didn't wait for her to initiate the conversation, but rather immediately barked, "Stand down and turn yourself in, Director Torov. A warrant for your arrest has been issued by the Tribunal."

Her face contorted into a snarl. "I don't think so. As the Undersecretary General, I am formally initiating a vote of no confidence in your leadership and demanding your immediate resignation."

An abrupt laugh escaped from Jed and he shook his head, "Misha, we found your little experiment. You've incurred so many human rights violations, you'll never see the light of day again." He paused and stared at her, shaking his head. "Once more, I'm asking you to stand down and turn yourself in."

She didn't answer Jed, but spoke to Vahn instead. "Initiate the override codes."

Vahn tapped his screen; looked up at Misha, puzzled; and went back to work. After two or three minutes, he turned and shook his head.

"Are you having trouble accessing our command systems?" Jed asked casually

Misha froze.

"We removed all the invasive programming," he said.

A cold fury crept up Misha's spine. Someone had given up that code. She caught Vahn's eye and he nodded with understanding. They'd deal with it later. Right now, her plan had just gotten more complicated.

Misha narrowed her eyes at Jed. "You won't have the stomach for this," she warned.

"Misha, please, just . . ."

But she cut the communication and turned to Vahn. "Engage the Defender."

5531.2.1
OPERATIONAL COMMAND CENTER
ALMAGEST JOINT MILITARY FORCES
BRASOV MILITARY BASE, AL AMAR PROVENCE

"Sir, we are detecting multiple incoming ships converging on the Defender," a junior officer reported.

"What is she doing?" Jed mumbled under his breath, and then turned to the base commander. "Put the whole fleet on high alert. Inform all divisions. Let's take them out quickly."

"Yes, sir."

"Sir, Defender is taking heavy fire." The pitch of the junior officer's voice had risen.

"Captain Reeves, report!" the base commander ordered.

Jed listened with increasing alarm as the battle escalated. Reeves launched Defender's fighter squadron and initiated onboard countermeasures, but Misha's attack had taken them by surprise. Defender suffered massive hull damage in the first volley, and to make matters even more dire, Misha's engineers had designed the Defender. She knew the large cruiser's every weakness.

Fifteen minutes after the first shot was fired, the battle ended. Stunned, Jed sank into his chair. "What just happened?" he whispered.

But he knew the answer. Outside, large chunks of burning metal plummeted from the sky, indiscriminate flaming missiles.

DEREK

CHAPTER 26

There were two soldiers posted outside his door, and unarmed, he was still working out how to get past them.

Earlier, Marcus had allowed Derek to accompany Drew and Alaric to *Eclipse*, but he could only watch as they loaded three unconscious bodies onto his ship. And when *Eclipse* powered up and effortlessly lifted off the launch deck, his eyes followed it streaking into the night sky from the open hangar bay. His new bodyguards joined him shortly thereafter, and hadn't let him out of their sight since.

Derek hoped Dorian had left his shift at the tavern and gone straight to the Stefans. He knew Lia would try to mislead Marcus the best she could, for as long as she could. But Marcus was both shrewd and paranoid, a dangerous combination, and Derek worried that time was running out for any resistance members still free inside the city.

He had to get to the Stefans, and he had to make contact with *Eclipse*.

Just as he was about to open the door and engage the guards, a plan he knew might end badly for him, the sound of two gunshots punctured the silence of the night. A furious pounding on his door followed. When he opened it, Jason stumbled in.

Derek caught him as he lurched forward. Still outside, another soldier leaned down to collect weapons off the fallen guards. When the other man hurried into the room, Derek recognized him from Caeli's memory.

"Jonah?" he asked.

Jonah looked at him, perplexed. "How do you know that?"

Derek shook his head. "That's a story for another time. But didn't Jason knock you into next week when he blew up the hangar?"

"Yeah, and he got caught because he came back to pull me out. He was my friend before this shit got really ugly, and he's still my friend."

"So you broke him out of Marcus's military prison?" Derek asked, incredulous, while maneuvering Jason onto his bunk.

"I had help," Jonah answered. And then, gesturing at Jason, he added, "He's in bad shape."

"I can see that."

Both of Jason's eyes were blackened and swollen, and one whole side of his face had bloomed into an array of purple bruises. When he tried to speak, a fine trickle of blood streaked down the corner of his mouth.

"That's not good," Derek mumbled under his breath.

"Lia questioned me," Jason managed to gasp out. "We didn't name any civilians, but we had to give Marcus something. I gave up some of the guys in my unit who were feeding us intel." When he shut his eyes and winced, Derek suspected it wasn't only from the physical pain.

Jonah stood nervously by the door, his eyes darting from the window to Derek and back again. "We need to get out of here. Someone's going to see them," he said, pointing outside.

"Agreed. Let's go."

Jonah shouldered the extra weapons while Derek picked up his own gear and swung the bag onto his back. Then he carefully helped Jason to his feet. After only a few steps, Jason's knees buckled. Derek caught him, but it took both Derek and Jonah to half drag and half carry Jason's now barely conscious body.

They kept to back alleys while they made their way out of the town center. Amathi patrols interrupted the stillness of the sleeping city as armored vehicles cruised slowly through the streets. More than once Derek and Jonah had to crouch in the shadows, supporting Jason's limp form between them and waiting in tense silence for the soldiers to pass.

Derek's muscles were screaming and his clothing drenched when he finally banged on the Stefan's back door. A well-armed Gregor Stefan met them in moments. The startled expression on his face transformed quickly to concern when he saw Jason's condition. He ushered the small group inside.

"I need to use the radio," Derek said, once Jason was settled on the Stefan's spare bed.

"We've got a pile of people hiding out here," Gregor reported, as they walked from the house to the barn. "It feels like the last safe place. We're running out of time."

"I know," Derek agreed.

Gregor pulled up the trap door and waited for Derek to descend into the hidden space before he lumbered down. The large cellar was crowded. Bodies lay in corners, curled under blankets, and huddled together for warmth. A few small lanterns cast their glow over hay bales and farming tools. Roots hung from the ceiling and stocked barrels stood in rows.

"Well, they won't starve," Derek said, looking around.

Gregor chuckled. "Not on my watch."

Many people slept, but others sat in small groups, talking quietly. All conversation stopped when Derek and Gregor entered. Dorian stood from the center of one group and smiled widely at Derek.

"I'm really glad to see you here," Derek said as Dorian pulled him into a fierce hug.

"Likewise," Dorian agreed.

"I'm going to try to reach *Eclipse*, see if they found Caeli, Finn, and the rest of my team."

"Let's do that," Gregor said, opening a door to the back room where the radio sat quietly collecting dust.

Derek blew off the light coating and tapped the transmitter. "*Eclipse*, do you copy?"

In seconds, Alaric's welcoming voice answered back, "Yes, sir. Good to hear from you."

"Report?"

"We've got everyone," Alaric responded. Derek dropped his head into his hands.

"They were all in one section of the lab when the attack happened. They were able to hide and were heading toward Alamath when we found them. What do you want us to do, sir?"

"Keep the ship in stealth mode and head to the coordinates I'm going to send you. There's a small group of civilian resistance members hiding out here. We'll regroup," Derek added.

"You got it. We'll be there shortly," Alaric said and signed off.

"That's one piece of good news," Dorian said, clapping Derek on the shoulders. "With Jon dead and Erik captured, we need Finn back. And we need your whole team."

Derek nodded. "They'll be here soon. I'm going outside to get some air and wait for them."

"Want company?" Dorian asked.

"Yeah, I'd like that."

They wandered from the barn to a wide field at the backside of the property. He and Dorian found an overturned log and sat down. The silence of the night closed around Derek. He stared up at the unfamiliar constellation of stars peppering the sky and breathed in the cold air. No planet he'd ever visited felt like home, but this one was starting to.

When Caeli had healed him after his crash, and then shared her story directly into his mind rather than telling it to him, she'd warned him that the connection between them would be deeply intimate. He wanted it. He'd wanted to be as close to her as he could get. At the time, she'd been like finding water after wandering in a desert for days. Stranded, with his body broken, his whole world felt like a distant, strange memory.

Before the crash, he'd always cared about his missions, about the people he was trying to save, but not like this. When Caeli shared her memories with him, her feelings for her home and for her friends became inextricably intertwined with his own. He'd fallen completely in love with her *and* with her world. He was as invested in this fight as she was.

And they were losing.

Dorian didn't speak, but his presence kept Derek's thoughts from straying too far into desperation. When a patch of stars winked out overhead and a strong breeze blew in from the field, Derek stood. Ahead of them, a door appeared to materialize out of the darkness. Drew emerged first, followed by Kat, her arm protectively around one of the Novali girls. Tree and Kade each carried another. He greeted them all quietly and Dorian waved them toward the house.

Finn and Caeli stepped onto the extended gangway. Their

forms were dark silhouettes backlit by the ship, but even in the shadows Derek could see the exhaustion and defeat in their bodies. He rushed toward them. Placing a hand on Caeli's face, he looked to Finn. "We've got Jason."

He watched the lines on Finn's face relax. Finn clasped Derek's arm and then walked away, leaving Derek alone with Caeli.

He pulled her close and breathed in the familiar smell of her hair. She lifted her face to his and kissed him hard.

Behind them, Alaric cleared his throat and stepped out of the ship. "*Eclipse* is secure, sir."

"Thank you."

Alaric passed them with a grin. "You kids just shut the door and lock up when you're done."

Derek couldn't help but laugh, and he felt some of the tension drain out of Caeli's body. "I'd love nothing more than to spend some alone time with you on that ship, but Jason's in pretty bad shape. I don't know if his injuries are from being too close to the explosion or if they're courtesy of Marcus, but you should take a look."

He kissed her again before they walked to the house.

***

Caeli knelt at Jason's bedside, speaking to the young woman she'd introduced as Mariel. Derek leaned against the doorway, watching with interest.

Both Caeli and Mariel had their hands on Jason. "What do you see?" Caeli asked the younger woman.

"His lung is damaged. Some ribs are broken. His sternum is bruised."

"I agree," Caeli said. "It's most likely damage from the

explosion. What else?"

"There's a hairline fracture in his skull and he has some trauma to his face." Mariel paused, her eyes closed and forehead wrinkled with concentration. "Both wrists are broken. I think that's everything."

"That's what I see," Caeli agreed. "What are you going to do first?"

"Repair the lung?"

"It's the most critical, so yes. Can you do it?"

Mariel looked uncertain.

"I think you can, and I'll be right here with you," Caeli said encouragingly.

Mariel laid her hands back on Jason's bare, bruised chest and closed her eyes again. Jason moaned and his eyelids fluttered, but he'd drifted into unconsciousness hours earlier, and he didn't awaken now.

"Good. Now his head," Caeli coaxed.

Mariel placed her hands gently on Jason's temples. This time he did open his eyes, and they immediately filled with panic and disorientation. Mariel sat back, startled.

"Hey there," Caeli said, smiling down at him, her voice soft and comforting.

"Caeli?"

"You're at the Stefans'. You're safe."

He coughed painfully and winced, but Derek noticed there was no blood.

"Mariel is a healer too, and we need to finish treating you. Is that okay?" Caeli asked.

"Please," Jason answered. "I feel better already."

Mariel put her hands back on his face. When she finished, she looked at Caeli with concern. "His wrists?"

"I know," Caeli said. She turned to Derek, who still hovered by the door.

"I need your help," she said. He walked over to the bed and squatted next to Caeli.

She put a gentle hand on Jason's shoulder. "Both your wrists are broken," she explained. "And they've already started to heal incorrectly. I have to re-break them or you won't have full use of your hands."

"That doesn't sound like fun," Jason said. What little color he had in his face drained away.

"It's not going to be. But I promise you it will be quick, and once I repair the bone, the pain will be manageable." She looked at Derek. "I need you to hold him down. Mariel and I will do the rest."

Derek knew his own expression looked as pained as Jason's. "Shit. Sorry," he said to Jason.

Jason squeezed his eyes shut and groaned. "Do it," he said, between clenched teeth.

Derek positioned himself behind Caeli and Mariel, leaning over Jason and holding him by the shoulders, careful not to apply too much pressure to his newly healed chest.

"Hold here," Caeli instructed Mariel. The younger girl gripped Jason above and below his elbow, and Caeli grasped him at the wrist. In one fluid motion, Caeli snapped, pulled, and realigned the bones.

Derek's stomach lurched at the cracking sound and Jason cried out, his body jerking violently.

"Breathe, Jason," Caeli instructed in that calm, soothing voice she used when healing. Derek knew it well.

"She reset my femur once," Derek said, momentarily sitting back on his heels while Caeli finished with the right wrist. Jason panted, and sweat trickled down his forehead. Derek reached to the side table and wrung out a warm cloth that Caeli had placed there. He placed it on his friend's forehead.

Jason opened his eyes. "That must have sucked," he said, still breathing heavily.

Derek grinned and nodded. "It's how we met. I woke up with a pretty blonde wrenching my thigh bone back into place."

Jason laughed weakly.

"I thought maybe I'd died, and pretty blondes populated the afterlife. Maybe the leg torture was my penance."

"Other side," Caeli instructed.

Derek leaned back over Jason. "Almost done. You've got this," he said.

Another snap. Another scream. Derek blew out a hard breath.

Jason's face contorted in agony, but as Caeli held his bruised wrist in her hand, he slowly relaxed, his head sinking back onto the soft bedding.

"When did you figure out you were still alive?" Jason asked a few moments later, his eyes still closed.

"Not for a while. I passed out cold," Derek admitted.

***

Later, when Caeli lay curled next to him in the root cellar on a makeshift bed of hay and old blankets, she asked in a whisper, "You remember me setting your leg?"

"Yeah. It was sort of a hazy blur. I didn't know where I was, and everything hurt so badly." He paused, remembering the pain and fear with vivid clarity. "But when I saw your face, I remember thinking that whatever had happened, everything was going to be okay."

"It's not okay, though," Caeli said, her voice breaking.

He pulled her close.

"And you're here in this mess because of me."

"Maybe that's true. Maybe I am here because of you. Because your world is almost as important to me as it is to you. Because your people feel like my people as well. Because I'd die for you, Caeli." He stopped, a catch in his voice now too. "And maybe, if I'd never crashed, I'd have somehow ended up here anyway, because this is a worthy fight, and this is what I do. But I did crash, and you did save me, and every breath I've taken since then I owe to you. You were brave enough to pull me out of that wreck, when you had no idea who I was or why I was here, and you risked yourself to do it. I was *always* going to fight next to you."

She lifted her head, and even in the dim light of the barn, he could see the tears glistening at the corners of her eyes. "I love you, Derek."

CHAPTER 27

He woke at dawn, after only a few hours of sleep. Covering Caeli's still form with the blanket, he stepped cautiously around the other sleeping bodies and left the root cellar for the house. Gregor puttered in his kitchen, while his wife, a woman as slight as Gregor was burly, efficiently worked around him. The smell of freshly baked bread filled Derek's nostrils and made his mouth water. His stomach growled audibly.

"Sit," Gregor commanded. He cut a large chunk of bread off the loaf, lathered it with a wild berry jam, and placed it in front of Derek, who took a grateful bite.

"How's Jason?" he asked, between mouthfuls.

"Much better and sleeping comfortably. Mariel hasn't left his side," Gregor answered.

"Good. As soon as Finn wakes up, we need to start working out a plan. We don't know what Marcus knows, or how long we'll be safe here," Derek said.

"After you three made it to my front door last night and caught us off guard, I sent my boys out to take shifts on watch." Gregor's sons had been part of the raid at the Novali prison, and had proven themselves competent and reliable. Their group would have some warning, at least, if Amathi troops showed up.

"How's Finn?" Gregor asked.

"I'm not really sure. Losing Jon hit him hard, and with Anya captured, I imagine he's pretty distraught, but I've never seen him lose focus," Derek answered.

"He'll do what needs doing," Gregor agreed.

Within the hour, Derek's crew all made their way into the house.

"We've got people to feed," Gregor said, piling baskets with loaves of bread and heading back toward the barn. "Whatever you need from us, just ask," he said, leaving them around the kitchen table, yawning.

Derek held a steaming cup in his hand and leaned back in his chair. Caeli sat next to him, with their blanket from the barn wrapped around her shoulders. He looked at Finn and waited, hoping the younger man would prove him right and get his head back into the fight quickly.

After a few quiet moments, Finn looked up, cleared his throat, and said, "Ideas?"

Derek felt the energy in the room shift. Kat leaned forward in her chair, Drew started pacing around the table, and Caeli looked at Derek with the ghost of a smile on her face.

"How many people would you estimate made it here?" Drew asked.

"Not enough," Kat commented.

"Maybe fifty," Finn said.

"How about weapons? What do we have?" Drew continued.

"The Stefans have enough to arm double the number of people we've got left. This was one of our biggest stockpiles," Finn answered.

"Well, that's a start," Drew said.

"But Kat's right," Caeli said, her quiet voice capturing

everyone's attention. "There aren't enough of us left. We can't do this alone, and it isn't just our fight. Everyone has to take a stand, one way or another. No one should have the luxury of ignorance."

She looked around the room. Jason and Mariel had emerged from the bedroom and now stood together in the hallway.

Finn nodded at her. "Agreed. If the rest of Alamath didn't understand the stakes before, they must by now."

"There are more people who feel how we feel. I hear them talking. I see the fear and anger on their faces. This isn't the world we want to build," Dorian said.

"And Marcus made a grave mistake," Jason said. Everyone turned to look at him. "In an effort to appear benevolent, he allowed the Novali survivors to live with us. He allowed them to work next to us. He allowed them to heal us. And then he asked us to round them up like animals. There are soldiers who will turn on Marcus if they're given a chance."

"We need to give them an opportunity to do that," Finn said.

"And we need to give the people an opportunity to do it as well," Dorian added.

"Marcus is going to start public executions soon," Jason said, and the room fell quiet.

"Do you know when?" Finn finally asked.

"No. I think he wants to be satisfied that he's got as much information out of them as he can, but he's got a surplus of prisoners. Executing some of them will be good motivation. I don't think it will be long."

Finn's face began to lose its composure.

"It would be good to have some intel of our own," Derek said, not wanting to let the focus of the moment succumb to panic or indecision.

"If you find me someone who has information, I'll get it out of them," Caeli said.

Derek blinked at her and opened his mouth to speak, but the resolve in her expression stopped him.

"We need to stay hidden and get there quickly," Finn said, now wearing a look somewhere between hope and misery.

"I can help with that part too," Caeli said.

Finn nodded curtly. "You, me, and Derek."

Derek was glad Finn thought to include him. He was going anyway.

"We need to find someone loyal to Marcus, but not in his innermost circle. They have to know enough, but not be missed right away. It'll be change of shift soon. Gregor can get us into town without too much suspicion. He runs supplies back and forth to the base. I'll go let him know the plan," Finn said, standing up.

When Caeli started to follow, Derek stopped her. "Are you sure about this?" he asked. She'd told him what happened when she'd tried to hide the group during the Amathi raid.

"I have to do it," she said. "I'm scared, but I have to do it anyway."

He touched her cheek, and nodded.

"I managed with Finn when we were in Alamath last time. But in the lab, I could hear their voices in my head, cornered and terrified. I couldn't shut them out. It felt like the first time the soldiers rounded us all up." She stared past him, into the nightmare of her own memory, and for a moment he was afraid she was sinking back into the darkness. But when she looked at him again, her expression was filled with a fierce resolve. "I have to do this."

***

A half hour later, concealed by Caeli's mind, they crouched near the military housing complex outside the main barracks. The morning sun crested over the distant mountain range and glinted off small windows in the neat row of apartments.

They were close enough to see the faces of an approaching group of young men. All wore military uniforms and carried their gear and weapons slung casually over their shoulders.

Derek felt Caeli tense next to him a second before he recognized one face in the crowd.

"Caeli?" Finn asked, concerned.

She just shook her head, still focused on keeping them hidden. They watched the group disband and head into their own separate accommodations. When they were out of site, Caeli exhaled her shaking breath and asked, "Will Matthews have the information we need?"

"Yes," answered Finn. "But so will this whole group."

"Take him," she demanded.

"Caeli, are you sure?"

"Yes," she answered resolutely.

Still shrouded in shadow, they approached the building. Derek paused at the door and then knocked loudly. When it opened a few seconds later, Matthews seemed to look right through them. Derek slammed his gun into the soldier's face, satisfied by the sound of crunching bone but wishing he could have shot him instead.

All three rushed into the room as the unconscious body fell backward onto the floor. Derek took a moment to be sure Caeli was okay. She knelt and stared at the young man with a puzzled look on her face, as if she were trying to reconcile something from her memory with the bleeding body in front of her.

"We need to move," he coaxed.

She glanced at him, then back to Matthews, and nodded wordlessly. Derek and Finn dragged him out the door and unceremoniously tossed him into the pile of hay in the back of Gregor's truck. Then all three climbed in, invisible to anyone who might have been watching. Derek rapped on the side door to give Gregor the all-clear signal, and they took off for the farm.

***

They decided to question Matthews in the storage cellar in Gregor's home rather than in the underground hideout. Neither Finn nor Derek thought it a good idea to announce the presence of their prisoner to the rest of the resistance. Tensions were high enough already, and until they had a plan, they weren't ready to address the larger group.

Matthews sat propped against a sturdy support beam, still unconscious but with his hands cuffed behind his back. His head hung, blood congealing on the front of his shirt. Derek watched Caeli lightly touch his face to heal the broken nose. Derek would have been just fine leaving it, but Caeli needed to do it. Maybe to prove to herself she could.

Finn leaned in the doorway behind Matthews, his arms crossed. He'd agreed Derek should lead the interrogation, and stayed out of the way. Finished with the healing, Caeli stood and stepped back while Derek squatted down and waited for Matthews to wake up. Almost immediately, the soldier startled awake and blinked in confusion.

He recognized Caeli and his eyes widened with surprise. He looked back and forth between Caeli and Derek, his gaze finally settling on Derek.

"There is no one I'd rather have in front of me right now than you," Derek said. His quiet tone didn't disguise the malice in his voice, and his cold grin did nothing to hide his violent intentions.

"Who are you?" Matthews asked.

"Doesn't matter," Derek answered. "Here's what I want to know, and one way or another, you're going to tell me." Derek nodded his head suggestively in Caeli's direction.

Matthews didn't move, but Derek watched the inner conflict play out over his face.

"Marcus is planning to publicly execute resistance members. What's his timeline?"

Matthews shook his head and remained silent. Caeli stepped forward and knelt so she was eye level with him. When she reached her hand out, he flinched and jerked his body away, as if she would burn him with her touch.

"Tomorrow," he blurted. Caeli pulled her hand away. "The first round of executions is scheduled for tomorrow. These will be people who don't know much and don't have any valuable intel."

Derek nodded his head. "Where?"

"Outside the barracks in the courtyard midmorning."

"Where is he keeping the prisoners? This is a large group. Are they in the underground bunker or somewhere else?"

Matthews hesitated. "I don't know."

"Yes, you do," Derek insisted.

Matthews glanced at Caeli again, and then closed his eyes and exhaled, looking every bit like an animal caught in a trap. "The only people in the bunker are the ones Marcus is actively interrogating. The others are being held in a converted warehouse. Kind of like the one used for the Novali, but closer to his command center."

"I think that's all for now," Derek said, standing and brushing the dirt off his pants. "I'll be back if I think of anything else."

From the doorway, Finn said, "We should keep a guard on him. I'll find someone." He headed up the stairs.

Derek ran a hand over his head. Caeli stood staring at Matthews again, her expression unreadable.

"Why don't we head upstairs?" he suggested.

She swallowed hard, but her gaze didn't move. "You go ahead. I just want a few minutes with him."

"Why, Caeli?"

She didn't answer the question. "Please."

He moved in front of her and touched his hand to her cheek. He knew she wouldn't be in any real danger. Caeli could kill Matthews with her touch if she wanted to. He worried that very thought might be going through her mind right now. Not that he would blame her if she wanted to end Matthews, but he knew her, and he knew she wouldn't be able to live with the guilt. He could, maybe, but not Caeli.

"We may still need him," Derek said.

She squinted at him, perplexed. "I know that."

He relaxed slightly, still not sure what she intended, but figuring she was at least owed this moment with Matthews if she wanted it.

"I'll be right upstairs," he promised.

She nodded absently, her attention already shifted back to the terrified soldier bound to the cement post.

CAELI

CHAPTER 28

He was younger than she remembered. Keeping her eyes locked on his, she moved closer and knelt in front of him again. His panic assaulted her. It burned her skin like a wave of heat, as if she were standing too close to a fire. Lightheaded, she closed her eyes.

This close to him, despite knowing he was powerless, her heart raced and she took quick gulps of air. Governing her own mind felt like grasping at a veil, a veil which now seemed to shred by the second.

As her memories pushed to the surface, they forced every trace of reality into a void. Nothing else existed. Only this.

She reached out to touch him, connecting to his mind instantly, without hesitation or conscience. Flashes of his thoughts fluttered next to hers. She plucked one. *Ethan.* His given name was Ethan. She whispered it, or thought she did. Then, instead of fighting the abyss, she flung herself into it and dragged him down with her.

She stood in line for water, tired and thirsty after a long day trekking in the heat. Her head ached, and it itched from the caked blood that had matted her hair to her scalp. When she turned, he was there, jeering at her, angry because she'd defied him to help another injured young woman.

She couldn't use her mind to fight him off and risk exposing her gift, and she couldn't run and sacrifice someone else's life for her own. Instead, she'd retreated deep into her mind, clinging to a sliver of sanity and hiding in the recesses of her own psyche. But a piece of her had always remained behind, unable to escape. Now she allowed the full force of memory to crash over her.

His hands were on her, pushing her onto the ground. She couldn't breathe from the weight of him holding her down. Instinctively she scratched his face. He hit her, stunning her motionless. Hot breath misted her cheek. The smell of sweat, his and hers, stung her nostrils and made her gag. He tugged her clothing out of the way. Undid his pants.

Afterward, she vomited, retching up water and bits of bread onto the dirt. Then, damp and shivering, she stumbled back to Lia. She curled next to her friend and fell into a fevered sleep.

When Caeli disconnected her mind from Ethan's, he slumped forward, arms still awkwardly bound behind him. It was as if she'd suddenly interrupted a current that had been running through him. His shirt clung to his body, drenched with sweat. Hot tears streamed down his face.

A wave of nausea threatened, but Caeli fought it back and sat still. Seconds, maybe minutes, passed. He was crying now. Loud choking sobs wracked his body. Finally, he looked up and their eyes locked. His gaze held a silent plea. Maybe he wanted forgiveness. Maybe he was so traumatized that he simply wanted out of his own misery. Caeli couldn't tell, and to her own horror, she found she didn't care.

***

Derek waited for her in the kitchen. He sat alone at the table, studying a map of the city proper. Something in her face must have alarmed him, and he nearly knocked the chair over to get to her.

She watched apprehension and uncertainty play across his features. "Are you okay?" he asked.

She didn't answer, and he stiffened.

"What happened?" he asked carefully.

She opened her mouth to answer, but couldn't form the words. When he reached for her, she fell against him.

"I've got you. I'm here," he said, holding her. She was so intimately connected to Derek now that she could feel him without any effort. She knew he'd have done anything to erase her suffering, including kill the soldier in the basement. His rage at Matthews competed with his desire to comfort Caeli, and she could feel the battle in his mind.

The weight of her own actions pressed down on her, squeezing the air from her chest. She knew she had to tell him. "I did something," she whispered.

He held her more tightly. "It's okay."

"No, it isn't."

"Tell me," he coaxed.

"I forced him to live it. I made him feel everything." Her voice broke and she sobbed into his chest.

Derek rubbed his hand up and down her back, attempting to soothe her. He kissed the top of her head and whispered that he loved her. When her sobs shifted to soft whimpers, she still gripped his shirt, like she was holding on for her life.

"What have I done?"

"Well, you didn't kill him. That shows restraint, I think," Derek answered. But it wasn't that simple and they both knew it.

"I think this was worse."

"Caeli, maybe this is what justice looks like," Derek offered, cupping her face in his hands and staring hard at her.

"Was it justice or vengeance?" she asked, even though she knew he couldn't give her an honest answer.

***

Derek insisted Caeli rest for a little while, and she didn't have the energy to argue. Sleep came easily, and when she awoke several hours later, she was grateful not to have been plagued by nightmares. Dusk had fallen by the time she wandered back into the kitchen, wrapped in a blanket to ward off the chill of the coming evening. A warm fire and the smell of dinner cooking offered false comfort.

Derek, Finn, Gregor, and Jason sat around the kitchen table, strategizing. The rest of Derek's team all piled into the room as well. They lounged on mismatched benches and cushions they'd stolen from various rooms in the house. Kat saw Caeli first and smiled, moving over on her bench and patting the space next to her.

Caeli joined the group. Gregor passed her a cup of steaming tea, and Derek tilted his head at her questioningly. She nodded at him and sipped from the cup. Kat gave her knee a comforting squeeze before they turned their attention back to the conversation.

"We know Marcus is going to execute the first round of prisoners tomorrow morning. We can't let that happen," Finn said.

"It's an opportunity," Derek added. "If we can coordinate an attack, we could simultaneously hit the prison barracks, save our people, and try to take out Marcus and his command structure."

Caeli could feel the energy of the room building.

"The resistance members we have left need to be armed and ready in the crowd tomorrow. And it would create an additional advantage if they could arm more citizens overnight tonight," Finn continued.

"It's risky sending them back out there," Jason warned.

"It is," Finn agreed. "But the endgame happens tomorrow. They only have to make it through the night. We're going to have a bloody street fight and we know it. They outnumber us and outgun us. So, we have to use everything at our disposal, and that includes *Eclipse*."

It was obvious to Caeli that Finn and Derek had already worked out some of this plan. Finn turned to Derek, who smoothly took over the conversation. "We'll need a couple of different teams, and our timing and coordination have to be perfect. We need a pilot for *Eclipse*. Air support will do a lot to even the odds on the ground, and hopefully we can wipe out some of their infrastructure." He held up a hand and began ticking off fingers as he mentioned each additional group. "We'll need two teams to breach the prison barracks for the Novali and the resistance members. And we need a team in the crowd at the execution site."

He paused, making eye contact around the table. "Thoughts?"

"What do we do with the people we're breaking out of prison?" Jason asked. "We have no idea what kind of condition they'll be in."

"True," Finn answered. "The resistance fighters and former soldiers will have to deal as best they can. And we'll try to get the Novali temporarily out of the way and into the woods again."

He paused and blew a long breath out before continuing. "We all know this is it. We don't have much left to give. Everyone has to fight if they can. By releasing the prisoners, we'll be dividing the army's attention, and we'll be giving them a shot at survival. Otherwise, they're dead anyway. It's only a matter of time."

Jason absently rubbed the fading bruises on his wrists and nodded slightly. "Yeah, I know."

"It would be great if we could get them some weapons, at least," Kat said. "Any way to do that?"

Derek looked to Finn and raised his eyebrows. "The biggest stockpile of stolen weapons is still here. We need most of it for ourselves and the civilians, but maybe we could siphon off a little?"

"I could bring a truckload into town tonight and stash them somewhere inconspicuously," Gregor offered.

"Jonah knows his way around that area well. He'd be a good one to take. Where is he, anyway?"

"In the barn, I think," Gregor answered.

"I think it's worth the risk. Most of the prisoners in that bunker are either soldiers or seasoned resistance members. We're going to need them," Finn said.

"Agreed. We should head out to the barn and get things rolling," Derek said.

As a group, they strode outside, Derek and Jason still deep in conversation. Caeli hung back briefly, staring up at the darkening sky. The brightest stars sparkled overhead, a necklace of lights twinkling against the fading blue backdrop. Her breath made a steaming cloud around her face, and she shivered in the brisk evening breeze. When Finn touched her arm, she startled.

"Sorry. I thought you saw me," he apologized.

"It's okay," she said, turning toward him. Even in the darkness, she could see his furrowed brow. "What is it?"

He blew out a long breath. "Jon was always the one who inspired us. He made us understand why turning away from this fight wasn't an option. He gave us a vision for a different kind of future. I can lead a squadron, and I can plan a battle, but I don't have the right words to motivate the people in that barn."

"You'll find the words, Finn," Caeli said with conviction.

"I've done inexcusable things. How do I stand in front of that group, knowing so many of them won't survive the next twenty-four hours, and tell them I know what's right?"

"Because this cause *is* right, and you know it. War is ugly. It's horrifying. But this regime, this destructive, genocidal regime, has to be stopped. You know that better than anyone. Speak from your heart, they'll listen."

He held her gaze for a moment longer, and then they went inside.

In the root cellar, Finn jumped onto a hay bale and called the group to attention. Caeli found Derek and stood next to him, reaching for his hand. Warm lantern light danced off expectant faces. The crowd hushed when Finn began to speak.

"I was a soldier in the Amathi army. Most of you know that. I joined because Marcus had a vision, a vision that we could be a strong, modern civilization, like we once were. I believed in that. I still do. But instead of empowering our people, he took that power for himself. Instead of building hope, he fed our fears. Instead of leading, he ruled. And we allowed him to do it. We had enough to eat. We had work. We had our families."

Finn paused and, looking down at his feet, cleared his throat. "One day, he ordered his troops to do the unthinkable. He ordered me to do the unthinkable. We went to Novalis and we destroyed our neighbors' homes. We annihilated most of the population. We took their children." He looked back up into the crowd, then pointedly at Caeli. "I have spent every moment of every day trying to make up for that. And I know I never will."

Hot tears streaked down Caeli's cheeks. Derek squeezed her hand.

"Then I met Jon. He saw through Marcus from the beginning, knew the kind of tyrant Marcus would become. He asked me to join his cause. He asked all of you the same. And here we are, desperate and out of time, but here." Finn waved his hand out toward the crowd. "You are the best of us. You took a stand when others couldn't, or wouldn't. And now we have to take that stand one last time. Others have seen this evil. They've lived with it for a long time now. If you know anyone who will fight with us tomorrow, go to them tonight. If not, stay here. Rest. Tomorrow we meet at the square and we end this."

The group didn't cheer as they might have months ago, before dying children, before the bitter winter, before sickness, hunger, and fatigue wore them thin. But Caeli could feel resolve settle over the room. She saw it in the steadfast faces staring up at Finn. She saw it in the way they stood a little straighter, in the way they nodded at their neighbors, and in the fierce determination that lit their eyes.

DEREK

CHAPTER 29

No one was sleeping. Small bands of people huddled together, checking their weapons, talking quietly, and drinking sparingly but appreciatively from a cask of ale Gregor had stored in the cellar.

Derek planned to leave at dawn. All the teams needed to be in place before the day's gruesome activities began, but the civilian resistance fighters would inconspicuously trickle into town when the rest of the crowd assembled.

He and Caeli sat against a wall in the cellar. She'd tucked herself next to him as if she couldn't get close enough. The agonizing thought that these might be the last few moments they'd ever spend together felt like a knife twisting in his gut. He wished they were alone. He wanted to touch every part of her just so her skin would be the last thing he felt. But all he could do was turn and bury his face in her hair, inhaling the familiar scent.

"Tell me what our life will be like when this is over," she asked.

The longing in her voice broke his heart. He pulled her onto his lap and held her against him. "We'll have a house near the river so you can always hear the water rushing by. Every wall will have windows to let in the light. At night, we'll sit outside and look at the stars. You'll be able to walk to the clinic. And I . . . well . . . I don't know what I'll be doing. Fishing maybe?"

She laughed. "You'll fly. You'll run the first shuttle service between Alamath and the rest of the galaxy."

"Brilliant," he agreed. "And we'll have babies. Lots of babies. They will all look like small versions of you, and I'll give them anything they want because I won't be able to resist their big blue eyes."

"And we'll visit your parents. They'll even get to come stay with us here," she added enthusiastically.

"Definitely."

Before she could speak again, he kissed her, the tenderness of it rapidly transforming to urgency. "When this is over, I'm going to do all kinds of things to you," he said, imagining them alone, naked, his mouth trailing from her lips to her belly, then to the sweet spot between her legs. He knew she was there in his head with him.

"Promise?"

"Yes."

Her cheeks were flushed pink and her eyes closed when he finally pulled away. Both their hearts raced.

"That was an excellent distraction," she said, smiling up at him.

"I try."

She sighed, resting her head on his chest and tracing her fingers down his arm.

If he could stop time, he would. If he could snap his fingers and transport her to another place, he would. If he could die right now to assure she'd survive, he'd do that too. Instead, he held her close and hoped with all his being that they would live through tomorrow.

***

Faint light dusted the horizon with an orange pink haze. Derek watched Caeli, Jason, and Drew disappear around the corner. Caeli would give them the advantage of invisibility as their team breached the Amathi prison.

For that same reason, he'd assigned Noah to Alaric's team, who had already headed toward the Novali prison camp. Once the Novali children were safely stashed out of harm's way, anyone capable of fighting would rendezvous back in town.

Tree silently put a hand on his shoulder, and Derek appreciated the fact that he didn't offer empty words.

"As soon as everyone else is away, get *Eclipse* in the air," Derek said. "We're going to need that air support, especially if Marcus uses his own ships."

"I'll be there," Tree promised.

Finn joined Derek and Tree in the doorway, staring stone-faced at the rising sun. Finn believed Anya would be in the first round of prisoners facing execution, and there was no way he'd be anywhere else but in the square come midmorning.

"Ready?" Derek asked.

Finn nodded and Derek shrugged into one of Gregor Stefan's large overcoats. Derek matched Gregor in height but not in girth, and the coat hung loosely off him, but it did its job concealing the impressive array of weapons he carried. Hats pulled down on their heads and bodies bundled against the cold, Finn and Derek could have been any two men walking to work together at the start of the day.

He gave a quick wave to Kat and Dorian, who, similarly clad, took off in the opposite direction. Derek had almost assigned Kat to pilot *Eclipse*, but she was a quick thinker and an excellent shot, and he thought she'd be most useful on the ground.

Having spent enough time in the town center, Derek knew where he needed to be in order to have a clear vantage point, and eventually a clear shot, at the staging area where Marcus planned to execute the prisoners.

Dorian had given him a key to the tavern. As he and Finn approached the building, Finn split off to head closer to the plaza while Derek circled around, unlocked the back door nearest the loading dock, and slipped inside.

He passed through the darkened storage room to the bar, where the pungent odor of cleaning products only partially hid the sour undertone of ale. Stools and chairs stacked atop tables cast their oversized shadows on the polished floor, silent guests in the otherwise empty room.

A creaking staircase in the far corner of the room opened into the attic. Derek had to crouch while he navigated his way through a maze of boxes and pallets to the window overlooking the square.

He tossed off Gregor's coat and placed the gun he'd been carrying over his shoulder on top of it. He took off his hat, rubbing a hand through his thick, dark hair. It hadn't grown out this long in years. Neither had his beard, for that matter. When he caught a glimpse of his reflection in the glass, he barely recognized himself.

"All teams, report," he ordered quietly into his com, settling himself against the wall. He'd set the transmitter function so that he could establish two-way communication with the other team leaders when necessary, but maintain an open com with his own team.

"We're at the warehouse," Drew answered first.

"All set by the Novali prison camp," Alaric said.

"Kat?" Derek asked.

"Almost," she answered, slightly out of breath. She'd be taking the highest position on the rooftop of the school building.

"I'm just outside the square, hidden, but nice and close," Finn said.

"Good," Derek acknowledged. "Tree?"

"The first group of civilians are heading to town now," Tree answered.

"Okay. Everyone sit tight. We've got about an hour. Stay alert."

As he waited, he shimmied the attic window open and sighted his gun toward the square, then calculated the distance to the raised platform where, in just a little while, terrified prisoners would stand waiting to be shot.

Slowly, as the sun crept higher in the cloudless blue sky, the square began to fill.

And then, over the hum of the burgeoning crowd, another sound rose in crescendo. Derek hesitated to stick his head out the window and risk being seen.

"Kat?" he barked into the com.

"I hear it," she said.

"See anything?"

"No. Wait. Yes. Three aircraft. Here they come," she said.

"I have a shitty feeling about this," he said as they passed overhead and away from the town center.

"Me too," she agreed.

They waited in tense silence until Tree's alarmed voice roared in his ear, "They're firing on us!"

"Can you get to *Eclipse*?" Derek asked, gripping his gun so tightly that his knuckles turned white.

"They're blanket bombing everything!" Tree answered. "I'm going to try and make a run for the yard."

Through the com, Derek heard screams, gunfire, and explosions. He felt the walls around him rattle from the distant impacts.

"I'm almost there!" Tree yelled over the chaos. "I don't think *Eclipse* has been hit. Shit! They're coming in for another pass. I . . ."

When Tree's voice cut out suddenly, Derek slammed his fist against the wall and closed his eyes. The silence over his com was deafening. He sagged backward, heart thudding against his ribs and the blood pulsing through his temples.

His brain wasn't processing the information that flooded it. *Not Tree*, he repeated in his mind. Leaning forward, he crawled back to the edge of the window, where he sucked in the cold morning air. All the muscles in his body felt heavy, sluggish, unwilling to respond to the commands given by his mind.

But he had to move, and he had to get his people ready to move. Not only was Tree likely dead, so were most of the people who would have been staging the offensive in the square.

"Everyone hold your positions. We just lost the safe house and *Eclipse*," he informed his team, with as much composure as he could manufacture.

"No," Kat said, the anguish in her voice matching his own.

"Damn it," Drew said.

Scattered over the town, his stunned crew would need to quickly process this latest loss. "We have to keep our heads in the game," he said.

After a few heartbeats, Kat said, "They knew where we were."

"It was Jonah," Finn added, his voice flat but convincing.

"He risked his life to break Jason out of prison. You really think?" Kat asked.

"Maybe they let him, so that Jason would lead him back to the hideout. Gregor Stefan's was the last real safe house. Marcus knew we were crippled, but not broken completely," Finn said.

Derek's mind raced. "Gregor never did find Jonah to make that weapons run into town."

"Assuming it was Jonah, what else did he know for sure? What else could be compromised?" Kat asked, her mind heading in the same direction as Derek's.

"He knows we want to stop the executions. And he knows we'll try to go after our people," Finn said.

"He was gone before we worked out the details, but I bet they know we're out here somewhere, and I bet they're ready for us to make a move against the prisons. Drew, Alaric, that means your operations are likely compromised," Derek added.

"We still have to do this," Finn said. "We're out of options and we're out of time."

"Agreed," Derek answered. "Everyone just stay alert and . . ."

"There's movement from the barracks," Kat interrupted.

At this, Derek repositioned himself in front of the window and watched as well armed Amathi troops marched a group of about twenty-five prisoners toward the stage near the far end of the square.

"All teams, engage when ready, and good luck," he said, before tapping off the com link with everyone but Kat and Finn and turning his full attention to the scene unfolding on the stage below.

CAELI

CHAPTER 30

Caeli stared blankly at Drew, whose face had gone ashen, and slid down the wall onto the cold ground. "Tree," she whispered.

Drew inhaled sharply, struggling to compose his face, and then knelt in front of Caeli. "We have to keep going," he said.

"I can't," she answered.

"You can. If you stop, they win," he said simply.

The feeling of shock and gut-wrenching loss was now so familiar to Caeli that it was like a chronic illness whose pain she feared but had also learned to expect. She closed her eyes and forced herself to wall it off. If she allowed any of her grief to seep through now, she wouldn't be able to take another step.

When she opened her eyes again, Drew searched her face. She didn't speak, but instead hauled her pack back over her shoulder and nodded at him.

"Okay, let's do this," Drew said, before any of them could sink too far into their own despair.

***

Shrouded in shadow, Caeli and Drew crept around the prison building. They'd left the rest of the group dispersed in various hiding places near the warehouse. As Drew reminded her, there weren't any guarantees working with explosives. If something went wrong, they'd never know it, but the fewer people they put at risk, the better.

Caeli had worked with Drew the previous year on Tharsis. Instead of arming explosives, they'd been locating and disarming them. She marveled at his composure, then and now. Singularly focused on his task, the only sign that he felt any stress at all was the fine sheen of sweat coating his forehead.

His emotions ran much deeper than he let on, though. Caeli had healed him once, and in doing so had brushed against the essence of his mind. There was a trove of love, hurt, anger, and conviction buried deep in his consciousness. She knew the source of some of it, but not all, and she imagined it would take years of friendship and trust to get at any more.

"You holding up okay?" he asked, pressing a charge onto one of the cargo entrances. He'd taken these thermal bombs from *Eclipse*'s store before they'd left the Stefans' earlier.

"Yes," she answered. This was it. Today they either won or lost. And if they lost, she'd be dead. Her fear of living without the people she loved, of existing in a constant state of terror, and of being subjugated at the hands of this genocidal regime now outweighed her fear of death. The feeling was strangely liberating.

When Drew finished setting the charges, he and Caeli rejoined their group and got set to enter the north end of the building. Five more resistance members would rush in from the south side. Jason and the third group would remain outside and hidden.

After an audible countdown, Drew hit the detonator and the cargo doors exploded into rubble.

"On me!" Drew ordered, and Caeli kept pace behind him.

When they entered the building, Drew cut down the guards, his weapon firing in quick, even bursts. Caeli ran toward the cage-like gate that separated the prisoners from their jailors. She hit it with the butt of her gun, and when the lock didn't give, she stood back and shot it open. Behind the gate, dazed faces stared back at her.

Caeli recognized one face in the crowd. "Ben!" she shouted.

He pushed his way forward. "Do you know what happened to Lia and the baby?" he asked, his desperation and fear bleeding into her own mind.

"I don't know, but we have people at the Novali prison camp right now. We'll find them, Ben," she promised, hoping she spoke the truth.

Over the com, Jason yelled, "Troops are approaching both entrances!"

"Jason, don't move. South team, engage the hostiles and hold them off for as long as you can," Drew ordered.

He and Caeli handed the few extra weapons they carried to Ben and the other healthiest looking prisoners in the group. "Keep them from getting inside. The rest of you stay down and wait for me," Drew said. Ragged prisoners gripped the guns and rushed to join the fighters defending the north entrance.

"Come on," Drew said to Caeli. They ran through the makeshift kitchen area to the far west end of the building. Drew set down his bag and handed Caeli his remaining gun.

"Three should do it," he mumbled to himself as he pulled the charges out of his bag and set them on the wall in a semicircle. With a satisfied nod, he ushered Caeli behind a large refrigeration unit.

"Jason, engage the north side now!" he shouted. From the outside, Jason's team would pin the Amathi soldiers to the building, at least for a few precious moments.

"Fire in the hole," he said to Caeli. They ducked and he hit the detonator.

When the smoke and debris cleared, a neat gap pierced the wall.

"South team, retreat and draw them in. Caeli, go now. Lead the prisoners here," Drew said.

Caeli took off back through the kitchen and into the main holding area. Her ears rang from the blast, and from the gunfire peppering the air. She shouted over the turmoil and gestured at the prisoners. "Come on! Through the kitchen! Run!" she urged.

She stood her ground and waved them past her. Over the com, someone from the south team said in a panic, "They're in!"

"Everyone, retreat to my location. Jason, back off and rendezvous by the weapons stash," Drew ordered.

Caeli waited until all the prisoners were ahead of her and then fell in behind them. A few resistance fighters still engaged at the rear to slow the troops. When she reached Drew, he stood directing the prisoners out through the hole in the building and across the lot to the farm truck full of guns that Gregor Stefan had left hidden in an alleyway.

"Caeli, throw down a little cover for them," Drew said. "Just enough. I don't want to draw extra attention here."

She joined the swarm of bodies scrambling through the wall and forced her way outside. Squinting in the bright sun, she moved away from the surge and leaned against the chain link fence that enclosed the backside of the facility. She imaged the area devoid of people, with the sun reflecting off the hard-paved surface of the lot. And instead of a gaping crater on the side of the building, she visualized a neat wall of stone cinderblocks.

Out of the corner of her eye, she saw Jason with his group approach the alleyway and dive behind the truck. Only a small group of Amathi soldiers followed, and Jason made short work of cutting them down from behind the cover of the truck.

Screams echoed from inside the building. Caeli couldn't determine which were from resistance fighters and which from the Amathi soldiers.

"Drew!" she shouted.

He emerged from the hole holding something in his hand. "Out! Out! Everyone out!" he shouted as a few resistance fighters tumbled through behind him. While they all ran full speed across the lot, he hit the detonator, bringing the west side of the building crashing down in a torrent of crumbling rock.

DEREK

CHAPTER 31

Staring down the scope of his gun, the sea of soldiers resolved into individual faces and bodies. He didn't see Marcus yet, but Derek wasn't surprised. If Marcus thought he had a target on him today, he'd be well protected.

Blindfolded, with their hands bound behind them, the prisoners stumbled up onto the platform, manhandled by the soldiers who shoved them into place.

"Kat?" he said into his com.

"I'm ready," she answered.

As he scoured the faces on the platform, he recognized Captain James from Marcus's trusted inner circle, off to the right and seemingly in charge. James looked backward to the roadway, where seated in a military vehicle and barely visible through the armor-plated window, Marcus nodded.

"I've got James. Fire on my mark. Three, two, one . . ." he inhaled, held his breath for the briefest of seconds, and whispered, "Mark."

His shot blew off the top of James's head.

The crowd erupted in chaos as Kat and Derek methodically picked off the soldiers on the platform, the bodies jerking backward in a grotesque spray of blood and torn flesh. At the first shot, resistance members in the crowd threw off coats and wraps to reveal their hidden weapons.

"Finn!" Derek shouted through his com. "Get the prisoners off that stage."

Disoriented and surely terrified, the prisoners knelt frozen in place, ripe for becoming victims of the crossfire. Derek caught sight of Finn as he pushed his way forward to the stage and rushed up the stairs.

"Kat, lay cover fire in the direction of the bunker," he ordered.

Troops were pouring out of the building, splitting up, with some heading toward the stage and some circling around to flank the crowd.

While Finn maneuvered through the group of prisoners, removing blindfolds, cutting bindings, and shoving people over the side of the platform, Derek and Kat covered him until he freed the last person and leaped off the end of the stage.

"Finn, have you got Anya?" Derek asked.

"She's here!" Finn shouted.

"It won't take them long to figure out our positions," Kat said.

"Hold as long as you can," Derek answered between rounds.

Below him, piercing screams filled the air. A massive surge of bodies pushed out of the square and into the streets, trampling the fallen in their panic. When the flanking group of soldiers converged on the backside of the square, pinning the civilians in place, Derek refocused his firepower, cutting into their lines and giving the resistance fighters on the ground a chance to engage.

But Kat was right—it didn't take long for the soldiers to figure out Derek's position, and soon he was taking heavy fire.

Ducking under the windowsill, he barely dodged a round to the face. Wood splintered and glass shattered around him.

"I'm moving!" he yelled to Kat as he crawled toward the stairway.

"Me too," she answered back.

He had to make it out before they trapped him in the building. His adrenaline surged and his heart pounded in his chest. The urge to stand and run was powerful, but if he did, he'd be cut in half. He forced himself to stay down on all fours until he reached the staircase. Then, taking the stairs two at a time, he landed with a thud at the bottom. Gunfire shattered the front windows of the tavern and ricocheted off the wall. He ducked again, but it was only a few steps to the back corridor.

"Derek!" Kat screamed over the com. "Get out of there! Now! The planes!"

"Shit!"

He tore down the corridor. Against the steady chatter of gunfire, another sound grew louder, and just as he threw his entire bodyweight against the back door, the building exploded behind him.

CAELI

CHAPTER 32

In the alleyway behind the warehouse, they caught their breath. So far, the fighting they heard in the streets didn't extend out this far, but they all knew it wouldn't be long before someone realized the battle had gone badly for the Amathi at the prison warehouse and more soldiers were sent to deal with them. Drew made it clear they needed to be engaged elsewhere by then.

"We lost eight," he said, taking a count of his people.

"Damn," Jason said under his breath.

Drew acknowledged him with a curt nod. "Let's get the rest of these weapons handed out."

Caeli looked around at the group of battered prisoners with increasing alarm. "Where's Erik? Was he with the group they took to be executed?"

A young man, wearing the tattered remains of an Amathi uniform answered, "No. He and some of the high value prisoners were taken to the underground bunker."

"How many, do you think?" Drew asked.

"Maybe ten or fifteen."

"Caeli and I know our way around down there, at least better than most," Jason said.

Drew hesitated.

"We have to try," Caeli insisted.

"I know," Drew agreed, exhaling loudly. "But I've got no goodies left in my bag, we're down to one weapon each, and pretty soon this whole city is going to be fully engaged."

"Send this group into the fight, and we'll go. It's a long shot, but we might be able to sneak in and sneak out if everyone else is occupied," Jason suggested.

"Free the prisoners means free *all* the prisoners," Drew acknowledged with a tight smile.

He tapped his com. "Commander?"

No answer.

He tried again. Caeli frowned at him.

"Derek!" he finally shouted.

Caeli felt the air rush from her lungs. She opened her mind and was immediately assaulted by the panic and terror that filled the city. Searching, she tried to sift through the discordant noise and find him. Finally, she brushed against the faint hum of his consciousness. *Derek*, she whispered in her mind.

"He's alive," she said, collapsing onto her knees. "That's all I can tell from here."

"Caeli, we have to go," Drew said, placing a hand on her shoulder.

"What if he's hurt?" she pleaded.

"You'll never make it into the city, and we need you to help get the rest of the prisoners out," Drew said, his tone gentle but firm.

"I know," she whispered, conflicted.

"Lock it away. Focus right here, right now," Drew coaxed.

She told herself Derek was fine. She told herself he'd want her to save Erik and the others if she could. She told herself anything just to make her uncooperative body stand and put one shaking leg in front of the other.

Drew divided the newly liberated prisoners and the remaining resistance members from his team into several groups and sent them toward the fighting from different directions. "Shoot anyone wearing a clean Amathi uniform," he said in parting.

When he, Caeli, and Jason were alone in the alley, he ran a hand over his head and said, "Let's go."

They navigated the back streets of the city, following Jason's lead toward Marcus's command center. They didn't know for sure where Marcus might be hiding out, but the command center and underground bunker ranked at the top of their best guess list. Which meant that Marcus's most elite guards would likely be there to protect him and secure the facilities.

"Nothing about this is going to be easy," Drew said, as the three squatted a block from the command center and surveyed the heavily reinforced perimeter.

"The most direct route into the bunker is inside the command center, but there's another entrance," Jason said.

"We probably need to use that other entrance," Drew commented.

"It's through the research facility," Caeli added, remembering her own escape from the depths of that bunker.

Jason nodded. "It is."

"We'll follow your lead," Drew said to Jason.

They made a wide loop around the command center and cautiously approached the rear entrance of the research building.

"No security," Jason observed. "The guards here must have gotten called into the fight."

"Who works inside?" Drew asked.

"Mostly civilian engineers and scientists."

"Good for us," Drew said, and then to Caeli, "A little cover?"

She nodded, and the three approached the entrance unseen.

When they stood in front of it, Jason looked at them, shrugged his shoulders, and proceeded to knock loudly on the door. "This is Captain Jason Logan with the General's security detail. Open up!" he demanded in an aggressive, confident voice.

When the door slid sideways and a pair of frightened eyes peeked out, Jason jammed his foot in the opening and slammed his gun into the unsuspecting face. He elbowed it open far enough that he, Drew, and Caeli could squeeze through, and then slid it shut behind them.

The engineer who lay sprawled on the floor was an older man, thin and gaunt, with his face now a shattered, bleeding mess.

"Shit," Jason said under his breath.

The facility appeared vacant, but Caeli sensed the nervous energy of several people nearby. She searched the room with her mind and knelt next to the dazed man.

"In the office," she told Drew and Jason.

"Stay with Caeli," Drew said to Jason, and cautiously approached the enclosed office, weapon ready.

"I can fix this," Caeli said to the engineer. When he nodded, she put one hand on the side of his face and closed her eyes. His shattered nose required energy to heal that Caeli couldn't spare, but she did it anyway, and relief spread across his face.

From across the room, she heard Drew speak reassuringly to the group huddled in the office. Jason helped the engineer to his feet and ushered him into the room with the others. Caeli followed.

"Stay here. Stay hidden. One way or another, this will be

over soon," Drew finished, locking them into the room.

"Anyone in there we need to worry about?" Jason asked.

Drew turned to Caeli. She barely hesitated before sifting through the thoughts of the terrified group. The inner conflict she'd felt so keenly the first time she'd purposefully violated someone's mind was gone, and she worried that it might never return.

"No," she answered.

They left the scientists and followed Jason to a lift in the back corner of the main floor.

Jason touched a sensor panel and the door to the lift opened. "We're definitely going to run into trouble down here. Be ready," he said, and they stepped inside.

Caeli's stomach dropped as the lift plunged downward. When it came to a stop several levels below ground, Drew pushed Caeli behind him. Drew and Jason crouched to either side of the door, weapons ready, but when it slid open, only an empty corridor greeted them.

They crept into the quiet, dimly lit hall.

"This way," Jason whispered.

Caeli held a wavering shadow image over them as they followed Jason. She recognized this space. The memory of her last visit here made her shiver. In one of these rooms she'd witnessed Marcus interrogate and torture a young man and, when he was finished with the boy, shoot him in the head. If she closed her eyes right now, she'd be there again, locked in that room, watching helplessly.

"Caeli," Jason prodded.

She realized she'd stopped moving. "Sorry," she said, picking up her pace again.

They turned a corner and Caeli knew they'd found what

they were looking for. The hum of a dozen minds brushed her consciousness. "Here," she said.

The doors all had sensor panels with coded locks.

"We're going to have to shoot them open," Drew said.

"That won't attract any attention," Jason mumbled.

"Let's do it fast, before our luck runs out," Drew agreed.

All three frantically began firing at the locks and wrestling the heavy metal doors open. The ragged, weary prisoners they'd rescued in the warehouse looked robust compared to the emaciated, bruised bodies they found in the cells.

Caeli cried out when she saw Erik Kellan, his face barely recognizable. She knelt in front of him and, with trembling hands, touched his face. "Oh, Erik," she whispered.

He opened one swollen eye and managed a half-hearted grin.

"Let me help you." She searched his wounded body, her mind snagging on every broken bone and bruise. Focusing on the worst of his injuries, she healed his damaged kidney and his fractured skull. There was nothing she could do for dehydration, but she could fix a shattered knee and several ribs.

"Caeli, stop. You're going to wear yourself out. Leave me and help the others," he said, gripping her hands in his.

"No," she answered firmly. "I can do this."

Healing was the only thing she was sure of. The only thing that made any sense to her. Ignoring Erik's continued protests, she focused on the intricate web of vessels flowing through his body, allowed her mind to follow their pulsing currents.

"Caeli." A different voice pulled her back into herself.

Drew stood in the doorway. "Two are dead. One won't be able to move without some medical attention. The others are in rough shape, but we can get them out," he reported.

"Caeli, I'm okay," Erik said, using the wall to push himself up on shaking legs.

She stared at him numbly. The walls of the room closed in on her, choked her. Erik's blood, smeared in dry streaks across the floor, became Connor's, the boy Marcus had killed.

A split second after the gun fired, bits of his blood and brain sprayed Caeli's face and caught in her hair. The metallic smell stung her nostrils. She could taste it in the back of her throat. His scream of agony echoed through her mind, long after the room fell silent.

Absently, she wiped her hand along the side of her cheek.

"Caeli," Drew said again. Startled, she looked up.

He held out a hand to her, helped her to her feet. "Come on."

The other severely injured prisoner was Liam, the soldier who had accompanied Derek on the raid to the Amathi base. Instinct and years of training took over, and Caeli's cloudy mind refocused on her wounded patient. When she'd done enough to get him moving, she collapsed onto her hands and knees.

"I just need a minute," she said. The world spun around her and she shook her head. Her body was shutting down. It took her last reserve of energy to stay conscious. Drew squatted down and lifted her to her feet, his arm firmly around her waist. Dazed, she leaned against him, and they moved out of the cell.

They'd only taken a few steps when a familiar voice pierced through the chaos of her consciousness.

"Lia!" Caeli gasped. "Drew, Lia's down here somewhere!"

"Can you find her?" he asked.

She stopped and called out to her friend, stilling her mind to listen for the answer. "Around this corner."

When they forced open the door to Lia's cell, the baby began to cry. Lia gripped him and rushed forward. "Caeli!" she cried.

Caeli threw her arms around Lia and the baby, a single sob

escaping from her chest. Lia was thin and dirty, but she was in much better shape than the other prisoners. Her cell, unlike the others, contained a cot with a blanket. Crusts of bread and a jug of water sat in one corner of a wooden table, and a washbasin with cloth diapers piled neatly next to it sat in the other.

"We have to move," Drew said, ushering them forward.

The battered group moved slowly. Erik leaned on Jason, Drew had his arm around Caeli's waist again, and Liam limped along, supported by two of the healthier prisoners. They headed back down the corridor in the direction of the lift, but when they turned the corner, a well-armed garrison of Amathi soldiers waited for them.

"Jonah," Caeli whispered.

DEREK

CHAPTER 33

Something crushed his chest, prevented him from taking a deep breath. He tried to open his eyes, but the darkness pulled him down.

Later, a voice called to him, faint and distant. At first he thought it was Caeli, but the urgency grew along with the volume and he recognized Kat. She frantically dug him out of the rubble, flinging chunks of crumbled wall and splintered wood.

"Derek!"

Carefully she rolled him onto his back. He groaned, and took an inventory of his injuries. Broken ribs, and fuck, his head hurt.

"Derek!" Kat yelled at him again, her voice growing more panicked.

He squinted up at her, although his eyes begged to stay shut.

Kat exhaled in relief. "How bad?"

He tried to answer but coughed instead, and then nearly passed out from the pain.

"Not good," she muttered under her breath, and then with more force, "We have to get out of here."

Derek opened his eyes again. Although he and Kat were fairly obscured by piles of rubble and the remains of the building, the tavern itself was in the center of town. Gunfire and screams filled the air, growing closer.

"Come on," she said, helping him to sit up.

The world spun and the edges of his vision swam.

"Let's just try and make it to that alley, okay?" Kat said, looping her arm under his left shoulder and around his back. She hauled him to his feet and together they staggered into the adjacent alley.

Temporarily out of sight, Kat leaned him against the wall. When she let go, he promptly slid to the ground and landed on his ass.

"My gun's gone," he said, his head resting against the cold cement wall.

Kat pulled out her sidearm and handed it to him. "Better than nothing."

She squatted next to him and used her sleeve to wipe the blood from his face.

When he opened his mouth to speak, the roar of plane engines overhead drowned out the sound. Automatic gunfire followed, and then more screams as the rounds met their targets.

"I'm going to try Finn," he said, and then, speaking into his com, "Finn, it's Derek. Do you copy?"

"Derek?" an anxious voice replied. "We're taking heavy fire from the ground and from the planes. We aren't going to last long out there against the air strikes."

Eclipse wasn't coming to the rescue. There had to be something they could do.

"Kat, the experimental planes," he said, a spark of renewed life in his eyes.

She looked at Derek sideways.

"Think we can make it to those planes?" he asked.

She raised her eyebrows. "Maybe. But Derek, you can barely stand up."

"I'll be sitting, if we can get there. Can you fly one?" he asked.

"If it has wings, I can fly it," she answered.

He grinned at her.

"This is insane, even for you," Kat said, but she grinned back.

***

Derek led them, stumbling, through back alleyways and deserted streets, taking a slow, circuitous route to the hangar. Between his broken ribs and this latest concussion, Kat was right. He could barely stay on his feet. He pondered how many brain cells he'd permanently lost in the last year from various head injuries, but the thought was interrupted when one of the planes made a low pass on its way back to the town center and they had to duck into a doorway. His surging adrenaline temporarily masked the pain.

They turned a final corner and stopped across the street from the hangar. It appeared all but abandoned.

"Most of the troops must have been called into the fight," Derek said.

"Could we be so lucky?" Kat whispered.

"Still two guards, in the tower," he said pointing.

Kat balanced herself on one knee and sighted down her weapon. "I can make the shot," she said.

"Okay. As soon as they're down, we have to get inside that building quickly."

"Roger that," Kat agreed.

He held his breath while she counted down from three and then pulled the trigger. Two shots in quick succession, perfectly aimed, shattered the glass and sent both guards careening against the back window of the tower in an explosion of red.

Kat blinked once, and then she and Derek took off for the hangar.

They met no resistance and skidded to a stop at the door. "Open it. I'll go in first," Derek ordered.

Kat nodded and wrenched the door open. Derek stepped inside, crouching low, with Kat's sidearm up and ready. But there was no one inside.

The three fighters cast imposing shadows on the hangar floor. Derek scanned the room before he and Kat cautiously approached the closest plane.

Kat ran her hand along a sleek, silver wing and ducked underneath to get a better look at the propulsion engines. "Sleek design. But we need a runway for takeoff."

Derek moved to the opposite side of the building and hit a button on the wall. Large bay doors slid open to reveal a long, paved surface stretching from well beyond the east side of the hangar to a large field.

"Let's do this," he said.

Inside the cockpit, he pulled the helmet onto his head and switched on the ship-to-ship communications.

"Kat?"

"I'm in," she answered.

He familiarized himself with the instrument panel, recognizing much of it from his early flight training on planet-only craft on Erithos. But that had been well over a decade ago, and he'd been flying spacecraft for much longer. He hoped he could make the adjustment quickly and not crash the damn plane into the side of a building. He flipped a switch and the engines roared to life.

When he pushed the throttle forward from his position at the edge of the runway, the hangar became a blur in his peripheral vision as he blew by it. He knew the split second when the craft left the ground and there was nothing but air and power beneath him. The rush of flying never got old. For one brief moment, while the nose of the fighter tipped toward the blue sky, everything else slipped away.

As soon as he leveled out, he began testing the plane's responses and getting his head ready for the coming fight.

"She feels like the Raptors we used to train on in flight school," Kat said.

"Yeah, with a little more drag," he answered.

"The engines have good thrust, though," Kat said, and Derek could hear the enthusiasm in her voice.

He made a wide arc out over the field and then headed toward the town center.

"Stay tight until we make contact," he said.

"Will do. We've got the element of surprise on our side."

"And missiles," he added, noting that, in addition to the magnetic rail guns that dropped from below the wing, the craft carried two missiles. "My radar tracking is on. As soon as I see the first one, I'm going straight for a missile lock before they know we're even here."

"Enemy target. Coming in from the west," Kat said.

"Got him. Cover me. I'm going to intercept."

He banked left. The other craft was approaching from the west and would be back over the town in a matter of seconds. He had to catch it before then.

Against the blue backdrop of sky, the dark speck rapidly took shape as he closed in on it. Flipping another switch, he activated his missile system and chased down the Amathi fighter. It wavered in and out of his grid, and he fought to keep it centered long enough to get a lock. Finally, the tiny screen lit up red and blinking, and he hit the launch button, sending the first missile hurtling into the air. In seconds, the other plane exploded into a bright orange ball of fire.

"Nice shot," Kat said.

"Thanks. Now they know we're here though, so stay sharp," he warned.

He adjusted his heading and flew back toward the town center. "Try to draw them away from the city center. We can't use missiles in here to take them down. A hit *or* a miss will massacre civilians on the ground."

"Roger that. I have visual on a second fighter. He's going low. Heading to intercept," Kat said.

"Right behind you," Derek answered. "Wait. I see the third. I'm breaking off to go after him."

The third fighter was coming in from the east side of town, flying just over the grain silos and production facilities. Derek headed straight for him, head on.

The distance between them closed fast. An alarm rang out in the cockpit, warning Derek that the other craft had a radar lock on him. He didn't think the Amathi would fire a missile at him over the populated city, but he wasn't going to bet on it. He banked hard to port and back toward the hangar and field, hoping the other pilot would follow him rather than resume his ground assault.

It worked. The Amathi fighter was on his tail. He used every defensive maneuver he could think of to keep the other pilot from getting a lock on him, until he crossed the field and headed out over the forest. Then he increased his speed and straightened his course, forcing the Amathi pilot to do the same in order to stay with him.

When he was satisfied they were far enough from the city, he let his altitude drop, and gradually allowed the distance between them to close, so that he was within range of the rail guns but any missile fired on him would be less than accurate.

The rail guns did fire, their impact rattling his teeth. He had to make his move now, before his plane was shredded.

Taking a deep breath, he sent the nose of the plane vertical. His stomach dropped and his head swam as he fought to stay conscious. He counted to three and then looped backwards, dropping altitude until he settled directly behind the enemy plane. The blackness receded from the edge of his vision, but his extremities tingled and he shivered uncontrollably.

He couldn't afford to let precious seconds slip past, and he shook his head to clear it. The shooting pain that followed did the job. He focused on the plane in front of him, now engaged in some evasive maneuvering of its own.

But the pilot was inexperienced, and Derek anticipated his moves. Within seconds he had a lock and let the second missile fly. It made contact, blowing the plane out of the sky and raining chunks of burning metal down on the forest below.

CAELI

CHAPTER 34

Jason and Drew stood frozen, weapons pointed at the Amathi soldiers. But they were outgunned and they knew it.

It was Jason who took a single step forward and spoke. "Are you going to shoot me, Jonah? Or Caeli, who saved your miserable life when you were gutted like a fish? Because you'll have to. We aren't standing down," he said.

Lia's baby fussed, and she gathered him close.

Jonah's face was unreadable, but the group of soldiers shifted uncomfortably on their feet.

"How about the rest of you? Is this what you signed up for? I know I didn't. I thought we were building something. I thought we were creating a better future. I didn't plan on committing genocide."

He turned and pointed to Erik and Liam. "Who does this? Who tortures his own people in the name of progress?"

Silence filled the corridor. Caeli felt the soldiers' resolve falter. Jason took another step forward and continued. "Marcus is a monster. We all know it. And now you have a chance to do the right thing."

After a tense silence, one by one the soldiers put down their weapons. Eventually even Jonah faltered, lowering his eyes and his gun.

Caeli felt Jason's inner conflict, an overwhelming desire for vengeance at war with his deeply ingrained morals. He stepped forward and aimed his own gun directly at Jonah's head, his hand shaking and his finger twitching on the trigger.

Jonah stared back, a pained expression on his face. After several heartbeats, Jason lowered the gun. "I want him in a cell," he said, the anger in his voice laced with hurt and betrayal.

"Put them all in a cell," Drew ordered.

"Wait. Please," one of the soldiers said, pulling away from the group. "I want to fight with you."

A few others stepped forward, following suit.

Drew looked to Jason, who in turn gestured at Caeli.

Her mind was shutting down along with her body, and she couldn't dig as deeply into their thoughts as she would have liked. But even so, all the soldiers who'd stepped forward felt honest in their intentions and relieved to have been offered a different course.

Jason gave a curt nod, and then prodded the others back down the hall into Lia's old cell.

***

Back on the main floor of the research facility, the scientists and engineers still sat huddled in the locked office, right where Drew had left them. Drew ordered Lia and the baby to stay inside, but when he tried to convince Erik and Liam to join them, they adamantly refused.

As they stood by the door checking their weapons, the roar of jet engines shook the building. The ragged group hurried outside in time to watch one plane streak overhead, tailed closely by another, which was inexplicably firing on the first.

"Derek!" Caeli gasped.

Drew turned to her, eyebrows raised. "Are you sure?"

"Yes."

They lost sight of both craft as they sped out over the forest.

"Come on," Drew said, leading them around the facility and back in the direction of the command center. "We should try and confirm Marcus's whereabouts. If they've got a plane . . ."

Caeli followed his thinking immediately, as did Jason and Erik.

Jason turned to one of the Amathi soldiers who'd joined them. "Where is he?"

"The General sent us to intercept you, based on Jonah's conviction that you'd come rescue your people. He wasn't heading for the bunker when we left, and he won't want to be seen as weak or in hiding. My bet is he's gone to the command center."

"Let's make sure," Jason said.

"We have to stay out of sight, and I don't think I can help." Caeli looked at Jason, then Drew, knowing she probably looked as awful as she felt.

"That's okay. We'll do it the old fashioned way and sneak around," Drew said, throwing her a reassuring grin. "Once we have eyes on him, we'll need to surround the building and pin him inside," he continued, but his instructions were cut off by a deafening blast that shook the ground beneath them. He looked to Caeli, his eyes widening.

She stretched her mind out, and immediately felt Derek's pulsing life force resonate against her own. Sagging against Drew in relief, she nodded.

Before they could move any further, Erik pointed at the sky.

In the distance, two more planes engaged in a deadly game of chase. The lead craft executed a steep vertical climb, and the other followed. When they became mere black specks against the vivid blue sky, the first plane threw itself into a spiraling dive.

"Fucking Kat!" Drew yelled.

Caeli startled and Jason cast him a surprised glance.

"I'd recognize her brand of crazy anywhere," Drew said.

"What's she doing?" Caeli asked.

Drew didn't answer. All his attention was focused on the two planes hurtling toward the ground at mind-numbing speed.

"Come on, Kat," he whispered. "Pull up."

Caeli grabbed Drew's hand and squeezed.

"Now, Kat," he begged, willing her to do it.

At the last possible second, or so it seemed to Caeli, the lead plane banked hard and pulled out of the dive.

The other craft couldn't make the adjustment quickly enough, and another blast, closer than the first, punctured the air, sending tremors through the ground.

Drew stood still and closed his eyes, but his grip on Caeli's hand relaxed.

"Wow," Jason said.

"We have to move," Drew said finally, and the group cautiously made their way closer and closer to the command center. When they were positioned across from it, out of sight, Drew admitted reluctantly, "I'm not sure how we're going to get close enough. The building's surrounded."

"That probably means Marcus is inside," Jason said.

"Today 'probably' isn't good enough," Drew answered. Jason nodded his agreement.

"I'll go," an Amathi soldier said. It was the young man who first volunteered to join them.

All eyes turned to him. His youthful face carried a worn and tired look. "I'll be able to walk right in," he said.

"Talk to me," Drew demanded.

The soldier thought a moment. "We were sent to ambush you. I can report that the fight had been more difficult than we thought. I'll tell the guard that you all are locked back up, but we need a medical team for some injuries we sustained in the fight. I'll ask him directly if the General is inside and can spare a team. If he's in there, I'll point to the spot in the sky where the planes did their death spiral thing. That will be my signal to you. It'll be easy to work that into the conversation."

Drew gave him a long, measured look. "You could totally fuck us."

The young man swallowed hard. "But I won't," he whispered.

Drew looked at Caeli. "He won't," she said.

"Go," Jason ordered the Amathi.

When the soldier stood, Drew stopped him with a hand to the arm. "You know our intent is to blow that building?"

The soldier held Drew's gaze. "I'll try to get out again, but . . ." he hesitated. "But I know you have to do it anyway."

Drew nodded. "What's your name?"

"Private Brendan Curtis."

"Good luck, Private Curtis."

They watched him cross the street and approach a guard positioned at the main entrance. The two engaged in an animated conversation. When Curtis turned and pointed to the horizon, where moments before Kat's aerial acrobatic drama had unfolded, Drew rubbed a hand over his head. "Let me try to reach Derek again on the com," he said.

DEREK

CHAPTER 35

Trees burned below him as he circled around to look for Kat. He caught sight of the two fighters just as the first plane pulled out of a terrifying dive and led the second to its fiery end over a grain field.

He knew it was Kat who'd survived, even before her voice came back over his com. He'd flown with her a long time, and he knew that not many pilots could have pulled out of that dive in time.

"That was bold," he commented.

"I see you lost your tail too," she answered, slightly out of breath.

"I did. Now let's see if we can't find Finn and give him a hand," he said.

"Following you."

They came in from the west, looping the monorail station and grain silos. Derek banked the plane, tilting a wing toward the ground and peering down over the side. Civilian bodies, interspersed with uniformed soldiers, peppered the streets. Most buildings were still intact. Marcus wouldn't want to destroy his own infrastructure, just his people, Derek thought bitterly.

The battle on the ground raged at such close quarters that there was no way for Derek or Kat to engage without causing unacceptable collateral damage. Bands of soldiers chased down resistance fighters in alleyways and streets, and resistance fighters waited to ambush soldiers from behind vehicles and buildings.

"Commander, do you copy?" A voice broke in over his regular com.

"Drew? Is that you?"

"Yes, sir. I see we've got air support after all," Drew said.

"We do," Derek answered.

"Marcus is in the command center."

"Are you sure?" Derek asked.

"As sure as I can be. He must be getting nervous about losing his planes, and I don't want to give him a chance to move, but the building is surrounded by Amathi troops. We're completely outnumbered."

"Do what you can. We're on our way," Derek assured him and adjusted his heading.

He reached out to Finn again and told him to get to the command center.

"Kat, I'm out of missiles. I'll try and knock out the troops with the rail guns and cover you. You'll have to take the shots," he ordered.

"Roger that," she said.

Derek kept his com open and heard Drew order his team to engage the command center perimeter from all sides.

Weapons fire lit up the scene below him. He flew low and fired into the mass of soldiers. Automatic rounds from his guns sprayed in deadly bursts, piercing bodies and bursting them open like overripe fruit.

He didn't take them all out with his first pass, and any soldier left on the ground now turned their weapons on his plane. He lifted the nose and punched the throttle, but not before a few well-placed rounds damaged one of his engines.

"Kat, put one in!" he ordered.

"Firing!" she shouted back.

Alarms blared in his cockpit once again, and this time the starboard engine indicator light flashed a persistent warning. The plane dipped down and to the right. Derek quickly made an adjustment to compensate and switched all power to the port side engine. He leveled out and turned, making a wide arc back over the command center.

Below him, one half of the building smoldered. Debris and bodies littered that side of the street. In the ensuing chaos, soldiers poured out of from the back door, running for their lives.

Derek fired on them, any regret silenced by the thought of Marcus surviving for another day.

"Kat, finish it!" he ordered.

She fired the second missile. Debris erupted into the air, and then the command center collapsed on itself.

***

"I think we got him," Kat said, her voice laced with incredulousness.

"If he was in there, we got him," Derek agreed. "Kat, I have to land. I'm flying on one engine." And truthfully, he had to get the plane on the ground before he passed out. "Stay in the sky a little longer until we know for sure Marcus is dead. The Amathi on the ground must realize we've got the advantage now. If we can confirm the kill, the remainder should stand down."

"I'll see what I can see from up here," she answered.

He headed for the airstrip and landed, barely making it out of the cockpit before tearing his helmet off and vomiting. On his hands and knees, he took quick gulps of air.

Silence greeted him on the ground. A breeze blew in from the west, warmer than any he'd felt since he'd arrived. He squinted at the brilliant afternoon sunlight. As the adrenaline wore off, physical pain and exhaustion took its place. His head throbbed and his chest ached with every breath. But he thought of Caeli, still in danger, and pushed himself to his feet.

He kept Kat's borrowed sidearm up and ready as he staggered toward the command center. Distant, sporadic bursts of gunfire punctured the air, but he stayed out of sight.

"Finn?" he said into the com.

"I'm here. I've got Alaric and Noah with me. We're close. With the command center knocked out, none of the troops are receiving orders. They know something's wrong," Finn said.

Derek rounded the corner of an alleyway a block from the command-center-turned-rubble-heap and stopped. The first person he recognized was Drew, stepping carefully through debris. Emerging into view, Derek waved and shouted.

A grin split Drew's face, but before Derek could say anything else, Caeli appeared from behind another building. She took a shaking step toward him, calling his name, and then ran to him. When she threw her arms around him, he gasped painfully but pulled her into a tight embrace.

"You're hurt," she said, looking him up and down. He felt the familiar tingling sensation of her mind inside his body.

"And you're exhausted. Stop. I'll be okay," he said. When she didn't fight him, he knew how depleted she really was.

Jason joined them. "Nice flying," he said.

The worn group of prisoners wandered out from hiding, and Jason immediately ordered them to set up a perimeter around the decimated command center. Moments later, Finn also arrived, with Alaric, Noah, and a small group of resistance fighters in tow.

Anyone able began sifting through the wreckage. Noah located survivors. Caeli did what she could, but she could barely focus.

"If I can get to the hospital, I can bring help," Erik said. "And we're going to have to prepare for casualties on a large scale. I'll need to get things organized."

"Go," Finn said, and Erik set off.

"We've got more survivors buried over here!" Noah called from the south side of the building.

Derek left Caeli kneeling next to an Amathi soldier suffering a broken leg, and went to help move the rubble. His fractured ribs screamed as he heaved chunks of debris off pinned bodies, but when Derek removed a piece of wall from the pile, he froze. A few feet below, his face covered with blood and grime, Derek recognized Marcus. And he was alive.

"Finn! Over here!" he yelled.

Finn rushed over, with Noah right behind him. For a heartbeat, Finn stared down at Marcus, his hardened expression transforming into one of disillusionment and hurt.

"I believed in him once," Finn said, staring at Marcus. "I did things in the name of his vision . . ." He stopped and shook his head. "Let's get him out of there."

Marcus's legs were pinned by a heavy beam in the unstable alcove. Finn started to carefully climb down to reach him when Noah interrupted. "Let me stabilize him first."

Without waiting for an answer, Noah slid down into the

space next to Marcus and squatted by his head. He placed a hand on the General's shoulder.

"Both femurs are fractured and he's bleeding internally," Noah reported, his tone flat.

"All right. Do what you can," Finn said.

Noah didn't respond, but instead moved his hand to Marcus's temple and said, "You sold my sister."

Derek glanced at Finn, who looked back at him in confusion. "Noah, don't," Derek pleaded.

"You killed my parents," Noah continued, his voice breaking. "You destroyed everything and everyone I've ever loved."

Noah squeezed his eyes shut, and a single tear slid down his cheek.

Marcus gasped and tried to speak. His eyes widened and then rolled back in his head. All remaining color drained from his already ashen face. His lips turned blue and he convulsed once before falling still.

Derek and Finn didn't move for a several minutes, until Jason jogged over, stopping short to peer into the ditch.

Finn sat back on his heels, and without looking at Jason said, "Marcus was buried under here. We tried to dig him out, but it was too late. He's gone."

Finn and Derek exchanged a wordless glance, and Derek gave him a barely perceptible nod.

5535.4.2
UNDERGROUND BUNKER 232A
AL AMAR PROVENCE

Jed's oldest son was on the recon mission. He was comforted by the fact that Alana, now Major Darcy, was J.P.'s commanding officer, and they had a powerful group of Betas with them providing cover and rooting out hidden patrols.

Jed wished he were there, but his injuries were still too fresh. Rory had done an admirable job of patching him up with nothing more than his mind, but Jed was still healing, so instead of leading the team himself, he sat by the radio, chewing a fingernail and monitoring the com.

The team needed to gather accurate intel about this particular enemy base of operations. They knew if they could take it out, the tide of the war might turn. Something has to work, Jed thought.

5535.4.2
UNDERGROUND BUNKER 232A
AL AMAR PROVENCE

They chained the woman to the chair. She was smarter, faster, and stronger than anyone in the room.

Darcy's recon mission had provided more than just intel. When her team surprised a group of enemy fighters, she'd made the risky decision to ambush and capture one. Most decisions had to be bold now. With four years of war and two thirds of the population decimated, the time for caution and careful strategy was over.

Early on, before Misha discovered that Owen Gareth was a mole, he'd been able to send Jed detailed information on the key players in

Misha's army. As Commander Issin stared icily at the wall in front of her, Jed knew they'd just gotten very lucky.

Rory circled her. A streak of dirt marked his cheek and his clothing hung off his too-thin body. When he dropped to kneel before Issin, his hands shook slightly, but his expression was calm, determined. He touched her gently and her body jerked. Wide-eyed, she shook her head and struggled against her restraints.

Jed closed his eyes as Rory began to speak. Names, places, codes, and descriptions tumbled from his mouth. Issin began to scream.

5596.1.1
ABOARD THE INFINITY

Her shuttle made it past the limping remains of the Almagest fleet undetected. Infinity *waited, orbiting the planet's second moon.*

Misha's enhanced brain continuously calculated the odds of victory. And now, after the loss of Commander Issin's entire base of operations, she found those odds to be overwhelmingly against her.

She'd left a number of Nova behind, knowing Jed's army would soon wipe them out, but she couldn't risk broadcasting Infinity's *location, even over an encrypted channel.*

Her shuttle docked and Misha entered the bridge to assume command, with Vahn at the helm.

They'd need a place to hide and regroup. "Set a course for Nysarin, and send out a transmission coded for the Battle Cruiser Zafar," *she ordered. "If General Sarovan is still in command, he may be interested in renewing our relationship." Sarovan had kept their illicit dealings a secret when she'd needed a separate source of income. And back then, she was only offering him a synthetic pharmaceutical cocktail. Now, she had something much better.*

Her plan to take Almagest had failed, but Vahn was with her. Some of her best soldiers were with her. And eventually she could make more.

DEREK

CHAPTER 36

Derek held Caeli's sleeping form on a makeshift bed he'd created for them in a supply room. Once the clinic staff had treated them both, he'd found this spot out of the chaos. They weren't in nearly as bad shape as some of the incoming patients, and so they had both insisted on giving up their hospital beds. Now, Caeli lay curled next to him, her chest rising and falling rhythmically, the warmth of her body seeping into his.

Derek touched her face, still in awe that they'd both survived. He wished he could stay hidden away with her for days, but he knew as soon as she woke up, she'd throw herself back into the fray and work herself to exhaustion once again.

His task here was nearly done, but for Caeli and the resistance, winning the battle was just the beginning. Healing their wounds, reuniting a long-divided people, and rebuilding the government would be no easy tasks.

He often found war had a clarity to it that peacetime lacked.

There'd been a moment, in the silence following Marcus's death, when Finn looked at Derek and asked, "What do I do now?"

"Take charge and keep everyone busy. You can figure out the

rest later," Derek answered.

And so Finn, backed by the surviving resistance fighters, had rapidly and unequivocally taken control of the remainder of the Amathi troops. Derek sent Alaric and Kade to try and salvage the command center communications system and recall the remaining troops. He ordered Kat to land, and he left Drew to help with the search and rescue. And then he and Caeli stumbled to the clinic.

Now, in the isolated quiet, he waited for her to awaken.

***

First, they cared for the living. Derek joined the rescue operations and Caeli healed patients. But very soon, they had to bury their dead.

The Stefans' house and barn were little more than craters in the scorched earth. Derek held Caeli's hand tightly as they approached the property. Their military vehicle also carried Alaric, Kade, Kat, Drew, and Finn. A dozen more Amathi soldiers and civilians followed behind, all preparing for the grisly task that awaited them.

Kat had flown over the site before landing and she'd already let Derek know that the place had been decimated. Despite that, Finn ordered a search of the entire area, and when Noah volunteered, Finn let him go. But there wasn't a single survivor.

Although he knew the truth from the moment their coms cut out, Derek had held out a sliver of hope that Tree might still be alive. Now, knowing that he might not even find a body, he felt physically ill.

When they stood staring at the debris, Caeli sagged against him.

"I can't believe Gregor's entire family is gone. Yesterday, we sat at their kitchen table," she said, wrapping her arms around herself as if the gesture would ward off the horror.

The somber group began picking through rubble and carefully removing human remains. Most were unidentifiable, but Derek knew Tree had been making a run for *Eclipse* out back. He wandered in that direction, catching Drew's attention and motioning for him to follow.

They found Tree easily. The powerful rail guns had mangled his body, but not his face. In death, he looked youthful, at peace. Nothing in his frozen expression hinted at the violence he'd suffered.

Drew dropped to his knees. "I think it was quick for him," he said.

Derek put a hand on Drew's shoulder, not trusting himself to speak. Beside him, Kat appeared. Wordlessly, they wrapped Tree's body.

Ironically, Derek found *Eclipse* intact. Hidden by stealth shielding, and far enough from the house and barn to have avoided missile damage, the ship sat unblemished, a silent, indifferent witness to the surrounding carnage.

He and Kat entered the still cockpit and Derek powered up the auxiliary systems, enabling the long-range communications system. He recorded a brief message informing Captain Donovan that the conflict had ended and the resistance had won a costly victory.

"We lost Tree," he said, and then he stopped speaking for so long he had to pause the transmission.

Kat's hand rested on his shoulder, and Derek let his head sink onto the cockpit dash. "I'm tired, Kat," he said.

Finally, he turned the device back on and finished his report.

"Once a provisional government has been established here, I'll be back in contact."

They secured the ship and rejoined the work outside.

Most of the bodies were being pulled from the barn, where the hidden cellar was now a debris-filled pit thanks to a well-placed Amathi missile, but he found Caeli with Finn, digging through the rubble at the main house.

He gave Finn a puzzled look.

"Ethan Matthews was still tied up down there," Finn said, out of Caeli's earshot.

Caeli worked with dogged persistence, but when she removed a timber and found a boot, she sat back on her heels and stared at it vacantly. Several heartbeats later she looked up at Derek.

"I can't," she whispered.

"It's okay," he said, lifting her to her feet and settling her several yards away on a grassy patch of ground. Then he and Finn finished digging out the body by themselves.

When the late afternoon sun set behind the mountains, the small group followed Finn to the barracks, planning to spend the night there. But Caeli had patients she wanted to check on, so she and Derek returned to the hospital.

They spent another night in the supply room. Derek managed to find extra pillows and blankets, and he made them a comfortable bed, relatively speaking. The hospital also had showers. And a cafeteria. For a temporary arrangement, it wasn't so bad.

In the morning, the aroma of baking bread flooded the ground floor of the hospital. Breathing deeply, Derek felt the first glimmer of hope he'd had since landing on Alamath months ago.

Dorian Bell had returned to cooking. He fed the tired,

hungry staff, organized meals for the patients, and sent his own people out into the streets searching for anyone displaced by the fighting who needed food.

Derek insisted Caeli sit and eat after cleaning herself up. Left unchecked, she would work herself to exhaustion. Derek suspected she was in shock, and he knew that work was her coping mechanism. But she wouldn't be able to run from the trauma forever, and he couldn't carry the weight of the pain for her. All he could do was make sure she ate and slept. And sure as hell, he would be there when her protective wall crumbled and she couldn't outrun her emotions anymore.

***

Orange tendrils of flame licked the sky. With the blessing of the rest of the team, he'd decided to put Tree to rest the Novali way, on a pyre. Heat blasted his face and he had to take a step backward. Caeli caught his hand, squeezing it so tightly that he lost the feeling in his fingers. She still held herself together, by a thread, he suspected.

Kat, Drew, Alaric, and Kade stood to his left. Caeli, Finn, Dorian, and Jason to his right. A small crowd also gathered across from them. Derek recognized Lia and her family; Anya and her sister Cara; Liam, Noah, and Mariel among the faces.

The morning sun glistened off frosty blades of grass. White clouds lingered over treetops. The scene was pure in its beauty and impervious to his grief. Derek didn't know what he was going to say until the moment he began speaking. His words were for Tree's family somewhere across the vast expanse of space, but also for this grieving group right here in front of him.

"We're soldiers. We travel millions of miles from home,

and fight for worlds that most of us have never seen before, for people we don't even know. We all joined the Alliance for different reasons: for the science, the exploration, the rush of flying, to be part of something bigger than ourselves, to protect our homes and our families. I think Tree mentioned he joined because he lost a bet." Soft laughter spread through the small crowd. "But we stayed because of an ideal. The ideal that all people deserve freedom. Anywhere, on any world, if people are fighting for their right to exist, we took a vow to stand with them and defend them like they were our own.

"Many of us come from peaceful worlds, worlds that haven't faced the devastation of war for generations. And that's a good thing. Our job is to protect that peace, defend it. But it's also to help others find it.

"In all of human history, freedom has been costly. It's been costly to establish, and it's costly to preserve. We strive for it. We grasp it in our hands. And then we stumble. We fail. And we try again. It's our nature. The failures are painful and the price almost too much to bear, but the alternative is intolerable."

He paused for a moment and stared at the flaming pyre. "Matthew Kline was my friend. He was a soldier under my command. He was family. This wasn't his first fight, but it will be his last. And I think he'd say it was a good fight. One worthy of the sacrifice he made."

As the small group broke up, Lia approached Derek and Caeli. She started to speak, but her eyes filled and she simply threw her arms around Derek and hugged him.

When she finally pulled away, she said to them both, "Please come and stay with us. I need you close, Caeli."

Derek saw such a look of longing on Caeli's face that he answered quickly, "We'd love to. Thank you."

"Let's have dinner tonight. All of you are welcome," Lia hurried to add.

"I'll tell them. Really, Lia, thank you," he said.

"*She's not okay.*"

Derek blinked and realized that Lia had spoken directly into his mind. He raised his eyebrows in surprise, and then gave her a slight nod.

"I need to get back to the hospital. I'll see you tonight Lia," Caeli said.

Derek waved at Lia and followed Caeli.

***

That night he practically had to drag Caeli from the hospital. Dark circles rimmed her eyes and her skin was ashen.

"How was your day?" he asked. The strangely normal nature of the question gave him pause.

"Busy," she answered. "I think we have a handle on all the critical cases, and the inflow of new patients has stopped, but we're over capacity. Erik is working with Finn to create an effective system to reunite families."

"How are you doing?"

"Trying to keep up. Noah, Isa, Mia, and Mariel are all promising, but they're students really, so it takes me that extra bit of time to explain everything I'm doing, and to give them tasks that are useful, but also ones they can manage," she answered.

"Caeli, I mean how are *you* doing?" he asked, his tone gentle but insistent.

"I'm fine," she answered, but the words rang hollow.

He didn't push, and then they were at Lia and Ben's.

Laughter flowed from the kitchen. When they entered the room, his team was seated around the table, along with Ben, Lia, and Ben's parents. They all had full cups of ale, and were snacking on thin, flaky pieces of bread. Kat bounced Jamie on her lap, and Drew ripped tiny chunks of crust and fed them to the baby.

Kat caught Derek's incredulous stare and said, "What? I have three little brothers."

Drew ignored Derek and continued feeding the baby. Lia leaped up and pulled Caeli into a fierce hug. "Supplies are a little scarce, but Ben's parents kept a good bit in the storage cellar."

"I'm so glad they're okay," Derek overheard Caeli say to Lia.

"They were devastated when Marcus's troops came for me, and it nearly killed them when Ben had to escape with the baby. Ben was terrified that Marcus would have them arrested, but he never bothered with them, so they quietly lived their lives." Lia sighed. "They've aged, though. This has taken an awful toll on them."

"What about Ben's brother?" Caeli asked.

Lia looked at the ground. "He was killed when the troops fired into the crowd on the square. The same day Nina and Lily died."

"I'm sorry," Caeli whispered.

"We've all lost so much." Lia swiped a tear from her cheek. "But right now, we're going to have dinner. And we're going to drink," she said, handing Caeli her own cup.

The conversation was lively. Drew, Kat, Alaric, and Kade took turns telling stories about Tree. Caeli leaned into Derek and listened, the whisper of a sad smile on her face. Ben's parents fussed over the baby.

When the meal was long finished and a weary silence fell around the table, Lia offered to show Derek and Caeli to their room. She handed Derek a pile of extra blankets and two soft, fluffy pillows, then quietly shut the door on her way out.

"A bed," Derek said happily, tossing the bedding on top and pressing his hands appreciatively into the plush mattress. "It's been so long . . ."

But when he looked up, Caeli stared blankly past him. "Caeli?" he said, approaching her cautiously, as if she were a frightened animal.

Her gaze moved to his face, but she still lacked any expression. "I don't know how to do this," she said.

"What?" he coaxed.

"Live with it," she answered simply.

He didn't speak, but rather took her hand and led her to the bed, and then sat next to her and waited.

"I've gotten used to the nightmares. Now, even when I'm awake and I close my eyes, I see blood, bodies. I hear screaming. I can't make it stop," she said, her bottom lip trembling. "I feel numb, like I'm watching myself do things from a distance. I'm seeing these awful things in my mind, but it's like they aren't really my thoughts."

When she looked at him, panic filled her eyes and she began gasping for breath.

Derek gripped both her hands in his and held her gaze. "I'm right here."

Her shoulders shook and tears streamed unchecked down her cheeks.

"Just breathe," he said.

She gulped the air while her chest heaved. "I feel like I'm drowning."

"Breathe. I'm right here. You don't have to do this alone."

And then she was sobbing. The powerful convulsions wracked her thin body, and he held her until she had no tears left.

DEREK

CHAPTER 37

Derek and his team stayed during those early weeks immediately after the war, mostly to offer assistance during the recovery, but also to ensure that things didn't backslide. They'd sacrificed too much to leave before their mission had truly been accomplished. Almagest needed to establish a provisional government in order to petition the Alliance for temporary membership.

It was Erik, Finn, and Caeli who did much of the work organizing the reconstruction, and they naturally slid into temporary leadership roles. Caeli had been reluctant at first. She understood the enormity of the task, and she knew she'd have to put her practice of medicine on hold. But the coalition government that she herself helped to envision required representation from both the Amathi and the Novali. Erik had the mind for organizational structures, and Finn's command of the military had gone unchallenged, but neither could heal hearts and minds quite like Caeli could.

Derek watched her struggle in her new role, and he admired her perseverance. She'd spend long days trying to get a handle on the infrastructure of the city, and long evenings scouring the Alliance's library, researching governments that had been the most successful on other worlds.

She'd be so exhausted most nights that she'd fall asleep in moments. When nightmares interrupted her dreams, Derek would coax her awake only so she could cry herself back to sleep again. But over the weeks, the nightmares happened with less and less frequency.

And then Derek had to leave Almagest and finish his tour on *Horizon*. Technically, he had already finished it, but he still needed to debrief this mission, among other formalities. And he had to decide what to do next.

His conversation with Caeli the night before he left had nearly broken his heart.

"You can't stop doing what you love and what you believe in, because of me. You would never ask me to stop practicing medicine," she'd said.

"How will we do this if I'm gone for months, sometimes years, at a time?" he'd asked, not expecting any kind of useful answer.

She hadn't tried to give him one. "I love you, Derek. And if loving you means letting you go . . ." Her voice trailed off.

But he couldn't let *her* go. His work had been his entire life for more than a decade. Now, for the first time, he wanted a real life, whatever that meant. And he wanted it with Caeli.

Back onboard *Horizon*, he completed his mission reports, got his things in order, and promptly resigned his commission with the Alliance.

But Captain Donovan wouldn't accept it. "You don't do anything half-assed, do you?" he quipped.

Derek just shrugged and took a sip of the drink Donovan handed him.

"What are you going to do, take up farming?"

"I thought maybe fishing," Derek joked. Then, more seriously, he added, "Sir, she's the best thing in my world. I want a life with her."

Derek knew his captain was genuinely fond of Caeli. She'd earned his respect, and despite the fact that she was a civilian, she'd spent more time on *Horizon* than any civilian would have normally been allowed.

Donovan took a long swallow of his own drink. "Give me a little time before you officially submit this notice to Admiral Reyes, okay?"

Derek tilted his head and squinted at Donovan, but the captain waved his hand, indicating that this part of the conversation was over.

"How is Caeli?" he asked.

"Better," Derek answered. "She was in pretty bad shape right afterward. But she's strong, and determined, and now she's really, really busy."

"Good," Donovan answered, and they finished their drinks in silence.

A week later, Donovan called Derek into the conference room off the bridge. "I have Admiral Reyes."

Derek stood at attention as the three-dimensional image of the Admiral took shape in front of him.

"Commander Markham," the Admiral said by way of greeting.

"Sir."

"I've received your mission reports, and the Minister has received Almagest's petition for provisional membership. I wanted to tell you personally that the Inter-Planetary Alliance unanimously approved the request. The starship *Aquila* has been redeployed to the Almagest system as a first line of defense until such time as the planet can provide for its own."

"That's excellent, sir," Derek said. He knew the *Aquila*. She carried an extensive complement of fighters, long-range scout ships, and her own significant firepower. She wasn't as quick and stealthy as *Horizon*, but she'd been built for a different purpose.

"I agree," Reyes said, nodding. "The system's perimeter alert network will be enhanced first thing. Limited commerce will be authorized off and on the planet, and *Aquila* will provide security access through a checkpoint."

For all the bureaucracy that sometimes plagued the Alliance, they could be effective and efficient when they wanted to be. Derek appreciated that efficiency now.

"There's another item I wanted to discuss with you, Commander."

Derek raised his eyebrows. "Sir?"

"Almagest has to develop its own defense in a timely manner, and they need quite a lot of help to do it. The Alliance wants some of our people on the ground there to oversee the process. We have to assess their needs, help them interface and upgrade their tech and train them to use it, and create an air defense basically from scratch. This is a lengthy assignment. Five years minimum. I'd like to offer command of this operation to you." The Admiral said this last part smiling.

Derek opened his mouth to speak, but nothing came out. He cleared his throat. "Sir, yes, sir. That would be excellent." He cringed and wondered what had happened to his vocabulary.

Reyes laughed and Donovan clapped him on the back.

"You've been one of the Alliance's most effective field operatives and you'll be missed, but if it's a choice between losing you completely or repurposing your skills, I'd rather keep you. And you've earned this."

"Thank you. I . . . thank you, sir," he stammered.

"Good luck, commander. I expect regular reports and good progress down there."

"Yes, sir," Derek answered, and Admiral Reyes's image dissolved.

A month later, after a two-day shore leave and a drinking binge with his squadron, he said his goodbyes.

Kat flew him and his new ground team to Almagest. He'd sat in the copilot's seat next to her for the last part of the flight.

"It won't be the same without you," she said, a catch in her voice.

"I'll miss you too, Kat."

"But I want you to know, I'm really happy for you," she hurried to add.

"Thank you. That means a lot. And I know my team is in good hands, Commander Rowe," he said.

She smiled. "Thanks for the recommendation."

"It was always going to be you. You earned it."

"And you've earned this," she said, pointing out the window at the lovely blue and white planet growing larger by the second.

18 MONTHS LATER

He held Caeli's hand as they walked through the garden. Since he'd been back, it had become a routine. On her day off, they'd come here. At first it was to check progress on the construction of the memorial wall, but later it was simply to walk through the rows of flowering bushes or sit under the canopy of trees. Always she'd run her fingers over the names engraved on the wall, and always she'd speak a few out loud.

The cratered pit that had once been the Stefans' home had been covered over and seeded with wildflowers. A stone path now created a walkway around the property, and where the barn once stood, the memorial wall curved around the easternmost perimeter instead.

Of all the duties and tasks Caeli had undertaken since the war's end, Derek knew working on this project had helped her heal the most.

"I can't believe I leave tomorrow," she said.

"Are you excited?" he asked.

"Yes. But nervous, too," she admitted.

"You're going to be perfect. And it's just a formality anyway," he assured her.

She nodded and knelt down to pluck a few weeds from one of the beds. "We've come a long way," she said.

Almagest had just concluded its first free election and successful transition of leadership. Caeli's last act in her official capacity would be diplomatic in nature. In the morning, she'd leave for Cor Leon to request Almagest's full membership in the Inter-Planetary Alliance.

"You've done amazing work," Derek said, pride filling his voice.

"And I am so ready to be done with it," she answered, shaking her head and laughing. "Healing a compound femur fracture will feel easy in comparison."

She stood, dusting her pants. He laughed with her and then took her hands. He caught her gaze and held it, his look so intense that she tilted her head and furrowed her eyebrows. "What is it?" she asked.

"Marry me when you get back." His proposal sounded more like a command, and the shocked look on her face made him check himself and try again. Allowing his raw emotion to pour into her mind he whispered, "Caeli, I love you more than anything in this world, or any other. I'd die for you. Will you please be my wife?"

Derek knew he wasn't the first man to ask her. She'd been in love before, on the verge of starting a family and dreaming about a future, when her home had been destroyed. The loss of her fiancé, Daniel, had crushed her, and for a long time she hadn't wanted to survive it.

Derek had chosen this place to ask her, a place where Daniel's name was inscribed next to so many others, because he wanted to acknowledge her loss, acknowledge that it was part of her and always would be.

"You're thinking about Daniel?" she asked, smiling but with a slightly puzzled look on her face.

"Is that awkward?" he asked lightly.

She paused before answering, "No, I don't think so. He'd want me to be happy."

"I want you to be happy," he said, pulling her in for a long, heated kiss.

"I am happy," she said, when they came up for air. "Yes, I'll marry you."

In the early morning hours, Caeli boarded the *Carina*, the ship that would take her to Cor Leon. When she said goodbye to Derek, a bright, hopeful smile lit her face, and for the first time since he'd known her, it reached her eyes.

EPILOGUE

"Drop stealth shielding on my command," Daksha Karan barked.

"Yes, sir," his pilot answered.

The Almagest system was well protected, and they would have only a matter of minutes to act once the ship came within range.

"Target engines only."

"Ready on your order," the pilot said.

Standing, Karan turned to address the boarding party. "Kill the crew. Take only the woman. Understood?"

"Yes, sir."

The bridge crew waited in tense silence. Karan sat back down, his body still and his face expressionless.

After several long minutes, the pilot announced, "Sir, a ship."

"Confirm its identity."

"Long-range transport. Alliance insignia." The pilot turned and nodded at Karan. "Identity confirmed. It's the *Carina*."

"Drop shields and fire!" he ordered.

ACKNOWLEDGMENTS

I feel like we got the band back together for this book! Amanda Rutter, editor extraordinaire, took a manuscript full of potholes and helped shape it into something respectable. Steven Meyer-Rassow, artistic genius, designed another stunning cover. I have no words for his talent. And Laura Zats, publishing pro, once again guided me through the process from start to finish. I couldn't have done it without this amazing team.

Grateful thanks to my beta readers—Ron Delaney Jr., Amy Hawes, and Lisa Messina. I gave them a tight deadline, and they delivered! *Infinity* is a much better book because of their honesty and attention to detail.

Enormous thanks to my family: my mom and dad, who are two of my biggest fans; and my little sister, who is always just a phone call away. But I simply couldn't do this without my husband, Ray, and my kids: Nicholas, Noah, RJ, and Kyra. I love you all and appreciate the unending support and encouragement.

ABOUT THE AUTHOR

Tabitha currently lives in Rhode Island. She is married, has four great kids, two spoiled cats, and a lovable lab mix. She has a degree in Classics from College of the Holy Cross and previously taught Latin at an independent Waldorf school where she now serves on the Board of Trustees. Currently, she is a full-time writer. Her first novel, *Horizon*, was a finalist in the Next Generation Indie Awards and the National Indie Excellence Awards, and was the winner of the Writer's Digest Self-Published Book Awards in 2016.